Petals and Poison

Petals and Poison

JESS DYLAN

St. Martin's Paperbacks

This is a work of fiction. All of the characters, organizations, and events portrayed in this novel are either products of the author's imagination or are used fictitiously.

First published in the United States by St. Martin's Paperbacks, an imprint of St. Martin's Publishing Group.

PETALS AND POISON

Copyright © 2021 by Jennifer David Hesse.

For information, address St. Martin's Publishing Group, 120 Broadway, New York, NY 10271.

www.stmartins.com

ISBN: 978-1-250-76956-5

Our books may be purchased in bulk for promotional, educational, or business use. Please contact your local bookseller or the Macmillan Corporate and Premium Sales Department at 1-800-221-7945, ext. 5442, or by email at MacmillanSpecialMarkets@macmillan.com.

Printed in the United States of America

St. Martin's Paperbacks edition / December 2021

10 9 8 7 6 5 4 3 2 1

"And now my beauties, something with poison in it I think, with poison in it, but attractive to the eye and soothing to the smell. . . . Poppies, poppies, poppies will put them to sleep."

—*The Wicked Witch of the West,* The Wizard of Oz
(movie, released 1939)

Chapter 1

Something's missing. Frowning, I studied the array of flowers, greenery, and assorted decorations I'd arranged in the picture window. In the center, fresh bouquets of bright zinnias fairly burst with color and cheer. On one side, a stand of purple and pink phalaenopsis orchids called to mind luxury and elegance; on the other side, a tied bouquet of fat, luscious silk peonies sang of romance and riches. The pottery—glazed ceramics handcrafted by local artisans—added an upscale touch, while the garden art kept things playful—especially the chubby gnome, ladybug fairy hut, and rainbow-hued metal spinner. As a backdrop, trailing ivy and potted ferns brought a lush, vibrant greenness to the scene. I leaned over to straighten two small wooden signs (declaring *Welcome* and *Be Happy*), then stood back with hand on chin.

It all *looked* very nice. The overall effect was "secret garden meets enchanted forest." But was it attractive enough? Meaning, would it *attract* the good vibes, abundant customers, and business growth I was going for?

"Sierra Ravenswood! Are you *still* working on that display?" Deena Lee, my right-hand woman and new best

friend, breezed in from the back room, her skirt swishing
and heels clicking on the tile floor. We'd run in different
circles back in high school, but when we both returned
to our hometown of Aerieville, Tennessee, a decade
later, Deena and I found we had more in common than
we ever knew. I was still grateful she'd decided to stay
and work for me at the flower shop. She had a good eye
for beautiful designs. "It looks fine," she assured me. "It
looked fine half an hour ago."

"Yeah, maybe. But I'm trying something here."

"You know," she went on, "it's not like we get much
foot traffic on Oak Street anyway."

That was true. Flower House was in the old section
of town. We were one of a few converted Victorians in a
quiet, mostly residential, neighborhood. The only other
businesses on the block were a small bakery, a dusty antique shop, an accountant's office, and a volunteer-run,
rarely open historical society. At the end of the street was
a forgotten little park called Melody Gardens. All the
more reason to take extraordinary steps to lure in new
customers.

"This is more than an everyday window display," I
said. The one I'd just removed had been more traditional,
with lots of red, white, and blue in honor of Independ-
ence Day. Now that the holiday was over, I wanted to
go in another direction. "This is a vision board of sorts.
Everything I included is meant to symbolize abundance
and prosperity. Like the vines: fast-growing, because we
need to grow fast."

She gave me a bemused look. "That's why we're opening the café next weekend. People will come in to try
our edible flower goodies, then make a purchase while
they're here." Deena would be the chef in our new mini-
restaurant.

"I know. But it can't hurt to infuse the place with an extra bit of luck." I looked at the display again and tilted my head. Was that what was missing? A lucky charm?

"How about this?" said Deena, as if reading my mind. She took a potted bamboo plant off a nearby shelf and handed it to me. "Lucky bamboo."

"That's the spirit!" Nodding with approval, I took the plant from her and found a place for it in the display. "If it works for the Chinese, why not for us?"

"Not just the Chinese," she said. "Koreans too. My grandparents swear by it. Well, that and pigs. Pigs are even luckier than bamboo."

"Pigs? Really?" I looked around, as if I might find a pig figurine in the shop. There was none.

"Yeah." Deena laughed. "According to my grandmother anyway. Grandma Binna's almost as superstitious as your granny."

"No way," I said with a smile. "Granny Mae's whole life revolves around her superstitions."

"You'd be surprised. When I was in school, Grandma Binna always used to tell me not to wash my hair before a test. Otherwise I'd wash all my knowledge right down the drain."

"And did you listen to her?" Deena had been one of the prettiest, most popular girls in our class. I was quite sure she'd never come to school with unwashed hair.

"Of course! Why take chances?"

"Right." I smirked. "Could you imagine if Granny Mae met Grandma Binna? I'd love to be a fly on the wall for that conversation."

I loved my granny to pieces but could never understand why she put so much stock in superstitions that had no basis in fact nor science. I, on the other hand, based my beliefs on personal experience. At least, I tried to. In my view, it was true that certain symbols and images could hold positive energy and bring about change, but that was because of the viewer's own state of mind. It was the simple Law of Attraction.

Come to think of it, maybe Granny Mae and I weren't that different after all.

I'd been seeing a lot more of my granny lately, ever since she'd planted a patch of flowers and herbs out back near the greenhouse. She came down from her home in the mountains about once a week, hitching a ride with her neighbor, Wanda Milford, who was a few years younger than Granny. Wanda liked to come into town to grocery shop and get her hair done. Granny liked to impart home-spun wisdom and keep an eye on me.

Deena picked up a feather duster and ran it over a table holding glass vases and metal urns of fresh flowers. "Grandma Binna makes the trip from Seoul at least once a year," she said. "I'll have to bring her by next time."

"For sure. I'd love to meet her." I headed for the front door. "I'm gonna look at this display from outside now. I still think somethin's missing."

I plucked a mint leaf from the planter on the stoop and rubbed it between my thumb and forefinger. Walking to the front of the house, I sniffed the minty sweetness. *Good stuff*, I thought. *One of life's small pleasures.* If Deena saw me doing this, she might call me "Amélie," after the character in the French movie. I guessed I could be quirky and imaginative like that. Or maybe it was just because of my brunette hair and short bangs.

I took a gander at the window display, immediately noting where I needed to shift things around for better effect. But my attention soon wandered up the face of the building, from the baby blue and white trim to the dusty rose scalloped siding beneath the gable roof. Sunlight glinted off the single circular window at the top. All at once, I felt a jumble of emotions wash over me, foremost a blend of pride and satisfaction—tempered with a healthy dose of worry and angst.

The place was all mine. And it was all thanks to one impulsive decision by my old boss, Felix Maniford. He'd built this business from the ground up, together with his late wife Georgina. Flower House had become an institution, and not just in little ol' Aerieville. The Manifords became known far and wide for Georgina's collection of exotic orchids and Felix's hothouse roses, not to mention the special flair Felix always brought to his bouquet arrangements.

I was just a part-time helper—until Felix up and left one day. He'd set off on a folly of a treasure hunt somewhere out West. He was so intent on his new adventure, he'd left everything behind. And he'd given me his shop, to do with as I pleased.

"Talk about your mixed blessings," I muttered to myself. It was the career opportunity I never knew I wanted. I'd planned to be a professional singer-songwriter—in spite of my false start in Nashville a while back. I was going to travel, get rich and famous, meet exciting people, and find fantasy-worthy romance.

Instead I was here, firmly ensconced in my Appalachian hometown, trying to make it as a small business owner. So far, it was mostly fun and exciting—when it wasn't tiring or terrifying.

A sharp bark pulled me from my reverie. I turned to see my corgi, Gus (another gift from Felix), trotting up the sidewalk on stubby little legs. I had to grin at his eager mini-wolf face, big ears, and furry bread loaf of a body. Then I glanced up at the guy on the other end of the leash and my grin widened by a smidge. *Calvin.* My second employee and only tenant. He tended the plants we grew on site and helped with maintenance—and dog wrangling.

It was sweet of him to take Gus out of Flower House and for a walk. Cal had been working overtime in the greenhouse, helping to get ready for the grand opening of our café next Saturday. For that matter, he'd been working overtime at Flower House ever since he showed up here three months ago and moved into the upstairs apartment. He'd been an immense help to me. More than that, he'd also turned out to be a fun person to have around. And then some.

I watched as Gus led Calvin on a zigzaggy sniffing tour up the block. What was it about that guy that made my heart go flippity-flop? He was of average height and average build, on the thin side actually. Nothing like the bodybuilder physique of my dad and brother who, together with my mom, ran Dumbbells Gym downtown. He was kind of nerdy really, prone to making goofy puns, and *way* more into plants than your average gardener—which made sense, since he'd been an adjunct botany professor in Knoxville before moving to Aerieville.

Of course, he'd copped a nerdy persona on purpose when he'd first introduced himself to me. As he later confessed, he'd thought it would make him seem more trustworthy—and help conceal his real reason for being here.

To be honest, I still wasn't sure how well I knew the real Calvin Foxheart.

He looked up at me then, as he and Gus finally stepped onto the lawn in front of Flower House, and flashed a carefree smile. I realized then that there were a few things I *did* know for sure. I knew he had a nice face, with a masculine jawline and sparkling blue eyes.

I knew he was good with Gus. And I knew he was hard-working, generous, funny, and kind.

Still, it was hard to get past the fact that he hadn't been completely honest with me from the start. And I'd been burned by dishonest men before.

"Hey," he said casually. "What's on your mind? You look conflicted about something."

I started. Was I that transparent?

"Um . . . I am conflicted. I'm trying to decide if I should add a money tree to the display." I hooked my thumb toward the window behind me. "Deena suggested the lucky bamboo plant, and it got me thinking about other plants that symbolize prosperity. Bart is stopping by with a delivery sometime today. I could order the plant from him."

"Sure, why not?" said Calvin. "You said the display is meant to remind you of what you want, right? I say, go for it. Don't hold back." His expression was slightly amused, tinged with genuine curiosity.

"I know you view this as a case study," I said with a smile. "But this sort of thing has worked for me before. Plenty of times."

"Really?" He pursed his lips, as if pondering the possibilities. "Sounds like you hold a magic lamp, then. Like, with a genie who will grant all your wishes. But if it's that easy, then why not do it for everything you want?" He paused and cocked his head. "Or have you? Is everything in your life here now because you've attracted it?"

I shrugged, not bothered by the questions. "In a way, yes. I mean, it's a little more complicated than that. But in general, yes. This is true for everybody. Whatever we put our attention on, good or bad, conscious or not, is what we draw to us."

He nodded slowly, fixing me with an interested gaze.

A second went by, and I imagined I felt a charge pass between us. Was he training his attention on me because of what I'd just said? Was he trying to draw *me* to him?

A small smile played at his lips, and I realized he was teasing me.

"You don't believe it's true?" I asked.

"You know me. I'm a man of science. I like to see proof." He nodded toward the window. "We'll see if this little experiment of yours brings in an influx of money. Like, an unexpected amount of business growth. If it does, then we'll know. You'll have found the rainbow leading to a pot of gold."

I smiled again. "Well, I already know. But, yeah. Then you'll know too."

"Speaking of treasure," he said. "Hear anything from Felix lately?"

And there it was. The reason Calvin had shown up in my life in the first place—and possibly the reason he stayed: his intense interest in Felix's treasure hunt. The Arwin Treasure was purportedly hidden somewhere in the wilds out West by an eccentric, wealthy antique collector. A series of hidden riddles and clues had kept treasure seekers on the hunt for several years now.

"As a matter of fact, yes," I said. "He called me the other day to catch up." Actually, he'd wanted me to look up something in one of the many books he'd left behind.

"How's he doing? Getting any closer?"

I shook my head. "He didn't say. But I kind of doubt it. He mentioned he might come back to Aerieville for the winter if he hasn't found it before then." I hoped he *would* come back. There was so much I wanted to ask Felix about the business.

"I take it he hasn't been bothered by any of the other treasure hunters?" said Calvin.

"I asked, and he only laughed. He always laughs about that."

Before Calvin could pursue the subject any further, Gus jumped up and barked as a car swerved to a stop by the curb in front of the shop. It was an old Subaru Outback—Granny's car—driven by her friend Wanda. Though Wanda usually drove, they alternated between Granny's car and Wanda's SUV. Both ladies piled out of the Outback, Granny dressed for gardening in rolled-up jeans, a cotton shirt, and a floppy straw hat, and Wanda dressed for . . . Hawaii, apparently, in a floral print muumuu. As Granny lifted the hatchback and retrieved various bags and baskets, Wanda scurried up the sidewalk, frazzled and in a hurry.

"Hello, dear. Can I use your powder room? Yours is much nicer than the one at the salon."

"Of course," I said, as she was already halfway in the door.

Calvin handed me Gus's leash and hurried over to Granny to help carry her bags. I joined them on the sidewalk and gave Granny a kiss on the cheek.

"Don't mind her," said Granny. "Wanda got into a little tussle at the meat market. Bopped the butcher right on the head with a foot-long salami."

"What?" Surely, I hadn't heard her right.

Calvin laughed. "No kidding?"

Granny reached into a bag for a small piece of lunchmeat and gave it to Gus, who was sitting attentively right in front of her like a good boy. He knew what visits from Granny meant.

"Well, he'd been ignoring her," said Granny, presumably referring to the butcher. "Wanda doesn't like to be ignored. Can't really blame her. Folks are always ignoring us old ladies."

"She really hit him on the head?" I asked. "Not hard, I assume."

"Hard enough. I had to drag her out of there before she did it again. It's getting to be a habit with her."

"Hitting people on the head with salami?" asked Calvin.

"Not just salami. It all started with her no-good drunk of a husband many years ago. Rest his soul. She bopped him on the head with a frying pan. Of course, he deserved it and didn't press charges. Ever since then, that's been her MO." Granny scratched Gus behind the ears, as she squinted her eyes with something like worry. "Disrespect Wanda and watch out. You might get bopped on the head."

Calvin and I looked at each other, sharing equal parts shock and amusement. "Good to know," said Calvin. He headed up to the front door and held it open. "I promise I'll never disrespect Wanda."

Inside, Granny looked around and commented on how nice the shop looked. Deena waved from behind the wooden counter in the center of the front room, where she was on the phone by the cash register. Calvin took Granny's bags to the large kitchen in the back that doubled as our workroom.

"Why, what a pretty little space you've created," said Granny, peering through the arched entryway leading from the shop's main room to the café area on the left. When Felix abandoned his idea for a café after Georgina died, this area had become a cluttery, mish-mash of a room. It was mainly used for storage and occasional special events, such as the bouquet-arranging class I'd led in the spring. Unfortunately, that time around it had also become a murder scene. I shuddered at the memory.

"We've been working hard the past few weeks." The

place *did* look pretty, if I said so myself. Of course, there were flowers and plants galore. And we'd opted for a sort of rustic Parisian décor, with eclectic furniture and vintage botanical prints on the walls. In addition to four small round tables, we'd added a velvet couch along one wall, giving the space a cozy coffee shop vibe. We'd even found an old brass chandelier at the antique shop across the street. "We got all our permits squared away and the menu all planned. Now we just hope folks will come by."

"Well, I'm sure they will," said ever-supportive Granny. She was a nice counterbalance to her daughter. My mom couldn't seem to help offering dire warnings about how so many new small businesses fail within the first year. Especially restaurants. And how location plays a big part in that depressing statistic. She meant well.

Deena hung up the phone and joined us in the café. "We just received an order for a get-well bouquet. I can deliver it this afternoon. I'm supposed to meet my parents for dinner anyway." Deena's parents both worked at the county hospital, her mother as a healthcare manager and her father as a cardiologist.

"That's great!" At this point, every order was cause for celebration. "Maybe you could stop by the gift shop and ask them again if they'd consider doing business with us. We could easily keep them stocked in simple bouquets each week."

"I'll ask," Deena promised.

Granny turned to me. "Business is going well?" she asked.

"Yes, ma'am. We're doing great. Can't complain."

She continued to give me the eagle eye. Granny may have been kind and supportive, but she was also shrewd. There was no fooling Granny.

"I mean, we do a steady business, for the most part. We're getting orders every day."

"And?" she prodded.

"And . . . well, I do worry about cash flow now and then. You know, we had to spend a pretty penny restoring the place following the uh, incidents, last spring." Besides the murder, there'd been a fair amount of destruction and vandalism in both our shop and the greenhouse.

Granny nodded. "Your mama told me insurance covered most but not all of your losses."

"That's right. And then, of course, we had to buy some things to get the café ready. But I'm not worried *that* much. I think the café will boost our income. Plus, there's this!" I pointed to my window display. "It's meant to ensure good luck. See? We have lucky bamboo and fast-growing ivy. And these flowers are known to represent wealth and good fortune."

"Hmm," said Granny. "Is that right? I didn't know those were lucky flowers."

"Well, maybe it depends on who you ask. But they seem lucky to me."

"Where's your four-leaf clovers? Where's your acorns and lucky pennies?" She looked doubtfully at the bamboo plant. "Maybe some healing herbs would make more sense in these parts."

"Great idea!" I said quickly. Granny had been teaching me about bad omens and lucky charms my whole life. I hoped I didn't offend her by getting it all wrong. "I want to start incorporating herbs in some of our bouquet arrangements anyway. I think it fits with the edible flower theme."

Calvin came out of the backroom with Gus at his heels

and joined us up front. "Is anybody getting hungry for lunch yet? I couldn't help noticing Granny brought—"

He was interrupted by a shrill scream. We all jumped, and Gus barked, as Wanda came running out of the hall bathroom, covering her head with her hands.

"Land sakes! It came straight for my scalp!"

We all stared at her. "What did?" I asked. "Are you okay?"

"What happened?" said Granny.

"A bird! I don't know what kind. Some sort of mad, crazy bird!" Wanda was dancing in circles, as if trying to shake off the heebie-jeebies.

Granny rushed up to her and clasped both her arms, effectively halting her in place. "Take a breath, Wanda. Tell us what happened."

She took a deep, shuddering inhale and pointed to the bathroom door. "I opened the window in there. For fresh air, you know. I was just washing up, reapplying my lipstick and whatnot, when out of nowhere a bird flies in the window."

Granny paled at this news and let go of Wanda's arms.

"Is it still in there?" I asked. "The poor thing must be scared."

"I think it wanted my hair for its nest," said Wanda. "It flew right at me!"

Calvin grabbed a broom and headed for the bathroom.

"Don't hurt it!" I called after him.

"I'm just going to shoo it out the window," he said, closing the door behind him. Gus scratched at the closed door, evidently wanting to help.

"Why don't you sit down," suggested Deena to Wanda. "I'll get you a glass of water."

Wanda nodded and took a seat in the café room. I

set out glasses for both Wanda and Granny, while Deena took out a pitcher of lemon water from the fridge behind the small café counter.

"Are you okay, Granny?" I asked, leading her to the chair across from Wanda. For some reason, Granny now appeared more shaken than Wanda.

She removed her straw hat and wiped her forehead. "I'm fine." She took a sip of water, then directed a disapproving gaze at Wanda. "Why'd you have to go and open a window with no screen? It only invites trouble."

Wanda frowned right back at Granny. "It's not my fault that silly bird flew inside."

"Well, you know what it means, don't you?" said Granny.

At first, Deena and I followed their exchange in confusion. But with Granny's last words it was dawning on me what had her so upset.

"Oh," said Wanda shortly. "You don't think . . . ?" She trailed off and covered her mouth with her hand.

"I do think," said Granny soberly.

"But it's just an old wives' tale," protested Wanda.

"What is?" asked Deena. "What are you worried about?"

Granny shook her head, then looked from Wanda to Deena and me. "Sorry to say this, girls, but it's bad news. If a bird flies in the window, it means someone is going to die. Someone in this very house."

Chapter 2

Well, this was a fine pickle. How was I going to reassure Granny—and everyone else for that matter—that we were all perfectly safe and in no danger of dropping dead, without straight-up contradicting Granny's beliefs? I never want to disrespect my elders.

When Calvin joined us in the café room, after safely helping the bird fly out the window, Granny repeated her dire pronouncement. We all stared at one another without saying a word. Even Gus watched me expectantly. I reached down and absently petted his head.

"Now, Granny," I finally said, as gently as I could. "Surely, it's not a hard and fast rule. Maybe sometimes a bird is a portent, and other times it's just an unfortunate bird. Don't you think?"

Setting her jaw, she spoke in a low, sepulchral tone. "A bird flew in the window of Aunt Dottie's bedroom. Twelve hours later, she was dead."

"That was probably a coincidence," I insisted. "Wasn't she in her nineties and suffering from diabetes?"

"When I was a girl," Granny continued, "a bird flew

in a window at my grandpappy's cabin. A week later, he was dead."

Deena and Calvin looked to me for my response. I racked my brain. There must have been plenty of times where a bird flew into a house without dooming any of its occupants. Why couldn't I think of a single example?

Granny wasn't finished. "Frank's cousin's wife's brother—"

"Okay," I interrupted, placing my hand on Granny's. I had to put a stop to this. "How about if we counteract the bad luck? Maybe we can cancel it out with some good luck."

She brightened slightly. "It can't hurt, I suppose. You ought to put a horseshoe above the front door. I'll make flannel herb bags for everyone. In the meantime, we can mix salt and red clay and crumble some in our shoes."

"Good," I said, clapping the table and ignoring Deena's raised eyebrow. "We have a plan."

Wanda left for her hair appointment, and the rest of us had a bite to eat. Then Granny went outside to dig some clay and tend the garden, while Deena and I made flower arrangements in the kitchen.

Calvin planned to work outside as well. As he passed by me on his way to the back door, I reached out to touch his arm.

"Hey, Calvin?"

He met my eyes and gave me a reassuring smile. "I'll keep an eye on her."

"Thanks." I dropped my hand and grinned at his retreating back. Apparently, we were on the same wavelength.

The next hour passed quietly. Almost too quietly. The phone didn't ring once. That's not to say we didn't have interruptions. Granny kept coming in and out. First she came in for a container of salt, then she returned with her salt-clay mixture. She made us all remove our shoes, so she could sprinkle in her protective concoction. It didn't bother me much, since I was wearing socks and sneakers. Deena, on the other hand, wore sandals today. She grimaced as Granny coated the inner soles of her sandals, but she refrained from complaining. We all wanted Granny to have peace of mind.

After that, Granny still found excuses to come inside, whether to use the bathroom, get a drink, or borrow the phone to call my mom. Each time, she surveyed the kitchen for lurking dangers and cautioned us to be careful with every little sharp thing: floral scissors, shears, thorns. After the last interruption, I called Mom myself and filled her in on the situation.

"Good grief," she said. "I'll come and pick her up and bring her to Dumbbells for a while. I'll tell her I need her advice about an ant problem we have. Which is true, actually."

As a former cheerleader, current aerobics instructor, and co-business owner, my mom was firmly grounded in the practical and the physical. She didn't share either Granny's superstitions or my New Agey notions. Sometimes it was a source of friction. Other times, like now, it was a relief.

By three o'clock, Deena and I were alone in the quiet kitchen once more, putting the finishing touches on all our outstanding flower orders.

"What else do we need for Saturday?" she asked, referring to the grand opening of our café.

"I think we're pretty much set," I said. "Except for the centerpieces. I was thinking each table should have a small flower arrangement. Maybe colorful carnations in little glass jars?"

"Good idea. They hold up well, don't they?"

A loud tap on the back door broke into our conversation. I peered through the window and saw that it was Bart Hammerson with the bi-weekly shipment from our wholesaler, Pauly's Plants. Although Felix often sourced flowers from local growers (and cultivated some himself), there were some varieties that could only be imported. For as long as I could remember, it was Bart who dropped off these deliveries. Gruff, taciturn, stony-faced Bart.

I'd once asked Felix why Bart always seemed to have a chip on his shoulder. Felix had laughed. "Does he? What do you want him to do, come in singing a song?" Felix only cared that Bart was fast and reliable.

Over the past few months, since I'd taken over Flower House, I'd been trying to get the delivery man to open up. I'd been extra friendly, making small talk and offering him water and snacks. And it seemed to be working. The last two times, he'd seemed to soften a bit. Once he even cracked a joke.

Today, however, he seemed to be back in his usual sour mood.

"Hey there, Bart!" I held the door open wide and stepped back as he carried in a crate and set it on the floor by the cabinets. "How are you today?"

"Eh," he grunted.

"What's the matter? Too hot for you? At least last week's heat wave is over. The rain last night cooled things off nicely." *When in doubt, talk about the weather.*

Bart grunted again, then went out to his truck for another crate.

"Talkative guy," said Deena once he was out of earshot.

I shrugged. "Our interactions are usually pretty one-sided. I'm determined to draw him out, though. It's only a matter of time."

"Maybe he's just the strong, silent type," Deena suggested.

"Hmm," I said thoughtfully. "I wonder if he's married."

Deena gaped at me. "You're interested in *Bart*? He's got to be at least forty, don't you think?"

I peeked out the window to see Bart standing by his truck and glaring at his phone. He was stocky and nearly bald, with closely cropped fair hair and a farmer's tan. I couldn't really guess how old he was. His face was perpetually lined from all the frowning.

I turned back to Deena. "No. I'm not interested in him, at least not in the way you mean. I'm just curious. I wonder about his story."

"His story?"

"Yeah. Why is he always brooding? Maybe he has a sad, tragic past."

"Maybe he's just fed up with the state of the world today," said Deena.

Now my imagination was fired up. "Maybe he's an international spy!" I joked.

Deena rolled her eyes. "Maybe he's a criminal—" She broke off as Bart reentered the kitchen. I stifled a giggle.

He set the second crate beside the first one and picked up the clipboard he'd placed on top. Scowling, he pulled a pen from his pocket and scrawled on the paper.

"How's traffic today?" I asked.

"Terrible!" he responded.

"In Aerieville?" Deena looked surprised. She'd lived in Chicago before moving back home.

"Crazy drivers!" spat Bart. "They're the worst on the county roads. Either too slow or too fast. One van was so erratic, it clipped me as it passed. Drove me right off the road."

This was probably the biggest speech I'd ever heard Bart make. I was so stunned it took me a second to realize what he was saying. "Wait—you were in an accident? On your way here? Are you okay?"

He looked over at me and nodded. "I spun out but managed to keep from going in the ditch. Truck is dented but still drives. I only wish I'd got the van's plate number."

"That's terrible!" said Deena.

"Aren't you shaken?" I asked. "I'd be shaken."

Bart shrugged. "I was madder than anything. I tried to chase him down, but never caught up with 'em. They must've pulled off somewhere."

"Would you like to sit down, have a glass of water?"

Bart hesitated. "I'm waiting on my boss to call me back, so . . . okay. Do you have any iced tea?"

"I'll make some! You can have a seat in our new café. Follow me."

I led Bart up the hall to the café room and pulled out a ladder-back chair for him near the front window. "Would you like to try one of our herbal specials? We have chamomile-honey, peppermint-chocolate, and rose hips and lemon. Oh! A lavender-chamomile blend would be nice for soothing your nerves."

He narrowed his eyebrows, clearly not impressed.

"We have plain black, too," I said.

"I'll take plain black. Iced."

"Yes, sir." I started to salute him, then felt silly and dropped my hand. "Coming right up."

Deena was opening the crates when I reentered the kitchen. She'd already turned on the kettle for me.

"Thanks!" I said, as I checked to make sure we had plenty of ice. "I'm so nervous, for some reason. This is like having our first customer. Or a practice customer, anyway. Do we have any pansy cookies left?"

"A few." She pointed to a container on the counter. "I plan to make more at home tomorrow."

I prepared the tea, using the quick-chill method, with less water and lots of ice. Then I sweetened it up and placed it on a serving tray with a small plate of shortbread cookies with pansy blossoms pressed on top.

Bart was scowling at his phone again. He barely looked up when I set the plate and glass in front of him. At least he mumbled "Thanks."

Oh, well. I try not to let the bad moods of others affect me too much. If I'd learned anything from all my self-help books, it was the importance of watching where you place your attention. If you don't want to feel bad, then don't dwell on things that make you feel bad—unless, of course, it motivates you to make a change.

I wandered to the kitchenette on the far end of the café room and gave it a once-over. Seeing that we hadn't filled the napkin dispensers yet, I proceeded to do that. A few minutes later, Deena came in to let me know she'd finished unpacking the crates and was ready to head out.

"Thank you *so* much for all your help," I said. "I couldn't do any of this without you."

"Well, you are paying me, so it's kind of my job." She smiled. "And I'm having so much fun. Who would've thought?"

Calvin popped his head into the café, glanced at Bart, and gave me a questioning look. I beckoned him over with one finger. He joined me at the café bar, as Deena said goodbye. "I'll call you later," she said.

"Say 'hi' to your folks for me!" I answered.

Calvin leaned an elbow on the counter and spoke in a low voice. "I was wondering why the delivery truck is still here. What's going on?"

"He's waiting to hear from his boss," I whispered. "He—"

"Hey, Sierra," called Deena, cutting me off. She stood in the arched entryway to the café but was looking out the front window. "I think we're about to get a bunch of customers. Maybe I should stick around."

"Really?" I scooched around the bar and ran over to the window. Sure enough, a large white passenger van had parked in front of the shop, and at least half a dozen people had emerged. "Awesome!"

Calvin walked over to see for himself. "Are you sure they're coming here?" he asked.

"Of course they are!" I said brightly. "Why else would they park right in front?" I grabbed his arm and looked over at Deena. "Guys, you know what this means, don't you? It means my window vision board is working!"

Deena laughed. "Don't get too excited yet. They might not even buy anything."

I peered out the window again, wondering why it was taking them so long to come inside. They seemed to be milling about in the street and on the sidewalk. Some were stretching their arms and bouncing on their heels. One guy, in a wrinkled T-shirt and cut-off jean shorts, had lit a cigarette. I gathered they'd been on the road for a while.

"Looks like college students," Deena commented. "Must be some kind of field trip."

"I think you're right," I said. "Some of them are holding notebooks. That older guy must be the professor or chaperone." The older man, a lanky fellow with thinning silver hair, wire glasses, and a white goatee, slung a canteen over his shoulder and checked his watch.

"So, do you want me to stay?" Deena asked again.

"Nah. Cal and I can handle this. *If* they ever come in."

"Good luck," Deena said lightly, before heading toward the back.

I noticed Calvin had fallen silent. He continued to gaze out the window, only now he had a look of consternation. Before I could ask what was wrong, another car pulled up behind the school van. It was Wanda, back for Granny—who hadn't returned yet herself.

"What is *he* doing here?" Calvin muttered.

"He?"

Calvin nodded toward the older man. "I know him. It's Professor Lowry, from UT."

At that, Bart suddenly looked up from his phone. "Did you say UT? A UT van?" He scraped back his chair and stood up to look out the window. "That's him! That's the van that ran me off the road."

"Are you sure?" I asked.

Calvin straightened abruptly. "You know what? I don't want to talk to him. I'll be upstairs for a while."

Startled, I followed Calvin out of the café room and watched as he headed to the door at the end of the hall. It opened to stairs leading up to his apartment. Gus scurried out of the office where he'd been napping and slipped around Calvin's heels. The door shut behind them, leaving me to scratch my head in confusion.

Then I heard the jingle of the front door and whirled around. Bart was stalking outside. I ran to the doorway, as he stomped down the sidewalk with his fists clenched. He headed straight for the professor—who appeared to be talking to Wanda. Or was she yelling at him?

Why is Wanda *so upset with Professor Lowry?* I

couldn't make out her words, but her shrill tone was un-mistakable. She was really letting him have it.

He didn't seem to be fazed. If anything, he seemed slightly bewildered, and then mildly irritated. Mostly, he seemed to be distracted. He said something, then gave her a dismissive wave, as if swatting a fly. *Uh-oh*. Wanda wasn't going to like that. Sure enough, as soon as he turned away, she raised her handbag and swung back her arm.

A roar from Bart stopped her cold. It stopped Lowry too.

"You!" yelled Bart, so loudly I could hear him from across the front lawn. "You almost killed me! And these kids were your passengers? You might have killed them too!"

At first, Lowry seemed annoyed again. Maybe even bored? He pinched his forehead before glancing down the empty street. Then, in an instant, he seemed to come to some sort of decision. It was fascinating to watch. He changed his stance, hung his head, and pressed his hands together. Just like that, he'd gone from aloof to apologetic.

Bart continued to glare at him. Apparently, he had no interest in dropping the angry-bear posture. Now Wanda joined in, shaking her fist once again.

One of the students, the guy with the cigarette, called to the professor. He bowed to Bart and Wanda and backed away. After a quick word to the group, he strode up the brick walkway to Flower House.

Quickly, I tucked my hair behind my ears and stood a little taller. "Afternoon!" I chirped.

He offered a tight smile in return. "Hello. I wonder if I might use your restroom?"

My restroom? It was on the tip of my tongue to say, "Of course! Come on in!" Darn my good nature. I really couldn't help myself. But not this time. I needed to start thinking like a businesswoman. "Uh, the restroom is reserved for customers and employees."

"Hmm? Oh, sorry. Allow me to introduce myself. I'm Steve Lowry, Professor of Botany at the University of Tennessee, Knoxville. I'm here with the summer field program."

"That's nice." It didn't really explain anything, but it was nice.

He gestured toward the students still milling about behind him. "Well, half the program, anyway. The other van seems to have fallen behind. We're meeting them here."

"Here? At Flower House?"

He sighed impatiently. "Is Felix here? He's expecting us."

Felix. Of course. He'd done it to me again.

"I left him a voice message," he continued. "We stop by every July, on our way to the Great Smoky Mountains National Park." At my confused expression, he rolled his eyes. "Yes, it's out of the way, but we're here to see the orchid collection. Felix knows."

"I'm sorry. Felix retired recently, and he didn't tell me . . . never mind. I'm Sierra, the new owner. And I'm happy to have you view our orchids—and anything else you'd like. We grow our own hothouse roses, too."

"Wonderful," he said shortly. "Now, might I use your restroom?"

"Of course! Your students are welcome to come in too, and look around. Maybe they'd like to buy a souvenir or two?"

He turned and beckoned to the nearest student, a petite girl with long curly blonde hair. On his signal, she rounded up the others. Without another word, he brushed past me and headed toward the hall bathroom.

I stood back as the students filed in. "Hi there! Welcome to Flower House!"

There were seven of them in all, four guys and three girls. Chatting among themselves, they barely acknowledged me as they fanned out, filling all four corners of the shop.

I tried to direct their attention. "We have a gifts table over here. You'll find postcards, greeting cards, mugs. Lots of little things . . ." I trailed off. It was no use. I could barely keep track of them all, as they moved around, smelling flowers, flipping through books, picking things up and putting them down in the wrong places.

Two girls in particular were starting to worry me. They'd come in with large backpacks swung carelessly over one shoulder, and they didn't seem to be aware of how much space they took up. Another guy, evidently the class clown, kept cracking jokes. His voice grew louder and louder—which seemed to give the others permission to turn up their own volume.

That is, except for the blonde, curly-haired girl. She had eyes only for the guy in the denim cutoffs, who'd been smoking. He had thick, tousled dark hair and a lazy, too-cool-for-school attitude that reminded me of a 1950s biker—or a bad-boy of any era, really. A rebel without a cause. She stared at him with an intensity I couldn't help noticing. He, on the other hand, was oblivious to her. He sauntered up to another boy, a preppy-looking Black kid with short hair and a cute, dimpled face. The rebel lifted his chin in greeting to the preppy. In return, Mr. Preppy glanced over at Blondie, before turning his back to both of them.

Suddenly, the class clown called out from the café room. "Whoa! There's a restaurant in here!"

"No way!" said his buddy. "There's food? Where? I'm starving."

"You're always starving," answered one of the backpack girls.

I hurried over to the archway. "Sorry, everybody! The café isn't open."

"Then why does *he* have a drink?" said the hungry guy, with a note of accusation. He was pointing at Bart, who was once again staring morosely at his phone.

He must have slipped in behind the others, when I wasn't looking. *I wonder where Wanda got off to?* Without looking away from his phone, Bart slurped his iced tea, then ate a cookie in one bite.

"Can't we at least order drinks?" a girl whined from behind me.

"Uh, we're not really set up," I began. The sound of shattering glass pulled my attention from the café. I ran into the front room and found one of the backpack girls staring down at a broken ceramic vase on the tile floor.

"Oops," she said, with a giggle. "That just totally, like, fell off the table. I swear I didn't touch it."

"Careful!" I said, rushing forward to pick up the largest piece. As I did, I managed to slice my finger. I gasped from the sudden sting. *Dang it!* A tiny drop of crimson blood appeared on the side of my middle finger.

Just then, an excited barking filled the room.

Oh, jeez. "Everybody, stay away from the glass! I need to get a broom." And a bandage. And some backup.

Gus ran up to me and jumped on my legs.

"Aw, cute puppy!" said one of the girls.

Another voice yelled at me from the café. "Hey, can we get some service in here? I want to order an iced mocha latte."

Ignoring them all, I hurried down the hallway toward the kitchen. Halfway there, I bumped into Calvin. He was carrying a dog leash.

"Hey, sorry," he said. "I was gonna take Gus out, and he got away from me."

I held my injured hand in the air. "Hang on a minute," I said, dashing into the kitchen. I ripped a paper towel from the roll on the counter and quickly wadded it around my cut finger. Then I grabbed a broom and dustpan.

Back in the hall, I found that Calvin had leashed Gus and was now standing by the open door of the room that housed our orchid collection. Looking past him, I saw two students standing close together, engaged in a lively whispered conversation. It was Blondie and the cute preppy boy. Only, on second glance, it appeared the boy wasn't quite as engaged as the girl. She grabbed onto his polo shirt, and he only shook his head impassively. She let go, and he turned toward the orchids, pulling a small notebook and pencil from his pocket. She wrinkled her nose at him before turning to leave.

A clatter rang from the front of the shop, followed by a bellowed expletive and laughter.

"Ugh," I growled. "This is madness."

"What can I do?" asked Calvin.

"Just take Gus out of here. I'll deal with these hooligans."

I hurried to the front and almost tripped when a backpack girl stepped in front of me without looking.

"Sorry!" she said, twirling a single-stem pink rose.

"It's okay." I waved my paper-towel-wrapped hand toward the checkout counter. "Wait for me by the cash register, and I'll ring you up for the flower in just a minute."

"Is there a vending machine?" came another voice from the café.

For a split second, I stood rooted to the floor. I couldn't decide which direction to go. I needed to clean up the broken glass, check out the customers who were waiting for me, and eject everyone from the café.

From the corner of my eye, I saw the bathroom door opening. *Finally!* Professor Lowry needed to take control of his wild bunch.

Except, to my dismay, it wasn't the professor who emerged from the bathroom. It was the too-cool rebel guy . . . followed by Blondie. *She moves fast*, I thought.

I had no time to dwell on it. Another racket drew my attention to the café. When I got there, I saw that Bart was now gone—and the two rowdy guys were leaning over the bakery counter, as if they might find something to eat. Besides canisters of salt, sugar, and candied flowers, we stored tins of dried petals and seeds, as well as cinnamon, cloves, and other spices back here. There was nothing I could sell them.

"Hey!" I rapped the broom handle on the floor for attention. "I told you the café was closed!"

Looking slightly sheepish, they backed away from the counter.

"Sorry," muttered one.

"We're just really hungry," said the other.

"Listen, there's a bakery right next door. They have coffee and tea and all kinds of treats. Why don't you go over there?"

Looking at each other, they nodded as one.

"Yeah, sweet."

"Let's do it."

The loud clown led the way, calling out to the room

as he headed to the front door. "Food's next door! Who's with me?"

Several of the students followed him, including the girl with the pink rose. I let her go. I didn't have the energy to make a fuss. Instead, I righted a tipped-over tin bucket and swept up the broken glass, grateful for the momentary peace and quiet.

That finished, I finally found a Band-Aid behind the checkout counter and bandaged my finger. Then, I began straightening the shelves and putting things back in their proper places. Just as my breath had returned to a normal rate, I heard the click of Gus's nails as he skittered up the hallway.

"Hey, buddy," I said. "Where's Calvin?"

When there were customers in the store, we usually liked to keep Gus in the office or up in Calvin's apartment. At this point, I wasn't sure who, if anyone, was left in the shop. I didn't think all the students had left for the bakery, and I hadn't seen Professor Lowry since he first came in. I assumed they were either in the orchid room, or else had gone outside to view the greenhouse. Maybe Calvin had decided to talk to the professor after all.

Now that I could once again hear myself think, I felt bad about how I'd handled the unruly students. Or, rather, *failed* to handle them. *I should have roped off the café. I should have required the students to check their bags or else leave them in their van. I should've been more assertive.*

Granted, their behavior, on the whole, was appalling.

The front door jingled open and Granny bustled inside. "I'm finally back!" she announced. "Land sakes, can your mama talk. I didn't think I was ever going to get her to stop gabbing and bring me back. Where's Wanda?"

"I'm not sure. Maybe in back looking at the garden."

We headed down the hall toward the kitchen and the back door. We met Calvin coming down from his apartment.

"Hiding again?" I teased.

"Gus and I just got back from our walk. I ran upstairs to get his treat ball." He held up the toy as evidence. "Where *is* the little guy? In the office?"

"He was just here," I said looking around.

Calvin gave the toy a shake. "Gus!" he called.

The corgi barked in reply from somewhere within Flower House. "At least he didn't sneak outside," I said with relief.

He barked again, in short high-pitched yelps. Something about it sounded different.

"Where is he?" I asked.

"Did he get himself shut in the bathroom?" said Granny. She went to check. "Not here!" she hollered. "But the window is open again. I'll close it."

Meanwhile, Calvin and I followed the sound of Gus's barking to the small storeroom off the kitchen. The door was ajar and, sure enough, Gus was inside.

"Augustus! What are you doing in there?" I said.

Instead of running up to us as he usually did, Gus remained sitting on the floor next to some boxes and crates. He looked up at us, then looked at a spot behind the boxes and whimpered.

"What's the matter, buddy?" said Calvin.

"Why is he acting so strange?" I said quietly. Something was definitely off.

Calvin and I stepped inside together and approached the small dog. Once we reached him, we could see the area that had his attention behind the boxes.

"Oh, my God!" I grabbed onto Calvin, as I felt my knees begin to buckle.

"Jeez!" Calvin quickly placed a supportive hand under my arm, as he cursed under his breath. But he wasn't cursing because of me. It was the sight of the body on the floor.

It was the professor, crumpled in a heap. A puddle of blood oozed from a gash on the back of his head. And his glassy eyes stared straight ahead, seeing nothing.

Chapter 3

If I thought things were chaotic before finding Professor Lowry's body, what happened next took chaos to a whole new level. Police swarming, neighbors gawking, students crying and screaming . . . it was all too awful. And overwhelming. Flower House overflowed with people coming and going. Every room of the shop, every inch of the grounds outside, even the street and sidewalks up and down the block—they were all fairly crawling with people.

I realized later that the moments right before and after the grisly discovery were the calm before the storm. I'd stared at the body for a moment, disbelieving. There was something off about the man's appearance, and not just the fact that he was dead. I couldn't put my finger on it, but I wasn't about to stand there and study him. As soon as Calvin and I had ascertained that the professor was beyond help, we'd grabbed Gus and backed out of the storeroom. Then immediately, instinctually, we turned to each other and embraced in a tight hug.

At least one of us was trembling; I couldn't have said which. As for me, I felt a tightness in my chest, like a dam barely holding back a surging wave of panic. *How did this happen? Could it have been an accident? Something heavy fell . . . or the professor fell . . . or—why was he in the storeroom in the first place?* Disconnected thoughts flashed through my mind, but one thing was clear. Someone must have whacked the professor on the back of the head.

Not again. How can this be happening again? Only three months earlier, another man had suffered a violent death in this shop. I'd worked so hard to bury that terrible chapter and get folks to associate Flower House with a more positive image. *So much for our grand opening.*

The instant that selfish thought cropped up, I felt a kick of remorse. A man was *dead*, for crying out loud!

The hug with Calvin lasted only a few seconds. In that time, I became aware of two things: One, it felt *really* good to be this close to Calvin. And two, he was whispering something in my ear. As I focused in on what he was saying, I became increasingly alarmed.

"I'd *just* seen him. I *hated* him. He didn't deserve this. Or maybe he did. I should have talked to him. I might have prevented this. I'd *just* seen him."

Gently, I pulled back and searched Calvin's face. Was he okay? As if waking from a dream, he looked into my eyes, then seemed to focus in on my expression of concern. Clearing his throat, he dropped his arms.

"Are you—are you okay?" he asked, echoing my thoughts about him.

I nodded and took a deep breath. "More or less," I answered hoarsely.

"Land sakes!" cried Granny. "I knew it! Didn't I say that bird was an omen?"

I looked over to see Granny appear in the doorway of

the storeroom. She must have slipped past us while we were hugging.

"It's a good thing I made you all put red clay 'n' salt in your shoes," she said, before turning back to the store-room. "Come here, Gus!"

Evidently, Gus had snuck past us too. At Granny's urging, he came out of the storeroom and crawled under a chair. *I feel ya, Gus.* I wished I could hide under a chair too.

"Well," said Granny, shutting the door to the store-room, "I don't know who he is, but he ain't gonna get any deader. Where's a phone?"

"Oh, Granny." I felt tears spring to my eyes and swal-lowed the lump in my throat.

She came over and patted my shoulder, then picked up the cell phone I'd left on the counter. As I watched, she dialed 9-1-1. Then she pushed open the door from the kitchen to the hallway and left the room, calmly report-ing that there was a dead man at Flower House.

"I need some air," I said, moving to open the back door.

"Me too," said Calvin.

He grabbed a leash from the hook by the door and leaned down to coax Gus from under the chair.

"Come here, buddy," he said. And then, "What's in your mouth?"

I turned swiftly to see Calvin pry open Gus's jaws. "What is it?" I asked. We were careful not to let Gus in the workroom while we prepared flower arrangements, in case we dropped any clippings on the floor. The room was clean now, but it was always possible the pup could have found a stray leaf or petal.

"It's a piece of paper," said Calvin. "Or part of one anyway." He handed me a wet, half-eaten wad of paper.

Wrinkling my nose, I set the thing on the worktable and dabbed it with a paper towel. Calvin leaned over my shoulder. "Looks like a receipt," he said. "From 'something Mini-Mart.'"

"Must be Marla's Mini-Mart," I said. "That's the gas station on the west side of town. The date and time are gone, but this seems to be a receipt for sunflower seeds. The price was ninety-nine cents."

"Huh," said Calvin. "That's not something you or Deena would've bought, is it?"

"No. We still have a bunch of the sunflower seeds Granny brought us from last fall's harvest. Plus, that gas station isn't very convenient, unless you're on your way in or out of town."

Granny came back into the kitchen and handed me my phone. "Where's Wanda?" she asked.

"I don't know. I haven't seen her in a while." I briefly explained to Granny about the appearance of the university van and all the hubbub that followed.

"Good grief," she said.

Calvin helped himself to some water from the refrigerator. I noticed him mop his forehead with his shirt sleeve.

"Let's step outside," I said, picking up Gus's leash from where Calvin had dropped it on a chair.

"I'll wait on the front porch," said Granny.

I called to Gus and was surprised to find him once again playing with something in his mouth. "Now what?" Then I glanced at the worktable. The receipt was gone.

"Gus! What did you do?" I reached into his mouth and pulled out what was left of the receipt: a tiny corner with no writing. "Ugh. So much for that."

"Gus, you little scamp," said Calvin. "I guess the paper fell off the table, huh?"

"It must have. Probably when Granny swung open the hall door." I wiped my hands on a towel, while Calvin took the leash and clipped it to Gus's collar. They headed out the back door, with me close behind. I wanted to look around for a minute before joining Granny.

Cicadas were rattling in the trees, informing us how late it was getting. To my surprise, the green delivery truck was still parked in the driveway. Walking partway up to it, I saw Bart sitting behind the wheel and—what else—staring at his phone. Through the half-opened window, I heard strains of a sad old country tune.

Gus pulled Calvin in the other direction, toward the garden. I went with them and spotted three students lounging over by the greenhouse. The one I'd nicknamed the rebel was smoking another cigarette and staring absently into the distance, as he paced back and forth. The curly haired blonde sat on the ground scrolling through her phone, while the cute preppy boy leaned against the greenhouse wall with his eyes closed.

"Should we tell them?" I said softly.

"We should probably wait for the police," said Calvin.

We continued around the side of the house, letting Gus sniff the bushes along the way. I thought again about the receipt the corgi had eaten. Where had he found it? Of course, anyone could have tracked it in on the bottom of a shoe or dropped it from a pocket. But wouldn't I have noticed a piece of litter on the floor? Besides that, Gus had it right after Granny shooed him from the storeroom.

I grabbed Calvin's arm. "Hey," I whispered. "Do you think Professor Lowry dropped that receipt Gus found?"

Calvin slowly shook his head. "No way. He'd never eat sunflower seeds, not from a shell. He was too fastidious."

It struck me that Calvin must have known the professor

pretty well. I'd have to ask him about that later. "Then the killer dropped it?"

He looked doubtful. "Maybe?"

Shrugging, I walked on. I knew it was a stretch. So what if the killer had dropped the receipt? How would that help identify them? Even if the mini-mart purchase could be traced to a single person—a difficult proposition, considering we never saw a date or time, and the receipt was now gone—it was hardly a smoking gun. The killer could have ended up with the receipt in any number of ways.

Before I could speculate further, I spied Wanda ambling up the sidewalk. She had an odd expression on her face, as if she were upset or confused.

Calvin and I met her on the sidewalk.

"Where have you been, Wanda?" I asked.

She peered sharply at me. For a split second, I had the impression she didn't know who I was. Then her face cleared, and she waved vaguely in the direction behind her. "I went for a walk. I always forget what a pretty little spot Melody Gardens is." Dipping her chin, she gave me a knowing look, then winked at Calvin. "Perfect place for a lovers' whatchamacallit. A dusky-dark tryst?"

I glanced at Calvin to gauge his reaction. Under other circumstances, we might have laughed at Wanda's suggestion that we were a couple. He quirked his mouth in a sad half smile. Of course, it didn't matter. There would be no trysts tonight.

The sound of sirens pierced through the evening air.

"Something has happened, Wanda," I said. "Something bad."

I had to tell my story multiple times before the evening was out. The first telling, to the responding police officers, was a haphazard rush, as if I could speed the end of this nightmare by pelleting them with everything I knew in one fell swoop. The second time was in a slower, more methodical manner to Acting Chief of Police Renee Bradley.

I'd met Officer Bradley during the last investigation that took place at Flower House. She was a competent, middle-aged policewoman, with short blonde hair and a pleasant demeanor. In fact, I'd found her easier to get along with than Police Chief Walt Walden. She'd been promoted to Deputy Chief and was filling in for him now, since he was still on medical leave. I was glad to learn he would make a full recovery following an incident last spring (especially since he was a friend of my dad's), but I was secretly happy Officer Bradley was now in charge. She was way less intimidating than Walt Walden. She was thorough, too. She had me write down my entire statement, and then carefully went over it with me to ensure I'd left nothing out.

We were sitting in the café room, just me, Acting Chief Bradley, and a second officer. Another pair of officers was interviewing the students, one at a time, over at Bread n' Butter. Outside, a beat cop (a dark-haired officer named Davy Wills, who I recognized as a former classmate of Rocky's) watched over everyone else as they waited their turn. They were directed not to talk to one another. Evidently, the police wanted to hear each person's firsthand observations before they could be influenced by what other folks said.

Before I was called in, I'd held onto Gus on the front stoop. I couldn't stay inside, because the place was overrun with investigators and forensics experts taking photos and gathering evidence. Granny got to go first, because she'd made the 9-1-1 call—and also because she insisted.

As I waited, I tried to make sense of what had happened. All I could think of was how disliked the professor had seemed to be. I felt kind of guilty about the uncharitable thought, but it was true. Bart and Wanda had both yelled at him. None of his students had interacted with him, as far as I could tell. Calvin clearly didn't like him.

Calvin was called into the café after Granny. I was surprised at how long his interview took. When he came out to get Gus, he seemed rather pale and a little dazed. After my turn in the "interrogation café," I thought I knew why. Deputy Chief Bradley asked me more questions about Calvin than about Professor Lowry and his students.

"How well do you know Calvin Foxheart?" she asked.

"Calvin?" I said, startled at the question. "I see him almost every day. He takes care of the greenhouse and helps out around the shop. He also rents the apartment upstairs and helps look after Gus. He's a nice guy."

I realized I hadn't answered her question, and for some reason I felt my face grow warm. Wasn't it just this morning that I, myself, was questioning how well I knew Calvin?

"He's new in town, isn't he?" said Bradley. "At least, he was new last time I was here, in April."

If she already knew the answer, why did she ask the question? What was she getting at?

She continued as if we were having a friendly conversation. "He told me he was a teacher at UT in Knoxville. Do you know why he left that job?"

"He'd met Felix online, and they struck up a friendship," I said. "I think Felix sold him on Aerieville and offered him the apartment. They shared a love of plants." Well, plants and geocaching, and an interest in the Arwin Treasure. But I still didn't see the relevance of any of this.

"Did Calvin ever mention anything about Professor Steve Lowry?"

I shook my head. "Not before today. Why?"

"He never said anything about a professor at UT stealing his research and having him fired?"

Now I could only stare, stunned by the news.

"He was quite candid about it just now," Officer Bradley said calmly. "He admitted he still harbored a lot of resentment toward the professor."

"I had no idea."

"When was the last time you saw Calvin today, before the two of you found the professor's body?"

"Um, I don't know. Let me think. He went upstairs before the professor came in. Then he came down to take Gus out, and I saw him in the hallway. That was probably twenty minutes or so before I saw him in the hallway again, right before we heard Gus barking from the storeroom."

"Did you actually see Calvin take the dog outside?"

I crinkled my eyes, not at all liking the direction of this conversation. "No. I went back to the front of the shop, and he took Gus out the back door. I assume. I mean, I believe he did."

There was a knock on the side of the archway between the café and the shop floor. It was Officer Dakin, a young ginger-haired cop I recognized from the last investigation. He held up a large clear plastic evidence bag.

"What ya got?" asked Officer Bradley.

"Thought you'd want to see this," Dakin said, approaching the table. "We found it in the garbage bin in the kitchen." *The garbage bin in the kitchen? He must mean the large plastic can we use to collect flower trimmings and other plant debris. What did they find in there?*

Bradley took the bag and set it on the table between us. She tilted it to give me a better view. "Have you seen this before?"

It was an ornate silver candlestick. There was another one just like it on a shelf in the orchid room. Only this one seemed to have a dark substance caked on the sconce end of the candle holder.

A wave of nausea washed over me. Swallowing hard, I sat back in my chair. It was the murder weapon. If this situation had seemed unreal before, it suddenly felt a whole lot realer.

I found Granny talking to the coroner in the driveway behind Flower House. It sounded like she was instructing him on how the body should be removed from the house—no doubt due to one of her superstitions. As I walked up to them, she shifted her attention to me, and the coroner made his escape.

"Soon as the police finish talking to Wanda, I'm gonna get her home," said Granny. "She's had a rough time of it today."

I nodded sympathetically. "When she got here earlier, she had some words with the professor out in the street. She was upset with him for some reason. Did she tell you why?"

"I haven't been allowed to talk to her yet," said Granny. "I'll find out later, I'm sure."

It was on the tip my tongue to say something about Wanda's habit of hitting men upside the head, but I thought better of it. This was no laughing matter. Besides, Granny might think it rude of me to even hint at the suggestion that Wanda might have killed the professor. There was no way little old Wanda Milford could have clobbered the tall professor hard enough to knock him out, let alone deliver a death blow. The idea was preposterous.

Wasn't it?

"Now listen," said Granny. "You better call your mama before she hears about all this nasty business through the rumor mill."

I winced. She was right. Heck, the way news traveled in this town, there was a good bet my mom had already heard and was even now on her way to Flower House.

"I don't suppose you want to call her," I ventured.

Granny laughed softly. "No, thanks. I've had quite enough of Mandy's loving concern for one day."

Officer Dakin came out the back door and walked up to Bart's truck. With all the commotion, I hadn't had a chance to speak to the delivery man. I'd been vaguely aware that he'd climbed out of the cab of his truck when the police first arrived. After being informed about what had happened, he was then allowed to wait in his vehicle until it was time for him to make his statement. Now, as he followed Dakin into the house, Bart looked over at me. His expression was inscrutable, but his eyes stayed locked on me for several seconds. Something about his penetrating gaze made goose bumps prickle along my arms.

"They must be done with Wanda," said Granny.

"Huh?" I said, turning to Granny. "Oh, right." I shook off the odd feeling and walked with Granny around to the front of the house.

Wanda seemed subdued when she emerged through the front door. Her new hairdo had fallen, and her lipstick was smeared. She was a far cry from her usual fiery self.

"Come on, Mae," she grumbled to Granny. "It's suppertime, and my dogs are tired."

I hugged Granny goodbye and stood on the sidewalk

as they drove away. No sooner had they left, when another vehicle rolled slowly down the street and pulled into the space they'd just vacated. It was a UT van, just like the one still parked in front of Flower House. Through the van windows, I saw half a dozen shell-shocked college kids. They must've heard the news from the other students, I surmised.

The driver's side door opened, and a woman stepped out into the street. She was dressed for hiking, in tan cargo pants, a tank top, and boots. From what I could tell, she seemed to be a fit and trim thirty-something Black woman, with chic ultra-short hair. Her expression was somber and worried. For a moment, she stood in the road, looking from Flower House to Bread n' Butter, apparently not knowing where to go. I started to approach her. At the same time, a cop stepped out of a patrol car across the street and waved at her.

"Sheila Washington?"

"Yes." Her voice was tight, as if it was all she could do to keep it together. My heart went out to her.

He joined her a few steps from the van. I stayed on the sidewalk, unsure what to do.

The cop placed a palm on his chest. "I'm Officer Wills. My condolences, ma'am."

She hugged her arms in a protective gesture. "What happened?" she asked bluntly. "Someone attacked Steve in the flower shop?"

"That's what we're trying to determine, ma'am. This is an open homicide investigation. We're still putting the pieces together."

"Unbelievable," she murmured. The crease between her eyebrows deepened as the news sank in.

"The deceased, Mr. Lowry, was your friend?"

Unless I was mistaken, she seemed to hesitate before

answering. "He was my colleague. We're—we *were* co-teaching a summer botany field course."

"Can you help us locate his next of kin?"

"I can give you the name of our department head. Steve wasn't married, and I'm not aware of any close family he had." She glanced over at Bread n' Butter. "Where are the students from his group? Are they free to leave?"

"Some of them are."

"What do you mean?"

"We've been able to clear four of the students. They were at the bakery at the time of death."

Tilting her head, she gave him a curious look. "How can you pinpoint the time of death without an autopsy?"

Quietly, I took half a step closer and leaned in. I was curious about that too.

"There's a short window," said the officer, "between the last time the deceased was seen or heard alive and the time his body was found."

Oh. Of course.

"Heard?" said Sheila.

"On the phone," explained Officer Wills. "The individuals at the bakery told the owner, Flo Morrison, that their teacher would pay for everything." He chuckled softly. "I guess she didn't want to take their word for it. One of the girls called Mr. Lowry and spoke to him, before handing her cell phone to Flo. Flo confirmed that Lowry said he'd be right over. And we verified the call was received on Lowry's cell phone."

She nodded. "I see. And the other three students?"

He pulled a notebook from his pocket and flipped it open. "Yes. April, Vince, and Isaiah," he read, then looked up. "They were still at the flower shop."

Her frown held a shade of impatience. "Who else was there? Surely you don't think one of the students did this."

I took another step forward. What *did* the police think?

Officer Wills was noncommittal. "We're speaking with a number of individuals, and working as hard as we can to get to the bottom of this. In the meantime, we'd like those three students to stick around town. I can give you directions to the local motel."

Closing her eyes, she sighed in resignation. "Guess that means I'll be staying too. I'll let my grad assistant drive the others back to Knoxville now, if that's okay."

"Yes, ma'am—in just a minute. I need to gather the names and contact info for everyone on the field trip. Also, do you or your assistant know a former teacher named Calvin Foxheart?"

I must've made a noise, because Sheila and Officer Wills turned sharply toward me. Without realizing it, I'd inched right up next to them. I smiled sheepishly.

"Hello," I said, thinking fast. "Sorry to interrupt. I, uh, just wanted to mention that there's a nice bed and breakfast not far from here. Much nicer than the motel. It's run by a friend of mine."

A B&B would certainly be nicer for Sheila and the students. This particular one would also be more convenient—for *me* to keep tabs on this investigation.

Chapter 4

It was dark by the time everyone finally left Flower House. I'd missed dinner, but I still didn't have an appetite. Sitting in the shop's office, a small study with an unused fireplace and floor-to-ceiling shelves filled with Felix's books and fishing paraphernalia, I forced myself to eat a granola bar. If anything, it should at least ward off lightheadedness. I'd just gotten off the phone with my mom—a taxing conversation, considering I had no answers for most of her questions. I didn't know the professor's backstory or why he was in the storeroom. And I had no idea what all this meant for the shop . . . or for me personally. I didn't even know what I should do next. I was thinking about knocking on Calvin's door, when I heard Gus skittering down the hall. That noise was followed by Calvin's much slower footsteps.

"In here!" I called, swiveling in the desk chair.

Gus ran in and jumped on my legs. I scratched the top of his head and looked up as Calvin appeared in the doorway. His face was drawn, and his hair was mussed, as if he'd been repeatedly running his fingers through it.

"Hey," he said simply.

"Hey," I returned.

"I fed Gus," he said.

"Thank you."

For a moment, Calvin studied the floor, not saying a word. It was so quiet, I could hear the clock ticking on the mantel. Two lamps gave the room a cozy, orange glow.

"Why don't you sit down?" I said, nodding toward an upholstered chair in the corner.

He complied, sitting heavily in the chair, and dropped his head into his hands. "This is a nightmare," he mumbled.

"It's bizarre, is what it is," I said. "I mean, this guy shows up out of nowhere with a van full of college kids—and acting sort of entitled and snobby, if you ask me. He apparently manages to offend everyone he meets, disappears into the bathroom for an inordinate amount of time, and then . . . somebody clobbers him over the head. And suddenly he's dead!" I laughed humorlessly. "I mean, *what* in the heck just happened here?"

Calvin looked up and gave me the faintest of smiles. "Sounds typical for Lowry. Except for the dying part."

"You mentioned you'd just seen him before . . . well, before we found him. Did you mean outside, when he arrived?"

"No, after that, too. Before I took Gus for a walk, I saw him in the orchid room talking to some students."

"What were they talking about? Did you tell Bradley?"

"Yeah, I told her, but I don't know what they were talking about. They were on the far side of the room, and I didn't go in. I didn't want to talk to him."

I waited for Calvin to go on. As far as I was concerned, he had a lot of explaining to do. Right after we'd found the professor's body, Calvin had said he'd *hated* the man.

Those were strong words. And Officer Bradley told me Lowry had stolen something of Calvin's and cost him his job. There was no denying that the cops were very interested in Calvin's relationship with the dead man.

Was I really going to have to pry it out of him?

"Calvin," I began. "If you tell me everything, I might be able to help."

He met my eyes for an instant before looking away again. "I wanted to keep my past in the past. I wanted to forget the whole dismal, humiliating affair."

"A humiliating past? Remind me to tell you about my stint in Nashville." I kept my voice light in an effort to put him at ease. "I gave my heart to a moody playwright, who turned out to be a liar and a cheat. I started out with high hopes and a promising music career—and ended up with an empty bank account, a broken leg, and a dream deferred. We all have pasts we'd rather forget."

He grinned in spite of himself. "I will definitely remind you to fill in the blanks there. You can count on it."

I smiled back at him. "So, Knoxville? The University of Tennessee?"

"Yeah." He sat back and gazed at the ceiling. "A few years ago, I was Professor Lowry's grad assistant. I looked up to him. He was basically a mentor to me, and we became friends. After I earned my master's degree, he got me hired as an adjunct in his department."

He paused, as if collecting his thoughts. I leaned down and nudged Gus, who had been lying on my feet. "Get Calvin!" I whispered.

The pup obediently hopped up and leaped onto Calvin's lap. Smiling briefly, Calvin ruffled Gus's fur.

"So, I was teaching a couple classes," he continued, "and, at the same time, working toward my doctorate. The university has state-of-the-art labs, a huge greenhouse, and several acres of land for Ag. Studies. Steve let me have free rein. I conducted experiments and developed a nice body of plant research. My aim was to find optimal growing conditions for the fastest growing edible plants—and, ultimately, you know, stamp out world hunger." His eyes sparkled. "It might have been a tad ambitious."

"I think it's amazing," I said, truly impressed. I'd known Calvin was smart, but I had no idea the extent of his talents. "So, what happened?" I asked, echoing the question of the day.

He shook his head. "Something happened with Lowry. I couldn't say exactly what or when, but he changed. I guess it was gradual."

"He stopped being your friend?"

"Yeah, but it wasn't obvious at first. He'd always been aloof and arrogant. Difficult. He was a strict teacher, but most students loved him anyway."

"It sounds like he was respected."

"Yeah. He had a reputation for brilliance—and for passing some of that brilliance along to a select group of students. There was an unofficial club, known as 'Lowry's Leaders.' He'd nurture and guide them, teach them how to think like him. Most importantly, he'd write letters of recommendation for them." Calvin paused, squinting his eyes at the memory. "I guess I was part of that group as an undergrad, but it turned into something else later. The new crop of students became his disciples."

I pictured the professor as he looked this afternoon, with his wire-rimmed glasses and white goatee. He'd seemed distracted and impatient, with a definite air of authority. This tracked with how Calvin described him.

"It must've been early last fall when he started flaking

on me," said Calvin. "He stopped returning my calls. We'd make plans to meet for lunch or coffee, and he'd fail to show up. At first, I took it personally, until I realized he was doing it to others. He even missed a class or two. I heard the department chair had to have a talk with him."

"Was there something going on in his personal life?"

"I have no idea. For all I thought I knew him, he was really a very private man. As the weeks went by, it seemed the only people he'd talk to outside of class were his inner circle of student followers."

"Lowry's Leaders," I said.

"More like Lowry's Lackeys. From what I could tell, it seemed like he was using the students as his personal assistants, making them run errands for him, do his chores."

I recalled the students on the field trip. At least half of them had seemed too self-absorbed to make very good assistants. "Did you recognize any of the people here today? Were they part of the professor's inner circle?"

"Yeah, I did see a couple of them. That guy we saw smoking outside. His name is Vince Gonzalez. And the bookish-looking guy in the orchid room, Isaiah Adams." *Ah, the rebel and the preppy.*

"What about the blonde girl?" I asked. "I saw her with both of those guys at different times."

"Oh, yeah. Her too. April Finley. I never had her in class, but I saw her hanging out in the science building with the others."

I thought about what Calvin had said. Was Professor Lowry using the kids? Could they have resented him for it? It seemed unlikely. If anything, it sounded like they had a mutually beneficial arrangement.

As Calvin talked, his voice had dropped in volume. I'd rolled my chair closer to his, so I could hear him better. By this time, our knees were nearly touching. It was such a cozy, intimate moment, with the soft light and quiet darkness beyond—and Gus snoozing peacefully in the chair beside Calvin. Almost without thinking, I reached out and rested the back of my hand on Calvin's knee.

"So, what happened with your research?" I asked gently.

"Hmm?" He was momentarily distracted, but quickly cleared his throat. "Oh, that. That's the shortest part of this story. I showed up at school one morning, all set to put the finishing touches on my research paper. Lowry was going to help me get it published. But the buzz on campus that day was all about an article Lowry had just published. I got a hold of a copy, and . . . yeah. It was mine. Word for word."

I winced in sympathy. "Didn't you have proof it was yours? I don't see how he could get away with that."

Calvin shook his head, continuing in a despondent tone. "He took everything and then some. Whenever I tried to tell anyone the truth, he managed to twist it around and make *me* look like the bad guy. Like I was jealous and trying to take credit for his work."

"Wow," I said. "That must've really hurt." I remembered the other professor, Sheila Washington, and asked if she might have known about Calvin's research.

"Unfortunately, no. She's fairly new to the school, and I never interacted with her much."

"That's too bad." I didn't know what else to say.

"I was pretty much done after that," Calvin continued. "Lowry recommended my classes be cut the following semester, and they were. He also said he could no longer be my faculty advisor. Just like that, I was out of a job and a career."

"I'm so sorry."

"It was a real blow," said Calvin. He rested his hand on mine, and I curled my fingers around his. I was touched he was opening up to me like this. I'd never felt closer to him.

Calvin sighed. "It was around this time Felix was telling me about Aerieville and Flower House. About how beautiful and friendly it is here. I needed a fresh start. So . . . here I am."

"I'm glad you're here," I said softly. "UT's loss is my gain—I mean, our gain. You do so much around here . . ." I trailed off, feeling self-conscious and hyper-aware of his touch.

His eyes fluttered to my face, lingering in my gaze, then dropping to my lips. My heart skipped ahead, as I imagined what it would feel like to kiss him. Our knees met, and, slowly, we leaned toward one other.

Our faces were inches apart, when Gus erupted in a deafening bark. We jumped back, as the dog jumped to the floor and flew out the door.

"Jeez, Gus!" said Calvin, bounding to his feet.

I held my hand to my heart, as I rolled my chair back and stood up, laughing nervously. "He's louder than a fire alarm!"

We followed Gus to the front of the shop. He'd stopped barking and was now emitting a low growl at the front door. Calvin looked out the window before opening the door, and we both peered outside. There was nothing to see.

"Must've been an animal," Calvin guessed.

"Yeah," I agreed. "Good boy, Gus. Way to protect us from cats and raccoons."

All was quiet again as Calvin closed the door. Part of me wanted to suggest we go back to the study and pick up where we left off, but the moment had passed. The spell was broken. It was time for Gus and me to go home.

It was after nine when I arrived home at my tiny cottage on the edge of town. My mom had nicknamed my place the "dollhouse" because of its gingerbread trim and overall cuteness. In fact, it was barely bigger than a child's playhouse, with one small bedroom, an eat-in kitchen, a living room, and a bathroom. The décor was simple, eclectic, and bright—kind of like me. And every free surface held a vase of slightly damaged, but still pretty, flowers I'd brought home from work.

I loved it. It was my haven and my hideaway. Only now, as I parked my car on the street, it seemed to be occupied. At least half the lights were on.

"Looks like we have company," I said to Gus, as we walked up to the house. I wasn't worried. I'd recognized Deena's car. I'd recently given her a spare key—not specifically so that she could be there to greet me after I'd discovered a body, but her instincts were right on.

I let myself in and kicked off my shoes. Gus ran straight for the kitchen. He greeted Deena with a friendly, excited bark, and I called out, "Honey, I'm home!"

She poked her head around the corner and gave me a questioning look. She wore a flour-spattered apron and a scarf around her glossy black hair. "I'm glad you're in a chipper mood," she said. "I expected . . . the opposite."

"You heard the news then?" I joined her in the kitchen and sat down at the table, which was covered with mixing bowls, cookie sheets, and containers of baking ingredients.

"Oh, yeah," she said. "My parents and I had finished

dinner and were leaving Augie's when we ran into Nell Cusley in the parking lot. Actually, I think she spotted us and pulled in specifically to share the newsflash." Nell Cusley, the owner of Nell's Diner downtown, was essentially Aerieville's town crier. She liked to be the first to break all big gossip, the worse the better.

"Figures," I said, reaching for a cookie. Deena had been experimenting with different flower recipes over the past month. This one was a version of her rose petal sugar cookies, made with rose water and bits of dried rose petals. "Mmm. This one is a keeper," I said, around a mouthful of cookie.

She shot me an incredulous stare, probably because of my nonchalant mood. To be honest, I wasn't really sure why I was so calm. Maybe I was in denial. Or maybe it had something to do with Calvin. We'd both been extra casual when I left, as if nothing had changed between us. But, of course, it had.

"What are you smiling at?" demanded Deena. "Was there *not* another murder at Flower House?"

"No, there was," I said, as I grabbed another cookie. "I'm just so tired and hungry, it's making me giddy, I guess."

"Hang on," she said. "Instead of gorging on cookies, try this." She opened my fridge and took out a large salad bowl filled with mixed greens, pink rose petals, purple chive flowers, and yellow marigold blossoms.

"Ooh, that looks beautiful! Almost too pretty to eat." I hopped up for a bowl and a fork.

Deena took a glass bottle from the refrigerator, shook it, and set it on the table next to a container of pepitas. "Raspberry vinaigrette," she said. "And pumpkin seeds for crunch."

I dressed the salad and dug in, as she used a spatula to carefully transfer the cookies into airtight containers.

"I drove straight to Flower House from the restaurant," she said. "At least, I tried to. The police turned me away at the end of the block. I guess they'd had enough with all the gawkers."

"It was a madhouse," I confirmed.

"That's when I decided to wait for you at your house," she said. "Plus, my kitchen is filled with so much food for the café, there's not much room left for baking."

I didn't respond. The day was finally catching up to me. And, while the salad was delicious, my mind was replaying the chaotic events of the afternoon. It had all happened so fast.

Deena fell silent and cleaned up the kitchen. Then she sat down across from me, as I ate my last bite.

"Okay, Sierra," she said. "Lay it on me. How bad is it? Do we need to postpone our grand opening?"

I shook my head, as the gravity of the situation finally sank in. "I don't know. Maybe. The shop is still technically a crime scene, and the storeroom is off-limits." The police had draped yellow tape across the entry to the storeroom. They'd told me it appeared Lowry had been hit in that room—rather than being placed there after the fact. "I have no idea how quickly the cops are going to solve this thing, but the grand opening isn't actually my biggest worry right now."

"Understandable," Deena said soberly. "A man has died."

"Yeah, that's terrible," I agreed. "But that's not what I meant. I'm more concerned that the police think Calvin had something to do with it."

She raised her eyebrows, and I told her everything I could remember, from the arrival of the UT van to

Calvin's account of his departure from the university. I skipped the part about holding his hand and (maybe? possibly?) almost kissing him. *Did that even happen?* It no longer seemed important.

Deena listened quietly. When I finished, she expressed sympathy but seemed more puzzled than anything. "It sounds like the police were quick to conclude there was foul play. How do they know it wasn't an accident? Maybe the man tripped, or something fell on his head."

I shook my head. "It was obvious he'd been struck from behind. Plus, the weapon was found, remember?"

"Okay. Then who did it? Could someone have come in off the street?" she asked. "The back door was unlocked when I left."

"Unlikely. Not without being seen." I'd wondered the same thing myself and rejected the possibility. "The timing is too narrow. The police established Lowry was alive just minutes before Gus led us to his body, and there were people all around. Some kids were next door at Bread n' Butter, and others were outside by the greenhouse. Bart was in his truck, and Wanda was . . . wandering around outside someplace. I think."

"What about Calvin?"

"He and Gus had gone for a walk. They returned, while I was up front cleaning. I know, because Gus ran in to greet me. Calvin had gone upstairs for a minute—and that must be when it happened. Somebody whacked Professor Lowry on the back of the head. In the storeroom. With the candlestick."

We both heard it: echoes from the game of Clue. Deena gave me a wry grin, and I covered my mouth to stifle a giggle. There was nothing funny about this situation, but I couldn't help it. The giddiness was back.

"Maybe they'll find fingerprints on the candlestick,"

said Deena. "If everything happened that quickly, the guilty person probably didn't have time to wipe it down."

"Maybe." I wanted to be optimistic. It would be great if the police could just solve the crime and be done with it. Yet somehow I doubted we'd be that lucky. If the killer had lured Lowry into the storeroom and hit him from behind, there must have been at least a little bit of planning. They'd also had enough time to throw the weapon in the trash, rather than drop it on the floor. It wasn't like they wanted to be caught.

A tap on the front door broke into my thoughts. Gus gave a bark and ran to see who it could be.

"Expecting someone?" asked Deena.

"Not really, but . . ." I trailed off, standing up. We went into the living room, and I looked out the window. "But I'm not surprised," I finished. "It's Rocky."

I opened the door to my brother, younger than me by four years but much larger in stature. He held a casserole dish, which was a little incongruous, considering he wore short-shorts and a bodybuilding tank top, both of which showcased his ample, sculpted muscles.

I took the pan and stood back to let him in. "Hey, bro. It's a little late for a drop-in, isn't it?"

"Hi, sis. I saw your lights were on." He reached down to scratch Gus behind the ears. "Hey, little buddy."

"And you just happened to have a casserole?"

Straightening up, he flashed me a grin. "You know it's from Mom. She's been bugging me all evening to come and check on you." Rocky lived in a small apartment above our parents' garage and usually had dinner with them. He was also a trainer at their gym, so he saw much more of our folks than I did. I was grateful for this arrangement. It made me feel slightly less guilty about my independent streak. I'd left town before and was liable to do it again. It was easier knowing my mom would still have one kid to fuss over—which she seemed intent on doing, no matter how old we got.

He nodded at Deena, who stood behind me. "Hey, Dee. How you holding up?"

"Me?" said Deena. "I'm fine. I missed all the excitement at the shop today."

I turned to her, with a sudden realization. "Yeah, but this affects you too," I said. Deena had a tendency to put on a cool, polished front, which often masked her insecurities. She must have been pretty scared and worried when she'd heard the news.

Deena shrugged, as she removed her apron and folded it neatly. "I'm fine," she repeated.

"Have a seat, both of you." I took the casserole into the kitchen and found a place for it in the refrigerator, then returned to the living room with a bottle of wine. "Nightcap, anyone?"

Rocky hesitated. As a calorie-counter, he wasn't a big drinker. Deena also appeared uncertain.

"Come on. It's just a light, white wine." I read the label. "A sauvignon blanc."

Deena checked her watch, then glanced at Rocky. "Maybe just half a glass," she said. "I should get going soon."

What was that look? Was I mistaken, or was there a hint of flirtation between Deena and my brother? I quirked an eyebrow but didn't say anything.

"Alright," agreed Rocky. He helped me pour the wine, and we found seats in the living room—Rocky and Deena on the couch and me on an oversized floor pillow.

"I was just telling Deena about everyone who was at the shop this afternoon," I said.

"And it's usually such a quiet place," Deena said ironically.

I filled Rocky in, sticking to the highlights. "Of course, Calvin had nothing to do with it," I concluded. "I saw his reaction when we found Lowry's body, and he was as shocked as I was."

Rocky's eyes flickered with a trace of doubt. He looked like he wanted to challenge my assertion, but Deena spoke up.

"You forgot to tell him about Bart's reaction to seeing the UT van. You said he really went after the professor." Deena turned to Rocky. "It sounded like a case of road rage to me."

"He was definitely mad," I said. "But does it count as road rage if it's after the fact? He should've had time to cool off."

"Maybe seeing the professor reignited his anger," Deena suggested.

"Bart Hammerson has always been a hothead," said Rocky. "At least, as long as I've known him."

"Wait. You know him?" I'd always assumed the deliveryman lived somewhere near our wholesaler—and Pauly's Plants was about forty miles west of Aerieville. Then again, as a truck driver, Bart could live anywhere. He could even work for more than one business. Either way, this was the first I'd ever heard my brother mention him.

"He's been coming to Dumbbells for years," said Rocky. "I worked with him as he was completing physical therapy after a car accident a while ago."

Deena and I spoke in unison. "Car accident?"

"Did he cause it?" Deena asked darkly. A flicker of fear shone in her brown eyes.

"Maybe that's why he's so sensitive about bad drivers,"

I speculated. That might explain his outsized anger at the professor.

Rocky played with his wine glass, which almost looked like a toy in his large hands. "I don't know the details. I only know he had acute back and neck pain from his injuries, but he eventually recovered. He generally works out two to three times a week now, mainly on the free weights and leg press."

I tried not to snicker. *Hard core.* "Why did you say he's a hothead?" I asked.

Rocky shrugged. "It was probably the pain. I've just seen him snap at people and get worked up easily. I've seen him at Cuties' Pool Hall too. He got kicked out once for starting a fight."

"Ha, I was right," said Deena. She nodded at me, then turned to Rocky. "Sierra thought Bart had some deep, dark secret, and I said he probably has a criminal past."

"Well, I don't think he was arrested," said Rocky. "But you might have something there."

"I'm gonna make sure Chief Bradley knows this next time I see her," I said, "which could be tomorrow. She said she'd be back."

Rocky finished his wine in one gulp and stood up. "I ought to go, sis. You need your sleep, and I'm sure Mom is waiting up for me. She'll want to hear my report on your state of mind."

Deena hopped up too. "I'll walk out with you." She grabbed her bag and patted my arm on her way to the door.

"What are you gonna tell Mom?" I asked. "I don't want her to worry."

"I'll say you were unfazed," said Rocky. "After all, this isn't your first murder. You're an old pro at it by now."

"Terrific," I muttered. I doubted that would reassure our mom very much. It certainly didn't make me feel any better.

The dollhouse seemed extra quiet after Deena and Rocky left. As I got ready for bed, Gus followed me around as usual, but he was clearly sleepy. When I finally pulled the covers back on my full-sized feather bed, he jumped to his place on the foot and promptly closed his eyes. It had been a long day for both of us.

I wished I could fall asleep as easily. Instead, open questions looped in my mind like a merry-go-round. *What was Lowry doing in the storeroom? Did someone lure him in there? And what was he doing in the bathroom for so long? Was he ill? What happened between the bathroom and the storeroom? And how did someone get him to turn his back?* Surely he hadn't seen the blow coming. From what I could tell, there was no indication that there had been a struggle.

As I finally drifted off to sleep, one more question surfaced from the abyss: *Where was Professor Lowry's canteen?*

Chapter 5

Sundays were the one day Flower House was closed to walk-ins. Everyone needed a day off now and then—if not two days. However, I often ended up going into work anyway. I wanted to be accommodating if anyone needed a last-minute delivery or, even better, wanted to consult with us about an event. Plus, there was always work to do in the garden and greenhouse.

Today, I'd planned to do more prep work for the café, by gathering and drying rose petals from the greenhouse. At this point, I had no idea if we'd be able to open as planned, but I figured it was best to proceed as if we would. After all, acting as if I already had what I wanted was one of the ways I'd learned to manifest some great things in my life. It was a basic Law of Attraction technique. *Fake it till you make it.*

After a quick shower, I pulled on some denim overall shorts over a lime green T-shirt and towel-dried my short, bobbed hair. I had a quick bite to eat, then poured some coffee in a to-go mug and hauled Gus out to my car, a bright orange hatchback Fiat. Even on gloomy days, I liked to bring a bit of sunshine wherever I went. Today wasn't gloomy yet—the morning sun shone brightly. But there was a chance of storms later.

When we arrived at Flower House, I opened the door slowly so the bell wouldn't jingle too loudly. Gus immediately ran to the back of the shop to sit at the door leading to Calvin's apartment.

"That's fine, Gus," I whispered. "You can wait for him, as long as you're quiet." I tried to be respectful of the fact that the place upstairs was Calvin's home. He was entitled to his privacy.

I set my purse on the kitchen counter and filled Gus's water bowl. Then, sipping my coffee, I walked slowly around the shop, letting my mind replay the craziness of the day before. I peeked in the café, noting the spot where Bart had sat staring at his phone and the table where the police had conducted interviews. I wandered through the front of the shop, where the college kids had touched all the merchandise and broken a vase.

In the hallway, I paused at the powder room door and looked inside. It was fairly tidy, considering how many people were in the shop yesterday. We didn't have a cleaning service, so that lovely task fell on my shoulders. *Might as well do it now.*

I left my coffee beside the cash register, donned a pair of rubber gloves, and then gathered some cleaning supplies from beneath the bathroom sink. As I cleaned and restocked the little room, I kept a sharp eye out for anything unusual—any small clue the police might have missed.

What was *the professor doing in here?* And those two students too—April and Vince. Were they sneaking a kiss? Or just having a private conversation? From what I observed, they hadn't acted like lovers. There were no

sly looks or secret smiles. If anything, they'd seemed unusually serious. *Hmm.*

I put the cleaning supplies away and washed my
hands. As I stepped out of the bathroom, I looked left and
right. Where had the professor gone from here? He didn't
come to the front of the shop—unless he did briefly while
I was in the café. Calvin would have kept the door to his
apartment locked. Likewise, we kept the doors to the
study and to the basement locked. Assuming the professor didn't go outside, the only other places he could have
gone were the orchid room and the kitchen. In fact, Calvin had mentioned seeing him in the orchid room.

Sliding open the pocket doors, I entered that room
now and walked around. It was an elegant space, with a
high ceiling and large windows on the south wall. Once
upon a time, this was probably a drawing room. Now it
contained tables and shelves of ten different varieties of
orchids, from colorful easy-growing moth orchids and
showy lady slippers to fluttery dancing dolls and exotic
hybrids.

I checked the water level in the humidifier and turned
a few of the plants, examining the health of their leaves
and root systems. Grabbing a water bottle from a hidden
cabinet, I also misted some of the leaves. As I strolled
around the room, I marveled at how I'd ended up here in
the first place. I'd never had any formal training as a florist. I'd never even considered myself much of a green
thumb. Still, I must've picked up a thing or two from
Granny over the years. And Felix had patiently showed
me how to work with different colors and shapes to create balanced and interesting floral arrangements. Beyond
that, I relied on instinct and intuition to come up with
designs I found pleasing. Fortunately, others seemed to
agree.

From the orchid room, I moved on to the kitchen. Gus watched me to make sure I wasn't going to leave the house, but he stayed at his station in the hallway.

Though there was still a stove, a refrigerator, and a large double sink, the kitchen was really more of a work-room than anything else. One wall held a glass refrigerator case for fresh flowers, while the other walls featured cabinets and drawers filled with florist supplies. In the center of the room, a large butcher-block table served as our work surface. On the floor at one end of the table was a tall, round garbage bin for all the stems, leaves, and other trimmings we regularly produced. It was empty now. After the police found the murder weapon in the bin, they'd taken the whole bag away with them.

I placed a new plastic bag in the bin, as I scanned the room. Nothing seemed out of place. For the heck of it, I tried the basement door. *Yep. Still locked.* Then I turned to the closed door in the far corner of the kitchen. It led to the storeroom. Taking a deep breath for courage, I reached over the yellow police tape, turned the doorknob, and gently pushed the door open. Staying behind the tape, I reached in and flipped on the light.

It was a deep, narrow room, formerly a walk-in pantry. Shelving from the center of the walls to the ceiling contained extra vases, baskets, and orchid supplies, including fertilizer, pots, potting media, and grow lights. On the floor beneath the shelves were boxes and crates, some empty, some filled with wire frames and other floristry materials we didn't use every day.

Of course, there was no chalk outline on the floor. I'd learned from the last death investigation here that cops only do that in the movies. Chalk could contaminate the scene and isn't even necessary. In real life, the police usually just take a bunch of pictures.

Anyway, I didn't need a chalk outline to remember where the body was. That image was emblazoned into my brain forever.

I roved the room with my eyes. What had Lowry been looking for in here? Maybe nothing. Maybe he'd been hiding or having a secret rendezvous with one of the students. I peered into the corners, again vainly hoping I'd spot a clue. No such luck. The police had done a clean sweep of the room.

Closing the door, I thought again about how the professor had looked when he came into Flower House. He'd had a canteen slung over his shoulder. Yet there was no canteen next to him when we'd found his body. I was sure of it.

I wonder . . . Thinking again about the bathroom, I remembered Granny had said the window was open. She'd shut it when we were looking for Gus. Could the professor have dropped or thrown his canteen out the window? It would be an odd thing to do, but I had to look.

Leaving Gus inside, I slipped out the back door and circled around to the side of the house. Landscaped shrubs bordered the long driveway, which separated the Flower House property from the grounds of the historical society next door. Directly beneath the bathroom window was a clump of overgrown juniper bushes. I examined the top of the bushes, then dropped to my hands and knees to look underneath.

There was no canteen. I kept looking anyway, hoping to find a cigarette butt or a crumpled note—anything to shed some light on what the professor or his students had been up to. I was about to give up when my persistence was rewarded. I spotted a tiny white circle of paper stuck to a branch of the bushes. Picking it off, I saw that it was a sticker: Made in the U.S.A. Before I could wonder where it had come from, I spotted something even more exciting: half a footprint in a patch of mud beside the house. Beyond this small section of bare earth was a grassy stretch of lawn, so there was no hope of finding further footprints. But this was definitely one—or part of one. And it must have been made relatively recently.

"Find anything?"

The voice startled me, though I quickly realized it was Calvin. I crawled backward and looked up, squinting at him in the sun. He appeared to be amused.

"How did you find me?" I asked.

"I didn't. Gus did."

Shielding my eyes, I now saw that Calvin was holding onto Gus's leash, preventing the pup from jumping on me. That was a good idea. As far as the corgi was concerned, why else would I be crawling on the ground if not to play?

Calvin held out a hand to me. I accepted and let him help me to my feet, while Gus barked excitedly. I shushed Gus and showed Calvin the sticker.

"I found this in the bush."

He took the sticker from me and read it out loud. "'Made in the U.S.A.'" Frowning, he shook his head. "That's not right."

"What do you mean?" I asked.

He gestured to the shrub behind me. "This is a Chinese juniper." Then he broke into a goofy grin. "The sticker lies."

"Very funny." I grinned in spite of myself, as I plucked the sticker out of Calvin's fingers. "Actually, I wondered if this might have come off of Professor Lowry's canteen." I showed Calvin the partial footprint and told him my theory about the professor dropping his canteen out the window—and someone else retrieving it later.

"You think the police found it?" he asked.

"It's possible, but I don't think so. If they'd found it, I think they would have asked me if I recognized it."

"You're probably right," he conceded.

"We should call them now. Can I borrow your phone? I left mine inside."

He handed me his cell phone, and I pulled up the number for the Aerieville police station. When the desk sergeant answered, I explained briefly why I was calling. She said she'd pass along the message to the investigators.

I looked at the partial footprint again, pondering what information it might hold. Because it wasn't complete, I couldn't get a good sense of the size. I couldn't even tell what kind of shoe had made it, other than one with treads.

"We should take a picture of this," I said. "Could we use your phone again?"

"Yes, ma'am." Calvin handed me Gus's leash and pulled out his phone.

As he squatted down to take the picture, it struck me that we made a pretty good team. My mind roamed back to the night before, and I felt a fuzzy warmth at the memory. What would have happened if Gus hadn't interrupted us? Then I thought of something else.

"Hey! Last night, when Gus heard something outside, maybe that was somebody out here looking for the canteen."

Calvin stood up and looked at me, as a small smile tugged his lips. Was he remembering the moment we shared too? Then he crinkled his forehead and looked away. "Hmm."

"What is it?"

"I just remembered something. When I saw Steve in the orchid room, I thought his face seemed a little flushed. And his stance was oddly loose and relaxed. Maybe there was alcohol in the canteen."

"Oh, wow. That could be important, couldn't it? Did you tell Chief Bradley?"

He shook his head. "I didn't know about the canteen at the time, and it had slipped my mind. I guess she had me a little rattled."

"Well, I suppose the autopsy will reveal if anything was in his system."

"Yeah, that's true."

Gus was tired of waiting and tugged on his leash. Calvin took it from me and strolled around the yard. I brushed off my pants and went back inside long enough to grab my purse (where I stashed the small sticker) and a large, plastic container. The other tools I needed were already in the greenhouse.

The glass building that dominated the rear portion of the land behind Flower House was divided into two climate-controlled rooms: one for tropical plants, including orchids and ferns, and one exclusively for roses. The rose room was cooler, which offered a welcome respite from the summer sun. Though it was still early, it was already shaping up to be a hot day.

Entering the rose room was always a feast for the senses. Surrounded by healthy plants bursting with soft-colored blooms, I had to pause, close my eyes, and inhale the luscious fragrance. *Mmm. Romance, enchantment, beauty . . . so many lovely feelings brought about by the scent alone.*

I grabbed a bucket from the floor and clippers from a wall hook and proceeded down the concrete aisles.

As a rule, it was best to pick fresh flowers early in the morning, when the stems were most firm and hydrated. But that didn't matter as much in the greenhouse, where a misting system kept the plants from drying out. My aim now was to select flowers that had fully opened and were still in their prime. Of course, we had been harvesting roses all summer, for both bouquets and for the petals. We'd made several jars of rose petal jam for the café and prepared dried petals for teas and other recipes. I planned to collect more petals today to add to our supply.

I snipped about a dozen stems and brought my collection to the workbench at the end of the center row. On a shelf under the bench was a stack of large trays. I set one on the table, then pulled up a tall stool and got to work. One flower at a time, I grasped the top of each stem and gently removed the entire head of the rose. Using my fingers, I carefully separated the soft petals and spread them in a single layer on the tray.

I had done only a couple of flowers when I heard the greenhouse door bang open. A minute later, Calvin and Gus joined me at the workbench.

"Want some help?" asked Calvin.

"Sure! There were more ready to pick than I'd expected."

Calvin opened the gate to a small pen we'd created in the corner, and Gus went right in. He knew this was his special area. It was padded with an old rope rug and outfitted with plenty of dog toys and treats. It was a convenient way to keep Gus out of trouble.

I moved the bucket of roses within Calvin's reach and brought out another drying tray. He sat on a stool on the other side of the workbench. Between the two of us, we made short work of removing all the petals.

Calvin was unusually quiet. I was sure he was think-ing about the professor's death and its aftermath. Maybe it was naïve of me to carry on as if nothing had happened, but I didn't know what else to do. To distract Calvin, I kept up a steady stream of chatter.

"Hey, I have an idea to run by you."

"Shoot."

"What do you think about creating little info cards about edible flowers? We could keep a stack in the café and hand one out with every purchase."

"Go on."

"Well, in addition to having our business info, the cards could list the most common edible flowers—and also include a big warning about not eating any ol' flow-ers, since some are poisonous."

"Good idea. We should also tell folks not to eat any flowers that have been sprayed with pesticides—which would include most flowers they get at a traditional flo-rist."

"Yes! Absolutely. And that gives us an opportunity to let them know our roses are all certified organic."

He smiled at my enthusiasm. "Good thinking."

"I'll ask Deena to mock up the cards. She's good at that sort of thing." Prior to moving back to Aerieville, Deena had been a long-time student in Chicago. She liked to call herself a "perpetual scholar," but I secretly felt she was just searching for her calling. Among her many de-grees, she'd studied anthropology, fashion, business, and communications. She'd been working toward a doctor-ate in business administration when her fiancé left her—providing the impetus for her to leave the city and her school behind. She said she was happier now. And I was sure happy to have her here.

"You're pretty creative too," said Calvin. "Take your

window display. It's very, um, unique." He had a teasing glint in his eye, which made me grin.

"Thank you!" I batted my eyelashes at him, before brushing all our stems back into the bucket. "To tell you the truth, I sometimes feel a little inferior since I didn't finish college. And, to think, between you and Deena, I've surrounded myself with over-educated—I, mean, highly educated—smart people."

He narrowed his eyes at me in mock annoyance. "There's no such thing as too much education. Hey, maybe you'll want to finish your degree someday. What were you studying?"

We'd both stood up and pushed our stools in. I carried one tray to a ledge along the wall, where the petals could dry out in the sun. "Um, I was undeclared."

He brought over another tray and set it next to mine. "Couldn't decide, huh?"

"Nope. But I believe in education too. It's called the school of life." I faced him with a playful smirk and waited expectantly.

He raised his eyebrows and opened his mouth, but I didn't get to hear his comeback. At that moment, there was a loud rapping on the greenhouse door.

Calvin frowned. "I'll get it."

Gus had started barking, so I went ahead and leashed him. We followed quickly behind Calvin. When we reached the exit, we found Calvin outside talking to Flo Morrison, co-owner of the bakery next door. She was neatly attired in slacks and a poplin blouse, calling to mind Martha Stewart in the kitchen. As usual, she wore her pale silver hair in a bun at the back of her neck.

"Hi, Flo." I stepped outside, shutting the greenhouse door behind me. "How are you?"

"I'm doing well. I saw your car and figured you were

back here." She lowered her chin and looked over her glasses to give me an appraising look. "I stopped by to see how you're holding up."

"She brought us cinnamon rolls," said Calvin, holding up a paper bag.

"How sweet." I paused, selecting my words carefully. Flo and her husband Bill were pillars of the community. Besides running Bread n' Butter Bakery for many years, they were active in just about every organization in town, from church and civic groups to Aerieville's tiny little arts council. I used to get along with them just fine, until I learned they wanted to drive me out of business. They coveted the Flower House property for their own purposes. When I accepted Felix's offer and decided to keep the shop running, they were none too pleased. They were even less enamored of me when they found out I planned to open a café. Now, every time I saw Flo, her pleasantries rang false. It was just a mite awkward.

"Had a bit of excitement around here yesterday, didn't we?" I said.

She arched her eyebrows. "'A bit of excitement'? Isn't that a *bit* of an understatement?"

"Well—"

"You must have been knocked for a loop," said Flo, cutting me off. "To think, you found a dead man in your kitchen! How ghastly that must have been."

"He was in the storeroom, not the kitchen," I said lamely. She continued to stare at me, until I added, "Which was bad enough."

"Weren't you planning on opening your little café next weekend? I suppose you'll not be able to now." She gave me a look I assumed was meant to convey compassion. "What a shame."

"I haven't actually decided yet. We might be able to go ahead as planned."

"Oh? Have the police caught the murderer?"

"Uh, I'm not sure. But—"

"I just can't believe it," she said, cutting me off again. "*Another* murder at Flower House. What are the odds? It almost makes you wonder if the place is cursed. Like somebody up there doesn't want you to stay open." She looked upward to the sky, then simpered, as if she were only joking.

"It's terrible, that's for sure," I muttered. Then I caught Calvin's eye and had to struggle to keep from laughing. He had stepped behind Flo and was making faces to mimic her saccharine expression.

The sound of tires crunching on the gravel driveway made us all turn our heads. It was a police car.

"Oh, good," I said. "They're probably here to remove the yellow tape from the storeroom. Excuse me, Flo."

I thought she would leave. Instead, she made a move as if to join me. "I'd like to hear what they have to say," she said. "I need to know if the neighborhood is safe."

I narrowed my eyes but held my tongue. In my mind, I was growling like Gus when another dog encroaches on his territory. I couldn't exactly blame Flo for her concern, but she didn't have to act so gleeful about the situation.

We started across the yard, but the police officers saw us and met us by the garden. It was Chief Bradley and Officer Dakin.

"Good morning," I said. "Would you like to take another look inside?" I started to head for the back door, hoping they would follow. I really wanted to go inside. Flo was making me nervous.

"Actually, we're here to speak to Mr. Foxheart," said Chief Bradley. Her voice was pleasant but firm.

"Calvin?" I said.

"Again?" he said.

"Mr. Foxheart, we have a few more questions for you. Would you please come with us to the station?"

Calvin visibly swallowed before nodding his head slowly. Flo didn't even try to cover her smirk.

Gus whimpered quietly—echoing my sentiments exactly.

Chapter 6

I was so upset after Calvin left with the police, I couldn't bear to be in the quiet shop alone. I'd forgotten to mention the footprint and the missing canteen. For all I knew, the police could have already found them. It wasn't my job to do their work for them. Surely they knew what they were doing. Right?

Poor Calvin. He didn't even get to have a cinnamon roll! I left the pastry bag in the café room and took off on a walk with Gus. Breezing past Bread n' Butter, I headed to Melody Gardens, hoping to soak up some peaceful vibes.

The park was home to plenty of scampering squirrels and twittering birds, but devoid of people. The solitude *was* peaceful. Yet, as we meandered along the flagstone path, past pine trees and flower beds, and around the rocky cascading water fountain, I barely noticed our surroundings. I was too preoccupied.

Why were the cops focusing on Calvin anyway? It was a waste of time. Shouldn't they be questioning the people who had arrived with the victim? If I were in charge of the investigation, I'd want to know what Lowry had been doing in the time leading up to his demise. What was his conversation about with the students in the orchid room? How about in the van before they showed up? Why was he driving erratically, as Bart had claimed?

Even earlier than that, what was going on in the professor's life that made him start missing appointments and classes and steal Calvin's research?

With these questions swirling in my mind, I circled around to exit the park. Without meaning to, I'd begun to formulate a plan. Why couldn't I go ahead and ask some of these questions myself?

On my way back to Flower House, I paused on the sidewalk and let Gus sniff the grass, while I made two phone calls: one to Rocky to see if he'd mind dog-sitting for a while (he never minded), and one to Deena. I needed a partner for this mission.

That done, I coaxed Gus along toward my car. We were still half a block from the shop, when I saw a vehicle pull out of the Flower House driveway. It was a Pauly's Plants delivery truck—unmistakable with its dark green paint and pink and yellow flower decals. It turned onto Oak Street and headed away from me, so I didn't get a good look at the driver. I assumed it was Bart.

I wonder what he wanted. We never received deliveries on Sundays. Maybe he just wanted to talk.

Come to think of it, I wouldn't mind having a chat with the man myself. Among my many questions were one or two for Bart Hammerson. He'd have to wait, though. For now, it was time to talk to some college students.

It was lunchtime when Deena and I convened at our friend Richard's B&B. We'd called ahead, so he knew to expect us. With open arms and a wide smile, he greeted us from the porch of the newly renovated farmhouse he'd inherited from his mother.

"It's my girls! It's about time you two came to see me. I know you've been busy with the flower shop, but I miss our gab fests."

"You've been busy too." Deena gestured toward the freshly painted sign in the front yard, declaring the house *Mountain View Bed & Breakfast—Richard Wales, proprietor.*

"The place looks great," I said, leaning in to let Richard kiss me on the cheek.

Tall and sandy-haired, Richard Wales was one of my first crushes as a young schoolgirl. Even after he came out as gay, I couldn't help pining after him just a smidge. He was just so darn attractive, funny, and handy. He represented what I always longed for in a romantic partner.

Now, he looked happier than I'd seen him in a long time. I knew he'd had a tough past couple of years, between caring for his sick mother, handling her affairs when she passed, and then losing his job as a bank teller. Of course, the job loss was his own fault after a series of bad decisions. He was lucky the job was all he'd lost. But he'd always been a good person at heart, and I was glad to see him doing well.

"Come in, come in." He led us through the living room, outfitted in a modern rustic style, with reclaimed wood floors, exposed beams, and a massive stone fireplace. Overstuffed chairs with earth-tone pillows and a comfy-looking sofa were arranged for conversation or kicking back. The adjoining dining room was equally inviting. A large picture window, with tied-back ruffled curtains, permitted an abundance of sunlight and a stellar view of the Smoky Mountains in the distance. In the center of the room was a long oval table covered in a cream-colored lacy cloth. The polished hickory sideboard was laden with platters of cut sandwiches, potato salad, and watermelon cubes, along with a crystal carafe of cucumber-infused ice water.

Richard handed us plates and told us to help ourselves. He filled his own plate and poured us drinks, before joining us at the table. Deena and I oohed and aahed over both the impressive spread and the beautiful renovations he'd made.

"It was a labor of love," he said, opening a gingham cloth napkin with a flourish. "I'm having so much fun with this new gig. And, Sierra, I have to thank you for the referral. Not many people know about me yet. All my rooms were empty until Sheila and crew arrived. Now all three of my guest rooms are full, and I actually have someone to cook for."

"Where are they now?" I asked, around a mouthful of cheese sandwich. "You don't provide lunch for your guests, do you?"

"No. Breakfast only, plus tea and treats in the afternoon. I have a catering deal with Tea for You."

Deena's eyes lit up, and I knew it wasn't just because she liked the tea offerings at Tea for You (even though she did). She was undoubtedly thinking we should ask Richard to serve some of our flower-themed treats. I had the same idea, though it wasn't my first priority at the moment.

"I imagine they'll be back soon," Richard continued. "They got up early for breakfast and went for a hike in the foothills."

I took a sip of water and glanced out the window. "I don't suppose you've talked much with them, have you?"

"Actually, yes. I ordered pizza last night, and we all hung out in the living room for a while. We had another nice chat this morning over breakfast. They're a delightful bunch."

Deena snorted, and I smirked, assuming he was being sarcastic. "Yeah, right."

Richard cocked his head curiously. "No, really. They're adorable. They've been cracking me up ever since they got here—with their memes and idealism and references I don't get. Like I said, they're totally cute."

Deena and I exchanged a look, and she raised an eyebrow. "That's not how you described them," she said to me.

I frowned, thrown by Richard's account of the students' personalities. "That's not how they appeared yesterday—even before their professor died. In fact, those three were the only students who weren't horsing around. They seemed sort of serious and aloof."

Richard shrugged. "I don't know what to tell you. Maybe it's the relaxing environment here."

Was that it? I wondered. Or could it have something to do with the death of their professor? Calvin had described Lowry as difficult. Maybe the students were tired of being "Lowry's Lackeys." Of course, that was hardly a strong motive for murder. As usual, I was letting my imagination get ahead of me.

Deena was bringing Richard up to speed on the progress of our new café. He promised to come and see it as soon as he could.

"Oh, and something else," he said. "Now that you've seen my place, I want to hire you to keep me stocked with fresh flower arrangements. What do you think? Is once a week doable?"

"Really?" I said. "I'd love to do that!"

"Perfect. Florist's choice. I trust you to put together something lovely with whatever flowers are in season."

"Do you have a certain number of bouquets in mind?" asked Deena. "Or certain locations? Maybe in the entry-way and living room?"

"I was thinking flowers in every room," said Richard. He winked at me and took a bite of watermelon.

Smiling, I finished off my own bowl of watermelon, savoring the juicy sweetness. Richard's buoyancy was rubbing off on me. He used to be a bit of a cynic. Now, he was Mr. Cheerful. If I didn't know any better, I might suspect the new B&B wasn't the only reason for his high spirits. Unless . . .

"Hey, Richard," I said suddenly. "Are you seeing any-one?"

He took a drink of water, giving me a sly look over the rim.

Deena put down her fork and looked at him in sur-prise. "Are you?" she demanded.

He made us wait, as he set his glass down and wiped his mouth. Then he grinned like the cat that ate the ca-nary. "I am."

"Why didn't you say anything?" said Deena, acting aggrieved, though smiling anyway. "That's wonderful!"

"Is it anyone we know?" I asked.

He paused again, apparently being coy. "Um, maybe."

"What do you mean 'maybe'?" said Deena.

"I'm afraid I can't share that information just yet." At our pouting expressions, he lifted his shoulders. "Sorry, ladies. He's not fully out of the closet. Hopefully, that'll change one day soon."

"Ah, okay," I said. It was understandable Richard would want to protect his new beau's privacy, especially considering not everyone was as open-minded as we were. Still, the situation would have made me a little sad, if not for the fact that Richard seemed to be having fun with his secret. And like he said, circumstances would hopefully change in the near future.

"Fine," said Deena. "But you know we wouldn't tell."

We finished our lunch, chatting about this and that, then helped Richard clear the table.

After putting away the last of the leftovers, I suggested a tour of the house. "We can scope out ideal spots for your flower arrangements. Deena can take pictures, if you don't mind."

"I don't mind at all," he said, ushering us to the living room. "But first, I have to ask you one thing."

"What is it?"

"Well, not to be ghoulish, but I thought you might tell me about finding a dead man in your kitchen."

"Storeroom," I corrected automatically. Whoever was spreading gossip around town had got that detail wrong.

"I'm surprised it took you so long to ask," Deena said.

"I thought I'd be civilized and wait 'til we'd finished eating."

"There's not a whole lot to tell," I said. "It happened pretty fast."

I dropped into one of the cozy armchairs and gave him the short version of yesterday's events. "Didn't your guests tell you all about it?"

"They acted like they were pretty in the dark about the whole thing. Of course, Sheila wasn't there when it happened. And April and the boys said they were outside. But they figured it could only have been one of two people who attacked their professor."

"Who?" said Deena. I didn't have to ask. I was already pretty sure I knew what he was going to say.

"They said it might have been a truck driver they'd encountered on the highway. They think the driver must have followed them, so he could confront the professor.

I guess he made quite the scene in the street, yelling and cursing?"

"Something like that," I said.

"But they were conflicted, because evidently their professor's nemesis happened to work at Flower House. I assumed they were talking about Calvin."

"Nemesis? I mean, yeah, Calvin had reason to be angry with Professor Lowry. But I don't think *nemesis* is the right word."

Deena looked thoughtful. "I'm kind of surprised the police didn't arrest Bart, the deliveryman, right then and there. He *does* seem to be the most obvious suspect."

I shook my head. "Guys, everyone there is a suspect. Including the three students."

Richard narrowed his eyebrows as if the idea hadn't occurred to him. "My guests? Those three nice kids? I don't think so."

"Isn't that why they're still here?" asked Deena.

"They stayed voluntarily," said Richard. "Sheila told me the university attorney recommended they cooperate. The police can't actually make them stay without charging them with something."

At that moment, a doorbell chimed throughout the house. "That must be them," said Richard, heading for the front door.

Deena and I hung back as Richard welcomed his returning guests. "Y'all made it!" he said. "See any bears or snakes?"

The group piled into the living room, dropping backpacks on the floor and removing their hiking boots. Several of them spoke at once.

"No bears, but we saw plenty of birds," said April. "I was glad I brought my binoculars." She appeared even more youthful today, with Swiss Miss–style braids and a cropped T-shirt. I guessed she must be eighteen years old. Her classmates seemed a little older. Isaiah, Mr. Preppy, was probably around twenty, I figured; while bad boy Vince might have been twenty-two or twenty-three. Their teacher, Sheila, appeared to be in her late thirties.

"It was lovely," said Sheila. "So good to be in the fresh air."

"Saw lots of interesting plants," said Isaiah, still looking preppy in walking shorts and a ringer tee. "I made good use of my plant ID app."

Vince lifted his white T-shirt to fan his midriff—and show off his surprisingly toned abs. "It's hotter 'n' Hades out there," he drawled. "I almost took a dip in the lake, but the others wouldn't let me."

"Come in and cool off," said Richard. "Who wants a cold drink? I've got cold water and iced tea. Or I could whip up some lemonade."

Deena regarded the students with interest. This was the first time she'd seen them up close. As for me, I was fascinated by the transformation. Richard was right. They came across as a fun-loving bunch. Not a mourner among them.

"Lemonade sounds yummy," said April.

"Got any beer?" asked Vince.

Sheila gave him a warning look. "What did I say last night? No alcohol. This is technically still a school-sponsored event."

Vince grinned impishly and shrugged. "Tea then."

"Tea for me too," said Isaiah.

"Tea for two," said Richard. "How about you, Sheila? Tea for three?"

"I think I'll hit the shower first. Thank you, though."
She picked up her boots from the floor and headed upstairs.

April and Isaiah had been shooting looks my way. I
couldn't tell if they were wary or merely curious.

Deena cleared her throat, reminding Richard of his
manners. "Oh!" he said. "Meet my friends. April, Isaiah,
Vince—this is Deena Lee and Sierra Ravenswood."

"Charmed," said Vince, shaking our hands in turn.
Something in the curl of his lips and the gaze of his deep
brown eyes screamed *sexy bad boy*. It would have been
amusing if it weren't so effective. I caught Deena's barely
raised eyebrows and hid a grin. On second thought, it was
still amusing.

"You were at the flower shop yesterday," said Isaiah,
addressing me.

"Yes, that's right. I own the place."

"I was hoping to get a better look at the orchid collection. Maybe we'll stop by tomorrow, if that's okay."

"Uh, yeah. Sure. I think that would be okay." I actually wasn't sure if the police would allow us to open,
but maybe I could let them in anyway. I welcomed the
opportunity to further observe and question the students.
So far, I couldn't bring myself to launch into the interrogation I'd imagined.

April draped her arm casually over Isaiah's shoulder.
"Always the nerd," she said playfully. "I love it."

Richard had left to prepare the drinks. He now
returned with a tray of tall, cold glasses, which he set
on the coffee table. The students helped themselves and
settled in on the sofa.

Deena was snapping pictures of possible bouquet
locations, including the fireplace mantel, end table, and
coffee table. When her camera faced the students, they

mugged for a shot. April, in the middle, rested her arms around the necks of both guys and puckered her lips. Vince made a sideways peace sign, while Isaiah smiled broadly.

"Adorable," said Richard. Then he patted me on the shoulder. "Come with me. I'll show you my bedroom."

One of the boys whistled, and the others laughed. Richard laughed along with them. Deena and I exchanged another look and followed Richard up the stairs.

The second floor featured four bedrooms, two on either side of a central hallway. At the end of the hall was a wood-framed mirror above an antique console table.

"This would be a nice spot for a bouquet," said Deena, snapping another picture.

"That's what I was thinking," said Richard. "Plus a small vase on each bedside table." He unlocked the door to his room, at the rear of the hallway on the left side. We admired his décor, while he explained that he had three bedrooms to let, a large one the size of his room and two smaller ones. Each bedroom had an en suite bathroom.

"Are the two boys sharing a room?" I asked.

"Yep," he said. "They're in the large room across the hall. It has two double beds. April and Sheila each have one of the smaller rooms."

When we went back downstairs, we found that Vince had disappeared, and April and Isaiah were head-to-head, leaning over a cell phone. I casually walked behind them and took a peek. They seemed to be perusing photos from their hike.

Richard wanted to show Deena and me his garage, which he'd transformed into a game room. He led us to the back door and outside across a brick inlay patio. Before we reached the garage door, I caught a whiff of cigarette smoke. *So, that's where Vince went.*

"Uh, you two go ahead," I said. "I'll join you in a minute."

"There's a half bath across from the kitchen, if you need it," said Richard.

As soon as they went into the garage, I slipped around the corner and found Vince standing on a slope behind the house, gazing toward the mountains.

"Hi," I said, walking up to him.

He nodded at me in greeting and held out a pack of cigarettes. After a brief hesitation, I reached out and took one from the pack. Smokers always seemed to share an instant bond, didn't they? It was the perfect excuse to strike up a conversation with someone.

I held the cigarette between two fingers and stared at it. *Now what?* Was I supposed to ask him for a light? The truth was, I had no idea how to smoke a cigarette.

I started giggling softly. Vince gave me a strange look, which made me laugh harder. *Get it together, Sierra!* Struggling for composure, I took a deep, ragged breath. Then I sheepishly handed the cigarette back to him.

"I don't actually smoke," I said. "Sorry."

"Okay," he said slowly. From the flicker in his eye, I could tell he thought I must be either crazy or ditzy. Maybe both.

"I just wanted to talk to you," I said, trying to sound more normal. After all, he was probably only five years younger than me. We were practically peers. "What happened yesterday was *insane*. How are you holding up?"

Instead of answering right away, he looked back toward the mountains. Was he trying to decide if he could trust me? I waited him out until he finally sighed.

"Yeah, it was shocking. Obviously. But I'm alright." He paused to take a drag on his cigarette. "It's not like this is my first encounter with death."

"Oh. I'm sorry."

He tilted his head in a gesture of acceptance. "That's life. Life means death. What are you gonna do?"

Huh. So, Vince was a philosopher. I never would have guessed.

"But," he continued quietly, "it can really mess a person up."

I wasn't quite sure what he meant. "Were you close with Professor Lowry?" I asked gently.

He looked at me askance. *Was that a weird thing for me to ask?* "Not particularly. He was my teacher."

"Oh, right." Trying to appear contemplative, I turned to gaze at the mountains too. "I just feel so bad. I've been trying to figure out how this could have happened. Do you, uh, have any idea what he was doing in the storeroom at my shop?"

"Not really. I assume he was forced in there, or lured somehow, by the person who hit him."

"Hmm. Was he acting strange on the drive? I heard he almost caused an accident. The delivery driver, Bart, said the professor was driving erratically."

Vince finished his cigarette and tossed the butt toward a patch of weeds. "If you ask me, that guy, Bart, seemed unhinged. Maybe he was the one driving erratically."

Maybe? Didn't Vince know? Also, he didn't really answer my question about the professor.

I snapped my fingers, as if I'd had a sudden thought. "Hey, by the way, do you know what became of the professor's canteen?"

Vince slowly swiveled his head to stare at me. "What?"

"He had a canteen when he came into Flower House, but it wasn't found in the storeroom or anywhere else in the shop."

I watched Vince with interest. On the surface, he

seemed as cool and smooth as ever—except for the tell-tale clench of his jaw.

"Someone must have picked it up," he said. "What's the big deal?"

"I don't know. I was just curious, that's all."

He moved closer, until he was standing right in front of me. With mouth twitching, he reached out and lightly tugged the ends of my hair flirtatiously—or trying to be. "Relax, cutie. No need to worry. The cops will catch the bad guy, and you can get back to making your pretty flower arrangements."

Startled, I stepped back an inch and plastered on a smile. "I know they will. I'm not worried."

Only, I really was. I was worried the truth about Professor Lowry might never come out—especially when the students closest to him apparently wanted to keep it hidden. As casual and playful as this one seemed, there was a hard glint in his eye that told another story.

Chapter 7

"I'm telling you, Deena, it was *strange*. One minute, he seemed almost sweet and vulnerable, as you might expect under the circumstances. The next, he was all cagey and guarded—and then he tried to flirt with me? I think?"

I still couldn't wrap my head around what had happened with Vince. I wanted to discuss it with Deena, so we made a plan to meet up again after leaving Richard's B&B. We'd come in separate cars, and she needed to run some errands, so I followed her downtown (a five-minute drive; everything in Aerieville is a five-minute drive) and parked next to her in the small municipal parking lot on the square.

Since it was Sunday, several places were closed, and the streets were half-empty. I was glad of that. At least we had a small measure of privacy, without being hounded by gossip-seekers. I tagged along as Deena made a stop at the drugstore and the walk-up ATM at the bank, and then picked up a dress at the dry cleaners. After all that, we bought double-scoop ice-cream cones at Tasty Cone: raspberry and mango sherbet for Deena, chocolate and mint-chocolate chip for me. We took our cones across the street, where we sat on a bench outside the darkened courthouse to finish our conversation.

Of everything I'd told Deena, she was most fixated on the last part.

"Maybe he likes older women," she said, barely hiding her grin.

"Older? I'm not that much older." I'd be turning twenty-nine in a couple of months—a fact I didn't particularly care to dwell on. I'd always thought I'd be so much further along in my life at this point—career-wise, relationship-wise, everything-wise.

"Well, he was definitely hitting on you," she said. "I think that little display of his six-pack abs was for your benefit too."

"C'mon," I said, waving away the idea. "We're getting off track here. The important thing is he was visibly rattled by my questions."

"So, now what?"

I sighed and licked my ice cream. "I don't know. I'd still like to talk to the others. We should make the flower arrangements for Richard and bring them to him tomorrow. He said he serves tea in the afternoons, right? If we time it right, maybe we can join them."

"That sounds good," said Deena, "assuming we don't have a lot of other orders to fill tomorrow."

We enjoyed our ice cream in silence for a moment, as we watched the sparse comings and goings on the quiet street. A gaggle of leotard-clad middle-school girls headed down the block toward Valerie Light's gymnastics and dance studio. A few minutes later, a couple of boys in baseball uniforms passed us going the other direction, toward the ball field. Cars driving by were few and far between. It was truly a lazy Sunday afternoon.

"Heads up," said Deena suddenly. "It's Nell Cusley, two o'clock."

I looked around. "Two o'clock?"

Deena pointed across the street. "Maybe it's one o'clock? Whatever, she's over there parking."

I checked my watch. I knew what Deena meant, but it still made me wonder about the time. It was actually almost four.

"Nell must have just closed her diner," I said. She was generally open for breakfast and lunch only. "What's she doing? Going to the drugstore?"

"I don't know," said Deena. "She's looking toward the parking lot, and now she's looking around."

"Oh, shoot." I hopped up and backed around the bench, out of her line of sight. "I bet she recognized my car." My electric orange Fiat was unmistakable. I'd bought it in Nashville, and it was definitely one of a kind in Aerieville.

"Let's walk around the block," said Deena. "I'm not in the mood for Nell's gossip."

"And I'm not keen to be *pumped* for gossip," I said.

As we cut across the lawn to the adjacent sidewalk, the sky grew dimmer under thickening clouds. A sudden breeze shook the branches of the poplar trees on the boulevard.

"I wonder how things went for Calvin at the police station," I said. "Hopefully, he's out of there by now."

"Why don't you call him?" said Deena.

I paused, popping the last bite of ice cream cone into my mouth. As I chewed, Deena handed me a paper napkin and raised one eyebrow. "You're worried about him, aren't you?"

Swallowing, I nodded my head. "Yeah, a little. It's so

unfair. Lowry victimized *him*, and now Calvin is being grilled about Lowry's death."

Deena put her hands on her hips. "I knew it. You really like him, don't you?"

"Well, sure. Don't you?"

"Sierra Ravenswood!" Deena used her mock-scolding tone. "Why have you been holding out on me? Haven't I been saying what a cute couple you and Calvin would make?"

I grinned in spite of myself. "Have you?"

"What's holding you back?" she asked. "Is it because he works for you?"

Now I dropped my smile. "Oh, gosh. I hadn't even thought of that, but you raise a good point. What if we started dating and things didn't work out? That could make it really uncomfortable at Flower House, and maybe even affect business."

"True," said Deena. "On the other hand, you're the one always talking about 'living in the now.' Life is short. Might as well seize the day—or seize the man, as the case may be."

For a moment, she directed a thoughtful gaze toward the sky, where puffy clouds threatened to build into a storm head. Was she thinking about a particular man, besides Calvin? She hadn't dated anyone herself, since breaking up with her fiancé and coming back to Aerieville.

Before I could ask her, she returned her attention to me. "You should ask him out."

"I dunno," I hedged. "There's a lot I really don't know about Calvin. I don't know anything about his childhood, or his past relationships, or—"

"Excuses, excuses," she interrupted. "If you ask him, he'll probably tell you anything you want to know."

"You're right," I said, making up my mind. "But I

think I'll text instead of calling. That way I won't put him on the spot."

I pulled out my phone, found his name in my contacts, and typed a short message: *So, are you in the slammer? Do I need to come up with some bail money?*

I pressed Send, then showed Deena the message, which made her laugh. Biting my lip, I paced in a circle as I waited. A few seconds later, he replied: *LOL. Thankfully, no. But not for the chief's lack of trying. BTW, know any good lawyers?*

Wincing, I showed Deena his response. "It doesn't sound great," I said.

"You could find out more over dinner," she nudged.

"Right." Quickly, before I could chicken out, I sent another message: *I have a homemade casserole in my fridge at home. Want to come over and help me eat it? We can discuss your legal defense strategy.*

Deena read my message and nodded her approval. "Good job."

We started walking again. "Looks like rain," I said, trying not to imagine what might be going through Calvin's mind.

Rounding the corner, we headed back toward Main Street. As we approached the intersection, we spotted Nell again, coming out of the drugstore across the street, half a block away.

"Jeez," said Deena. "It's like she has a sixth sense or something."

As we waited for the light to change, I felt my phone buzz. I grabbed it from my purse and read the text. My heart gave an excited flutter. "He said yes!"

"Of course he did," said Deena.

More specifically, he'd said, "Sounds good. What time?"

I hastily typed in *6:00* as the walk sign lit up. At the same time, Nell caught sight of us. "Well, hello there!" she hollered. Waving her arms, she hurried our way.

"Don't make eye contact!" Deena hissed.

Keeping our heads down, we jogged across the street and bolted for the parking lot. I stifled a giggle as we ran. Fortunately, we had a convenient reason for running away. The first fat raindrops splattered the pavement and pelted us like cold darts.

I didn't mind in the least. Calvin was coming to my house for dinner.

After picking up Gus from Rocky, I had just enough time to get home, dry Gus off from the rain, change into a cute sundress, and pop the casserole in the oven to warm it up. Calvin showed up at six o'clock on the dot.

Naturally, Gus was ecstatic to see him. He barked, wagged, and jumped on Calvin like he was a vet returning from war.

Calvin laughed at the attention. "I missed you too, buddy." When he managed to extricate himself from the onslaught of puppy love, he handed me a bottle of wine. "I wasn't sure what kind of wine goes with a casserole, so I brought a Chardonnay."

"That's perfect," I said. "Come on in and sit down."

I poured the wine and doled out what was left of the flower salad Deena had made. Then we tucked into the broccoli rice casserole my mom had sent over. As fitness enthusiasts, my family rarely ate foods with a lot of excess fat and salt. So, even though there was heavy cream and cheddar cheese in the dish, it was still on the healthy side, with fresh broccoli, wild mushrooms, and brown rice. Served with a side of crusty bread and butter, it was the perfect comfort food for a stormy evening.

Thunder rumbled in the distance as Calvin and I ate. I asked if he minded sharing what had happened at his police interview, and he shook his head.

"Not at all. Bradley and Dakin tried to get me to confess to the murder, and I kept telling them it wasn't me."

"Did they play good cop, bad cop?" I asked, trying to keep the mood light.

He smiled briefly. "Not quite. Bradley was polite and casual, like she always seems to be, and Dakin mostly held back and watched. After about an hour of back-and-forth nonsense, they finally let me go. They knew they didn't have a shred of evidence to hold me."

"I can't understand why they're so focused on you," I said, feeling indignant on Calvin's behalf. He seemed impressively patient about the whole thing.

"I do," he said. "They want a nice, tidy explanation. If they can pin me as a disgruntled employee or jealous rival, it makes their job a lot easier."

"I guess," I said, still not convinced.

"They also seem to think I knew Lowry was coming. This was a scheduled field trip, which supposedly happens every year. And I work at Flower House. They think I had the whole thing planned out." Calvin sounded so calm. But when he took a sip of wine, I noticed his hand trembling slightly. Maybe he was more nervous than he was letting on.

I took a sip of my own wine and pondered whether the murder was spontaneous or planned. I could imagine arguments for both scenarios.

"You know," I said, "maybe we should have told the police about that receipt Gus ate. It may not prove anything, but if it could exonerate you in any way . . ." I trailed off, as Calvin shook his head.

"I did tell them," he said, "and they weren't impressed. If anything, they seemed to suspect I made it up to deflect attention from myself."

I put down my fork, once again feeling piqued. What kind of detective was Acting Chief Bradley? I was rapidly losing respect for her.

"It's ironic," Calvin went on. "Even though I was in the Botany program for several years, I always spent summers working on my family's farm in Iowa. If I'd been around to participate in the summer field program, I might have met Felix much sooner. And you too."

I looked up with a jolt. Calvin had just revealed so much, I didn't know which part to follow up on: the mention of his family, the fact that he'd worked on a farm— or an admission that he might have feelings for me? After all, we hadn't technically said this was a date.

Momentarily flummoxed, I cleared my throat—and ultimately decided to stick with the topic at hand. "I didn't know about those field trips either," I said. "I only worked for Felix part-time in high school—thanks to Granny, who was friends with Felix's wife, Georgina. And I mainly arranged flowers or made deliveries. If Professor Lowry ever stopped by with a group of students, I probably wouldn't have seen him."

Calvin reached for the bottle of wine and topped off both of our glasses. "What were you like in high school?" he asked. "Were you always the optimistic dreamer? Always looking on the bright side and trying to influence things with your positivity, et cetera?" He smiled at me warmly, in spite of the teasing tone. Was he just trying to change the subject? Or did he really want to get to know me better? Either way, I didn't mind taking our conversation to a more personal level.

"I guess I've always been a dreamer," I admitted. "I wasn't the strongest student, academically, even though I read a lot. I was more interested in art and music."

"At least you get to use your creativity in floral design," he said. "Flower House seems like a good fit for you."

"Yeah. I've been lucky." I paused, reconsidering my words. "Actually, I believe we create our own luck, to a large extent. I think a person's outlook has a lot to do with their level of satisfaction. Know what I mean?"

For a moment, Calvin looked like he might be gearing up for a friendly debate. Then he tilted his head, as if reflecting on the idea. "That makes some sense," he said. "If you happen to be an open, positive person, you'll probably make more friends—and then have more opportunities come your way."

"For sure," I said. "You also have to be able to recognize opportunities for what they are—and grab them when you can. That's what I tried to do with Flower House. I saw its potential and decided to go for it."

A sudden flash of lightning lit up the darkness outside my kitchen windows. It was followed closely by a loud crash of thunder. Gus yelped in response.

"Yikes," I said. "Sounds like it's right on top of us."

"Yeah." Calvin pushed back his chair. "I looked at the radar before coming over here. There's a huge band of storms making its way across the state."

I took our plates to the sink and put the leftovers away, as Calvin comforted Gus. Then I joined them at the kitchen window to look outside. My side yard was engulfed in darkness, except for intermittent flashes of lightning. In those brief moments of illumination, we could see tree branches waving wildly in the wind.

"Guess we shouldn't be standing here," said Calvin, taking a step back.

"True," I said. "Do you want to sit in the living room?"

Before he could answer, there was another crack of thunder. This one shook the cottage and made me jump. In the next instant, the lights went out.

I gasped and reached for Calvin's hand in the darkness. With a quiet chuckle, he clasped my hand in a comforting grip and moved closer to me. I could feel the warmth radiating from his body. Gus barked again at our feet.

"Got any candles?" Calvin asked softly.

I laughed nervously. "Yeah, somewhere. Let me think a minute." The truth was, I was reluctant to leave Calvin's side. Not that I was afraid of the storm, or of the dark. I just wanted to enjoy this moment of intimacy while it lasted.

I started to turn toward Calvin, when another bolt of lightning flashed outside the window. In that second, I saw a dark-clad person leering from the gloom of my yard. I screamed in surprise and jumped backward. In the next flash of light, the figure was gone.

Chapter 8

Calvin wanted to go outside and search for the person lurking in the yard, but I wouldn't let him. It was raining buckets, and my electricity was still out. I'd found some candles and set them around the living room, creating a romantic, if spooky, atmosphere.

"Come and sit down," I urged, patting the sofa next to me. "I'm sure whoever it was is long gone by now." The sight had been startling for sure. But, in retrospect, maybe it wasn't as sinister as all that. From the glimpse I'd had, it seemed the person was wearing a raincoat and a sou'wester, like some kind of harmless fisherman.

Calvin dropped the curtain he'd been holding back and moved away from the window facing the backyard. "Maybe," he said. "But the storm didn't stop them from being out there in the first place. It could have been a Peeping Tom."

"It was probably just one of my neighbors," I said, trying to sound confident. "Or somebody looking for their dog or chasing something that had blown away in the wind." Those were plausible explanations, I thought.

Though I could very well be trying to convince myself as much as Calvin.

He slowly lowered himself onto the couch and reached down to pet Gus, who was hiding under the coffee table. "Your doors are all locked, right?" asked Calvin.

"Yes, of course. I always keep them locked."

"And your windows?"

"Yeah, I think—"

A loud knock on the front door made me forget what I was going to say. Calvin hopped up and moved to look out the peephole. I followed, standing close behind him.

"Oh," he said, relaxing his shoulders.

"Who is it?" I whispered.

He unlocked the door and threw it open to reveal my family—Mom, Dad, and Rocky—huddled under one large golf umbrella on my front stoop. They all appeared startled to see Calvin. He stood back to let them come in.

"Mom! Dad! What are you doing here?"

"We're here to check on you, what else?" said Mom, pulling off her galoshes. Dad shook the umbrella out the door before closing it. Rocky leaned down to greet Gus, who had run up to lick the rain off his bare legs. "Can you bring me a dish towel?" Mom asked.

I hurried to the kitchen and grabbed a stack of towels, then gave one to each of them.

"Hey, girlie," said Dad, pulling me into a damp, one-armed hug. "We thought you might stop by today."

"If the mountain won't come to Mohammed, Mohammed has to go to the mountain," said Mom. She moved to flick on the wall switch and found it didn't work. "No power?"

Rocky glanced at the candles, and shot me an apologetic look. I returned the look with a smirk.

Dad glanced from me to Calvin. "I hope we weren't interrupting something."

"No, sir," Calvin said quickly. "We were just talking."

I rolled my eyes. What were we, teenagers? Granted, I couldn't blame Calvin if he felt intimidated. As a former college football player and current health club owner, my dad cut an imposing figure. Between him and Rocky, who were both easily twice my weight, there was a lot of muscle crowding into the dollhouse. Add to that Mom's outsized personality, and anyone on the receiving end of my family's attention could easily feel overwhelmed.

"Did you check the fuse box?" asked Mom.

"It's not a fuse," I said. "It's the storm."

"Where's that heavy-duty flashlight I gave you?" asked Dad.

"It's in the closet, but I don't think we need it," I said. "Why don't we all have a seat in the living room? I can sit on the floor."

Ignoring the suggestion, my mom said, "We might have a camping lantern in the car."

Rocky headed to the kitchen, using his phone as a flashlight. "Got any of that casserole left?"

Calvin rocked back on his heels. "I should probably get going. I don't think the rain is going to let up for a while."

I threw up my hands in a gesture of defeat. Our date— if it could be called that—was over anyway. I knew my parents were here to grill me about the murder, and Calvin didn't need to sit through that. He'd already suffered through one interrogation today.

I walked him to the door, as my parents found a flashlight and went to check my fuse box.

"Sorry about all this," I said quietly.

"There's nothing to be sorry for," said Calvin. "I'm actually glad I'm not leaving you alone. I was starting to think I might have to sleep on your couch tonight."

I raised my eyebrows at that, and Calvin gave an embarrassed laugh. "Not that you're not capable of taking care of yourself. It's just been a weird night."

"Yeah, it has," I agreed. *Well, the last part anyway.*

He opened the door, then paused and leaned down to pick up something from the doormat outside. "Did you drop this? Looks like it got stepped on and soaked."

He handed me a bedraggled little bouquet of flowers. In the faint candlelight, they appeared to be red poppies, tied with a red string. I frowned. "How odd," I muttered. It almost reminded me of something a child might leave on May Day, except that this was the middle of July. Perhaps it came from one of my neighbors' grandchildren?

Calvin stepped outside and popped open his umbrella, then turned to give me a jaunty salute. "See ya tomorrow."

I smiled, tamping down a twinge of regret. "Have a good night, Calvin."

As I closed the door, I glanced at the poppies again. Their fragile, paperlike petals were soaked and crumpled, and many of their curly stems were broken. *What a shame.* I took them to the kitchen and tossed them in the trash can, before joining my family in the living room.

The rain had tapered to a gentle shower by the time I finally crawled into bed. My family had stayed until eleven, when the electricity finally came back on. In that time, my mom called the power company twice, my dad fixed a leaky faucet in the dark, and my brother finished off the casserole. It was like I'd never left home.

Of course, we'd also talked about the murder. Mom

was adamant that the incident would be terrible for business. She advised that I most definitely should postpone the café opening. Dad bemoaned the fact that his pal Walt Walden wasn't back on duty yet as the Chief of Police. He figured Walt would give him progress updates on the investigation. Dad wasn't sure what he thought of the acting chief. He thought she might feel as if she had something to prove, this being her first big case and all. I hadn't even thought of that—and wasn't sure what to make of it.

Mostly, though, my family was worried that the killer was still at large.

"The suspect list must be pretty small, huh?" said Rocky. "There weren't a lot of people at Flower House at the time, were there?"

"More than usual, actually," I said.

Mom paused in her pacing. She could never sit still for long. "*You're* not on that suspect list, are you?"

"No," I assured her. "I don't think so. I haven't been asked to come to the station for more questioning like Calvin was." The second I said it, I wished I'd held my tongue.

Dad narrowed his dark eyebrows. "The police are interested in Calvin?"

"Maybe it's not such a great idea to be inviting him to your home right now," said Mom.

"You know you can be too trusting sometimes, sis," said Rocky. *The traitor.*

Thinking about it now, hours later, it still raised my hackles. I'd had to both explain Calvin's connection to the murder victim *and* defend him from the implications. All in the same telling. And I probably didn't do a very good job of it.

I rolled over in bed and sighed. My folks meant well.

They were just concerned about me. I could hardly fault them for that. In fact, maybe they had reason to worry. Not about Calvin, of course, but there *was* still a murderer out there. With a shiver, I recalled the dark figure standing outside my window. Part of me even wondered if I'd imagined it. Or maybe that was wishful thinking.

I flipped my pillow over to the cool side and closed my eyes. Listening to the patter of the rain, I eventually began to relax. After all, the evening wasn't a complete bust. I'd enjoyed Calvin's company while it lasted. *I wonder if he had a good time.* He seemed to. Under different circumstances, he might have kissed me good night. I smiled at the thought.

Then I had another recollection. *Where had those poppies come from?*

Chapter 9

I rarely overslept. It hadn't happened in ages. So, I was all the more surprised when I squinted at my bedside clock and saw that it was after nine a.m.

"Gus! Why didn't you wake me up?"

The corgi perked up his head but remained spread out on his blanket at the foot of my bed. He was in no hurry to get up. The slate gray sky outside didn't help matters.

I rolled out of bed and padded to the kitchen to start the coffee maker. Then I brushed my teeth and took a quick shower. I was still in my robe when I returned to the kitchen to have breakfast. I'd just taken my first sip of coffee when my cell phone rang. It was Deena.

"Hey, sorry," I said, as soon as I picked up. "I haven't left home yet. I'll be in soon."

"You might want to reconsider that idea," she said.

"What? Why?"

Deena's voice was grim. "There's a line of satellite vans on the street in front of the shop. All the area TV stations finally caught wind of the murder. Turns out the brutal killing of a university professor is big news."

"Ugh. Of course it is." I should have anticipated this. Aerieville, sadly, had lost its local newspaper years ago, and the nearest TV and radio stations were based in bigger cities miles away. But the murder of a Knoxville college professor was definitely significant enough to warrant the trip.

"I didn't think I should talk to any reporters without clearing it with you," said Deena. "What should we say?"

"I have no idea." I pinched the bridge of my nose. What did one say in such situations? No comment? Condolences to the family of the deceased? Buy our flowers?

I shook myself. Definitely not the last thing. "Where are you?" I asked. "Have you talked to Calvin?"

"I'm at Coffee Art Café, trying to keep a low profile. I called Calvin first, because I thought he might have heard from you. He's basically hiding out in his apartment."

"Oh, jeez. I guess I'd better get over there and rescue him."

I heard voices in the background, before Deena responded. "Uh, yeah. You might as well give a statement. Then maybe the TV stations will stop replaying Flo's comments over and over again."

"What? Flo's been on the news already?" It just figured. *The one day I oversleep is when the news vultures descend.* And with Flo already primed to badmouth Flower House.

"It's pretty awful," said Deena. "She brought up the other murder."

"Of course."

"And she said Flower House ought to be called 'Poison House.'"

"Oh no! The nerve of that woman." I was fired up now. My annoyance with Flo overshadowed my usual shyness when it came to anything but my music. "I gotta go. I'll call you later."

Spurred to action, I dumped out my cereal, flew to my room, and threw open my closet. What to wear? Easy. I needed to dress for success. I needed to clothe myself to match how I wanted to feel. And, well, I needed to work with what I had. That meant off-white trousers and my one and only summer blazer over a floral-print satin top. With a touch of hair gloss and a dab of makeup, I was ready to face the masses. Or, at least, the TV cameras.

Calm, cool, and collected, I said to myself, as I leashed up Gus and shouldered my purse. *I am a confident businesswoman. I am composed and trustworthy and . . .*

My thoughts trailed off as I picked up my phone and saw a dozen missed calls. *Dang it.*

I dropped into a chair and began playing the messages. *Knowledge is power.* I needed to know what folks were saying.

A few of the calls were from reporters and busybodies. (How did Nell Cusley even get my cell phone number?) Two of the calls were hang-ups from unfamiliar numbers. But the rest were from people who were looking out for me, including my mom; Byron Atterly, Flower House's bookkeeper; and Calvin. The message from Calvin made the most sense.

"Hey, Sierra, listen up. If you're approached by any media people, you should say 'no comment.' Or, at least, say as little as possible. I spoke to a lawyer this morning, and that's what she advised me. If any of us ends up in court, our public statements will be picked apart and held against us. Sorry." With that, he hung up.

Gus, confused that we weren't leaving the house, whimpered at my feet. I absently patted his head, lost in thought. I needed a new plan.

Two hours later found me on the front steps of Flower House, facing a cluster of microphones and a horde of scary-looking video cameras. After hearing Calvin's warning, I'd called Deena back. "You were a communications major," I said. "What can we do that will paint us in the most favorable—or least damaging—light?"

"We take control," she said, after a moment's thought. "We schedule a press conference and give a prepared statement. Something short and sweet."

So, that's what we decided to do. Licking my lips, I took a deep breath and read the statement we'd written together.

"'On behalf of everyone here at Flower House, I would like to offer our deepest sympathy to the family and friends of Professor Steve Lowry. We are shocked and saddened that this tragic event occurred in our shop. We are fully cooperating with the authorities, and we feel confident that justice will be served. I'm sorry we can't offer any further comments, as the investigation is ongoing. Flower House will remain closed for the time being, except for online orders. This means we won't be opening our new café this Saturday as planned.'" It had pained me to make that decision, but I knew I didn't have much of a choice.

"'Thank you for your understanding,'" I concluded. On that note, I turned quickly and went inside the shop, shutting the door firmly behind me. When Deena had spoken with all the station representatives to set up the press event, she'd made it clear that I wouldn't be answering questions. Surprisingly, they all seemed to respect our decision.

Deena and Calvin were waiting for me in the café. "Good job!" said Deena. "That was perfect."

Calvin was slightly less enthusiastic. "You probably said more than the lawyers would've liked, but it sounded fine to me."

"Thanks." I peeked out the window and was heartened to see most of the reporters packing up and heading to their vans. "How about we take our minds off all this depressing stuff and get to work arranging flowers?"

"Don't you want to eat first?" asked Deena. She gestured to a spread of food Calvin had brought down from his apartment. It consisted mainly of oven-fresh frozen pizza, a premade mixed salad, and canned seltzer water. My stomach rumbled in response.

"As a matter of fact, yes," I said, laughing. "I haven't eaten much today."

We spoke little over lunch. Calvin seemed preoccupied with his thoughts, and Deena used the time to review our pending flower orders. I shot off a few texts to my family. I also let Richard know we still planned to stop by later.

For the rest of the afternoon, we worked together to prepare bouquets for delivery. First we arranged a get-well bouquet, a birthday basket, and anniversary roses, all of which Calvin offered to deliver. Then Deena and I designed the arrangements for Richard. We selected an assortment of vintage bowls and vases, ranging in size from the large centerpiece to small bedside jars. In the bottom of each vessel, we placed a metal flower frog to hold the flowers in place.

Based on the charming, mountain lodge aesthetic of Richard's home, I opted for elegant seasonal blooms in warm tones: chiefly two varieties of dahlias, in hues of

pale coral and brown sugar, and a few sprigs each of
peach spray roses and lavender-blue sweet pea. To offset
all the color, I interspersed several stems of silver dollar
eucalyptus. The result was beautiful and smelled amazing, if I said so myself.

As it happened, we had more work than I'd expected.
By the time Deena and I arrived at Richard's it was nearly
four o'clock. He came out to my car to help us carry in
the arrangements.

"Oh, my!" he said. "These are stunning."

"Thank you," I said, beaming. "We can always switch
things out next time. Let me know if there are any particular colors or varieties you'd like to try."

"I wouldn't change a thing. You perfectly captured
the vibe of Mountain View B&B—classy, welcoming,
charming." He pretended to polish his fingernails on his
shirt and laughed.

"I'm so glad," I said. Deena held up her palm for a
high five, which I returned with a grin.

"Speaking of classy," said Richard, "I saw you on the
breaking news. You looked terrific."

"Ugh." My smile transformed into a grimace. "I sure
wished I didn't have to do it."

He patted me on the shoulder. "This too shall pass."

Deena looked at Richard in surprise. "When did you
become so wise? Richard the sage."

"That's right. I've got the hard-earned wisdom of my
years. Getting older isn't all bad." He winked at us, still
in a good mood apparently.

We set the arrangements on the tables we'd previously selected: in the foyer, the dining room, and the living room. As I placed a bouquet on the console table, I
glanced at the staircase.

"I'm sorry we missed your afternoon tea," I said. "I

was hoping to chat with your guests. Are they all in their rooms?"

"Sheila is. The kids went for a bike ride."

"They brought bikes?" asked Deena.

"No, they're using mine. I have a bunch of old bicycles I fixed up for my guests' use. Just another perk here at Mountain View."

"Do you have time for a visit?" I asked.

"For you? Always. Shall I put the kettle back on?"

"Do you have chai tea?" asked Deena.

"You know I do." Richard disappeared into the kitchen.

I lined up the four bedroom posies on the coffee table for the time being and picked up the last centerpiece. "I'll go ahead and take this to the hall table upstairs."

Deena nodded, then called to Richard to offer help with the tea.

It was quiet upstairs. After setting the flowers on the table, I stood for a moment in the hallway, regarding the closed bedroom doors. It sure would be interesting to see what each person had in their room. Did someone have the professor's canteen, or a muddy boot matching the footprint I'd found? Or a package of ninety-nine-cent sunflower seeds?

In the midst of these ruminations, I was startled when a door opened and Sheila stepped out. She seemed equally surprised to find me loitering outside her room.

"Hello," she said shortly. At this vantage, I noticed her close-cropped brown hair had strands of silver. She was dressed casually in shorts and a Smoky Mountains T-shirt.

"Hi! I was just bringing up these flowers." I pointed to the bouquet on the table.

"They're lovely," she said. "I was going to ask Richard

for an extra towel. I don't suppose you know where he keeps them?"

"No, sorry. But he's right downstairs. We were about to have tea. Would you like to join us?"

She looked like she was about to decline, so I hastily added, "I was actually hoping to talk to you for a few minutes, if you don't mind."

After a brief hesitation, she shrugged. "Sure. I could use a break from reading anyway."

"This must be a strange situation for you," I said, as we headed down to the living room.

"It's definitely not the trip I thought I was signing up for," she said with a small sigh.

I gave her a sympathetic look. What an awful predicament to be in.

We took seats in front of the fireplace with Richard and Deena. Sheila waved away the hot tea, so Richard poured her a glass of iced lemon water from a crystal pitcher on the coffee table.

"The students seem to be coping well," I commented. "From what I could tell yesterday anyway."

"Mm-hmm," said Sheila. "These undergrads are tough. They've been through hard times before."

"More so than your average college kid?" asked Richard.

"I'd say so. I'm on the school scholarship committee, so I know a little about their backgrounds."

I remembered Vince mentioning this wasn't his first experience with death. Was that what Sheila was alluding to? I gave her an interested look, hoping she'd continue.

"I don't want to violate their privacy," she said. "But it *is* impressive how far they've come. Many of our scholarship recipients grew up in broken homes—or no homes, living in shelters or the foster system. One of our students served time in prison."

"Vince?" guessed Deena.

Sheila seemed almost to incline her head slightly before catching herself and saying, "I really can't say."

Deena slid her eyes toward me, as if to say, "Did you catch that?" I twitched my mouth and avoided looking at Deena. Of course, I had.

"Well, they seem like nice kids to me," said Richard. "That is, when they're not glued to their phones."

"They are definitely typical in that way." Sheila snickered lightly. "I swear, sometimes I think they're texting each other from the same room."

Richard smirked in agreement. "April was texting so fast and furious over breakfast, I thought she must be selling stocks on the New York exchange."

I had the urge to pull out my own phone to look these students up. I wondered which social media platforms they favored. It was hard to keep up. I made a mental note to search all the most popular ones the first chance I got.

A lull fell in our conversation, as we sipped our tea and water. Deena cleared her throat and shot me a significant glance. She was probably wondering why I hadn't asked Sheila about Professor Lowry. I was just gearing up to do so when Sheila beat me to the punch.

"So, you all work with Calvin Foxheart? You know, he was close to Steve Lowry at one time."

"Yes," I said. "Until the professor started acting strange and claimed Calvin's research as his own. Did you notice Lowry acting different last fall?"

She raised her eyebrows, apparently taken aback by my statement. "I only first met Steve at the end of last summer. I wouldn't know if he was acting differently than before."

I recalled Calvin saying Professor Washington was new to the school, but I'd hoped she could still corroborate the rumors Calvin had mentioned. "You didn't hear about him missing classes or being late for meetings?"

"I suppose he did seem distracted at times," she conceded. "I assumed it was because he was so focused on his research project. He was well-known to be a brilliant scientist."

The sound of the front door opening made us all turn our heads. The three students filed in, chatting loudly as usual. If I wasn't mistaken, both Isaiah and Vince seemed to stiffen when they caught sight of me. Why should my presence startle them so much?

"How was the ride?" asked Richard.

"Great!" said April. "We rode all over town. Aerieville is so cute."

Isaiah sat on the edge of a chair opposite the sofa and leaned forward to pour a glass of water from the pitcher on the coffee table. "Sorry we didn't make it to Flower House today," he said to me. "Maybe we'll get there tomorrow."

"That's okay," I said. "It was, uh, kind of busy today." I wondered if they'd caught my brief appearance on television.

"This town never seems to change," he continued. "It's always so quiet and old-school. And the amount of green space is amazing. I can see why Professor Foxheart moved here."

That was the first time I'd heard anyone refer to Calvin as "professor." It was interesting to think of him in that role. But more interesting to me was something else Isaiah had said.

"You've been here before?" I asked.

"This is my third summer taking the botany field program," Isaiah said.

"As you keep reminding us," said April, with a teasing grin. To me, she said, "This was my first time doing this trip. Isaiah is apparently such an expert on it, he could take Professor Lowry's place."

"That's *your* goal, not mine," he shot back. Something unspoken seemed to pass between them, as April subtly narrowed her eyes at him.

Vince came over and sat next to me on the couch. "This is my second time doing the trip," he interjected. I had the impression he was purposely deflecting attention away from his classmates. "I tried to get the school to pick a different location this year, like the Ozarks or the Black Hills. But nobody wanted to go that far away."

"This trip was a time-honored tradition," said Sheila.

For a moment, no one said anything. I wondered if everyone was thinking what I was thinking: that if they hadn't made this trip, Professor Lowry might still be alive.

Vince shifted in his seat. "Anyway, this is the first time any of us have spent this much time in Aerieville. What else is there to do around here, besides nature stuff?"

"There's a little bit of shopping," said Richard. "Though, admittedly, not a lot. There's a used bookstore just off the square downtown. And a little gift store next to that."

"It might seem like we're in a time capsule," Deena said, "but places open and close here just like everywhere. There used to be a nice dress shop and a department store on the square, but they both went out of business."

That sad reminder made me worry once again about the future of our flower-themed café. Would we ever attract enough customers to stay afloat?

"On the other hand," said Richard. "There's a new tea shop that seems to be doing well. It's where I get this delicious tea you've been enjoying."

"What about nightlife?" asked Vince.

"Cuties' Pool Hall is popular on the weekends," I said. "They have an attached restaurant, so they're family friendly before ten o'clock."

"I doubt if we'll still be here by the weekend," said Sheila. "God willing."

"The cops haven't even been by today, have they?" asked April.

Sheila shook her head. "I have to assume they're focusing their investigation . . . elsewhere." She glanced at me and looked away.

"I always kind of liked Professor Foxheart," Isaiah said thoughtfully. "I don't know exactly what happened between him and Professor Lowry, but he must have felt wronged. Or betrayed."

"It was probably a matter of honor," said Vince.

"Or revenge," said April.

I followed the exchange with growing dismay. Maybe I should've held my tongue, but I couldn't help myself. "Calvin didn't do it!"

Everyone stared at me in surprise.

"How do you know?" asked Isaiah. "Were you with him?"

"Who do you think did it?" asked Vince.

A chill fell over the room, as the university crew fixed me with stony glares. Were they daring me to accuse one of them? I gazed into my teacup and pretended to take a sip. I had no response to their questions. I wished I did, but I didn't.

Chapter 10

On our way back to Flower House, Deena and I compared notes on our impressions of the three college students. Richard had filled the awkward silence following my outburst and Vince's question with small talk, and shortly afterward we'd said our goodbyes. Deena and I had gathered our flower-transport boxes as quickly as we could and made our escape.

"They're so suspicious, all of them," I said. "Don't you think?"

Deena hesitated. "Are they?"

We were driving toward the square, with me behind the wheel. At a stop sign, I turned to look at her in surprise. "Don't you agree they're acting strange? You thought it was significant that Vince apparently served time in prison."

"I know. I'm just not sure it's enough to implicate them in the murder of their teacher. I mean, what motive could they possibly have?"

I drove past the courthouse and turned onto Main Street. A minute later, I slowed as we passed by the town park and ball field. Laughing children chased one another around the playground.

I knew Deena was right. It seemed ridiculous to imagine a college student intentionally killing their professor, especially on a voluntary field trip. But, to me, it was even more ridiculous to imagine Calvin doing it.

"Well, who do *you* think did it?" I asked.

"My money is still on Bart." She pulled down the visor to block the late-day sun, glaring brightly from the western sky. "Rocky said he's a hothead, and you saw him go after Lowry about his driving. Bart probably saw his chance and walloped the professor in a fit of rage."

I turned onto shady Oak Street and drove slowly toward Flower House. "With a candlestick?" I said. "He'd be more likely to punch the guy with his fists. Wouldn't he?"

Deena shrugged. "We don't know that. The guy is an enigma, remember?"

"True." In fact, I *had* been wanting to talk to the deliveryman. I wondered exactly where he'd been and what he'd seen during the few minutes between Lowry's last phone call and his last breath. If the three students were outside, Bart should have seen them.

"Should we stop by Dumbbells tonight?" asked Deena.

I pulled into the driveway alongside Flower House and parked near the back door of the shop. "I'll ask Rocky to let us know when Bart comes in," I said.

"Well, he did say Bart usually works out late on Monday evenings," said Deena.

"He did?" I cut the engine and frowned. "I don't remember that."

"Oh, maybe he just said it to me. We talked for a few minutes after we left your house the other night."

She got out of the car and shut the door, leaving me feeling strangely perplexed. Rocky only knew Deena through me, and I'd never known the two of them to chat much before. Not that there would be anything wrong with that.

Deena had grabbed some boxes from the back of my car and taken them inside. I gathered up the rest and joined her in the kitchen, where she was talking with Calvin. We briefly brought each other up to date, and Calvin agreed to keep Gus a while longer.

"What do you think, Sierra?" said Deena. "Meet at the gym at seven?"

"Let's make it ten after. That way my mom will already be leading her aerobics class." It would be hard enough to strike up a conversation with Bart in a public place, let alone within earshot of my overly protective family.

Oh well, I thought, as I filled Gus's water dish. *Might as well give it the old college try.* So to speak.

I had a little more than an hour to kill before meeting Deena at Dumbbells, so I went home to change and have a small bite to eat. It was strange being in the dollhouse without Gus. As I moved about, I kept expecting to see him at every turn. It was amazing how integral the pup had become to my life in just a few short months.

In fact, the lonely silence became so unsettling, I decided to head out early. Dressed in yoga shorts, a snug orange T-shirt, and sneakers, I locked up and took off. I thought I might drive around and reflect on recent events. But when I reached Main Street, I followed a whim and turned left instead of right. This route brought me to the west edge of town and Marla's Mini-Mart. A few minutes later, I pulled up to a gas pump and cut the engine.

As I filled the Fiat, a stout, whiskered man in grubby jeans and a stained T-shirt hefted himself from a bench next to the mini-mart. He approached me and flashed a toothless grin. "Warsh your winders?"

I hesitated a second, then shrugged. "Sure. Go ahead."

He smiled and got to work. "Name's Pete," he said amiably. "Where ya headed?"

"No place special. I live here." Once my tank was full, I fished a five-dollar bill from my purse. "Thanks, Pete," I said, handing him the money.

"God bless ya," he said, before returning to his place on the bench.

I moved my car to an angled parking space next to the little store and went inside. There was one other customer checking out and a long-haired teenage boy behind the counter. Browsing the snack aisle, I quickly found what I was looking for: a 99-cent package of sunflower seeds. As I figured, they were roasted and salted in their white-striped black shells.

When it was my turn to check out, I walked up to the counter and held up the little package. "Are these the only sunflower seeds you sell here?"

The clerk nodded. "Yes, ma'am. Will that be all?"

"I just have a quick question," I said, with what I hoped was an engaging smile. "Do you remember somebody buying a package of these sunflower seeds on Saturday?"

He scratched his head. "No, ma'am."

"Are you sure? It probably would have been around one or two o'clock."

"No, ma'am."

"Well, do you remember a white van from UT stopping by on Saturday? With a tall silver-haired driver and seven younger passengers?"

He shook his head again. "No, ma'am. I wasn't working here on Saturday."

Ugh. Why didn't he say that in the first place? I mentally slapped my forehead, as I fought to hide my impatience. "Who would've been here on Saturday?"

"Jimmy works weekends. He'll be here next Saturday."

I thanked the clerk and paid for the sunflower seeds. As I exited the store, Pete called out to me from his bench. "Spare some change, miss?"

I walked over to him and held out the sunflower seeds. "Would you like these?"

He grimaced and pointed to his gap-filled mouth. "I don't do so good with hard foods."

"Oh, I'm sorry—"

"But I'll take it anyway," he continued.

Feeling a bit sheepish, I handed him the snack. "Say, were you here a couple days ago, on Saturday?"

"I'm here ever' day."

"Do you remember seeing a white university van, probably around one o'clock or so?"

He surprised me by issuing forth a loud belly-jiggling chuckle. "Do I remember? Couldn't forget it. The driver—tall feller with a white goatee—he caused quite a scene right over yonder. 'Bout got hisself whupped." Pete pointed at a gas pump on the far side of the station.

"He almost got in a fight? With who?" I expected Pete to describe Bart. Maybe the deliveryman had followed Lowry's van off the highway after all.

"A little ol' lady!" Pete chortled again, as if this were the funniest thing he'd ever seen. "She drove in behind him in a ol' Subaru. He'd pulled in ahead o' her. I saw the whole thing."

"He cut her off?"

Pete rocked his whole body, as he continued to laugh. "Yeah, he did. And when she tried to give him what for, he turned his back on her. O' course, that only made her madder 'n' a old wet hen. What's that sayin' 'bout a woman scorned?"

I'd heard enough. At least now I knew why Wanda had been so upset with Lowry on the street outside Flower House. She probably didn't expect to encounter him again after he'd rebuffed her at the gas station. And that was after the butcher had slighted her that morning. Like Granny said, Wanda had had a rough day, and the more details I learned about it, the more like a suspect she seemed. It gave me a bad feeling in the pit of my stomach to think about Granny's friend like that, but part of me couldn't help it.

I started to back away, then paused. Might as well see what else Pete could tell me. "By the way, did you happen to notice anybody leaving the store with sunflower seeds on Saturday?"

He wrinkled his forehead, apparently stumped. "Most folks have their stuff in a bag or their pockets when they come out."

"That's okay. Never mind. Last question. Do you recall seeing a green delivery van for Pauly's Plants? It would've had pink and yellow flowers on the side."

Pete brightened. "Oh, yeah. That one I remember. Surly driver. Wouldn't give me the time a day."

Sounds like Bart.

"It weren't Saturday, though," Pete continued. "It was a day or two before that."

I found a ten-dollar bill in my purse and thanked Pete for all his help. Then I hurried back to my car. If I didn't get a move on, I'd be late for meeting Deena.

I felt rather pleased with myself, as I pulled out of the gas station and headed back toward the center of town. My little try at playing detective had paid off. I now knew that *all* of the suspects—except Calvin, of course—could have bought sunflower seeds from Marla's Mini-Mart.

However, my elation was short-lived. The information I'd learned didn't bring me any closer to solving the murder. I hadn't narrowed down the suspect list at all. I was just as baffled as ever.

As Granny liked to say, Dumbbells Gym was the baby my parents had before they had real babies. My folks, Hal and Mandy Ravenswood, had started their dream business right out of college—and had been running it, pretty much unchanged, ever since. It was a small facility, with two main workout rooms, one with exercise equipment and one for classes, both with rubber-mat flooring. Besides that, there were the locker rooms, a tiny office, and a small lobby. All the walls (except in the locker rooms, of course) featured glass pane windows, including the wall between the office and the lobby.

As kids, Rocky and I had spent so much time at Dumbbells, it was practically our second home. But, while Rocky would be challenging himself with every kind of free weight imaginable—and at ever-increasing weights and reps—I'd more likely be holed up in the office, writing songs or reading a mystery novel. Even today, exercising indoors wasn't really my thing.

Yet, as I parked on the street in front of the gym, I had to admit it was nice to have a place where I *could* work out anytime I wanted, if the mood should strike.

Granted, the mood hadn't struck in several weeks now, but I had a good excuse. I'd been busy trying to get my own small business off the ground.

Of course, that didn't stop Dad from making a big deal of it when I wandered into the lobby at a quarter past seven.

"Well, well, looky here! The prodigal daughter . . . in workout clothes? Will wonders never cease?" He stood up from behind the front desk and pretended to rub his eyes.

"Hi, Dad. Deena wanted to log some gym time, so I agreed to join her."

"She beat you here." He jerked his thumb toward the weight room. "Rocky's been giving her the intro to all the equipment." His eyes twinkled. "Maybe you need the intro again too, since you haven't been here in a blue moon."

"Har har." Though I rolled my eyes, I couldn't help grinning. "Got a towel back there for me? Or are you just gonna keep talking my ear off?"

He tossed me a white towel, which I caught in both hands. "Don't overdo it now," he said, serious this time. "Remember, quality over quantity."

"I know, Dad. You don't have to worry about me overdoing anything here."

Pushing open the glass double doors, I entered the weight room. Through the window to the adjoining room, I caught a glimpse of my mom, and about eight or ten other ladies and gents, twisting to the oldies. I weaved my way around the equipment in the opposite direction and spotted Rocky, leaning over Deena on the bench press. As I approached, she caught my eye and subtly pointed toward the far wall.

Ah, so Bart is here. He was using the rowing machine.

From the intensity of his expression, he might've been a Volga Boatman "yo-heave-hoing" against the flow of the river. With a curt nod at Deena, I made my way to one of the two treadmills along the outer windows. From this location, I could keep an eye on Bart—and hopefully be seen by him if he'd ever look around. I wanted our meeting here to appear accidental.

I set the treadmill to a moderate setting and began a brisk walk-in-place. I figured I might as well get a little cardio in. However, eight minutes later, Bart still hadn't noticed me. And when he finished with the rowing machine and moved on to leg extensions, I found myself tempted to decrease the resistance. A few more minutes of this and I was going to break a sweat. Not quite the goal today.

Looking around, I realized the floor stretch area might provide a good spot to run into Bart. It was a padded corner of the gym with a watercooler, a couple of balance balls, and a shelf of straps, smaller balls, and extra towels. Leaving the treadmill behind, I plopped myself down on the padded floor and reached for my toes.

What is my game plan, anyway? Bart had to be the least talkative person I knew. I wasn't sure what I expected to get out of him here. On the other hand, Deena was right. He was definitely a prime suspect.

I folded my legs into a butterfly pose and leaned down again. From what I'd read about road rage, it was usually triggered by stress. A driver's personal stress level compounded with the stress of driving could create a very short fuse. Aggressive drivers weren't necessarily bad people—they just had anger management problems. Once they cooled down, they probably felt bad about losing their temper.

Was that what had happened with Bart? If so, then

it would make sense that he'd be feeling remorse for his actions. Maybe my best course of action would be to appeal to his sense of decency. Then, maybe he'd own up to the crime.

A shadow fell over me, as someone walked over. Feeling a large presence, I looked up, expecting to see Rocky. Instead, it was Bart himself, squinting at me like I might be a mirage.

I jumped, startled at his sudden appearance. Turned out I got my "accidental meeting" after all. "Oh, hello!" I said.

"I thought that was you," he said. "I'm surprised I haven't seen you here before. I know your folks own the place."

"Yeah, well, I don't make it here as often as I'd like. How are you? Having a good workout?" I bit the inside of my cheek. *Having a good workout?* Why was I rambling like a nervous teenager?

"Pretty good," he said.

I extended one leg for another gentle stretch. "What a weekend, huh? Did you have to talk to the police again? They've been making the rounds." That was partly true.

"No. I told them everything I knew the first time." He walked over to the watercooler and filled a paper cup. I thought he might saunter away, but he stood nearby as he took a sip. I kept jabbering, as I switched legs.

"I keep thinking the whole thing must be some kind of terrible accident, you know? Like, maybe whoever hit the professor didn't really mean to hurt him."

Bart glanced down, searching my face. Had I struck a nerve? Or was he a little hard of hearing? It was so tough to get a read on him.

"I figure it had to be spontaneous," I went on. "Right? I mean, why else would someone do something like that with so many people around?" Bart didn't answer, so I kept rambling. "Plus, the guy was acting kind of weird. Did you notice that? Maybe he was high, or had some preexisting condition or something. Maybe that's why one conk on the head did him in."

I had no idea where I was coming up with this stuff. It was so irreverent and nonsensical. Instead of coaxing Bart to open up, I was probably scaring him away. He stared at me with his inscrutable eyes.

I held out my hand to him. "Help me up?"

He obliged, pulling me strongly to my feet. Then he cleared his throat. "I thought I'd get a drink after this. Want to come?"

My jaw dropped open, but I recovered quickly. "Sure! That would be nice."

My first thought was, *Yippee! My friendliness is finally paying off!* I mentally patted myself on the back—until I had my second thought.

What have I gotten myself into?

Chapter 11

The instant Bart excused himself to go change in one of the locker rooms, I dashed over to find Deena. She was sitting on the stationary bicycle, not moving her legs. "I've had enough exercise for a month," she groaned. "I'm sore in muscles I never even knew I had."

"Where's Rocky?" I hissed.

"I don't know. He had to help someone else." She gave me a curious look. "What happened with Bart? Did you get him to talk?"

"Not yet, but I will." I quickly filled her in. "You have to find Rocky and follow me, okay? I don't want to be alone with Bart, but I want to be alone with him."

"What?" She stared at me, incredulous. "You're not making sense."

I waved my hand, as if to erase what I'd said. "Oh, you know what I mean. I think there's a better chance he'll talk to me without an audience. But I'd like y'all nearby in case I need rescuing."

"Got it," said Deena, wincing as she climbed off the bicycle. "You're going on a date with him."

A date? I frowned. That wasn't what I had in mind. "No, no. It's just a drink. Just a friendly, impromptu—"

"Date," Deena supplied.

Ugh. "Never mind what it is. Just hurry!"

I headed to the ladies' locker room, where I finger-combed my hair and applied a touch of tinted lip balm. *Did Bart think we were going on a date?* I hadn't expected to have a full workout this evening, so I didn't bring a change of clothes. My shorts and T-shirt would have to do. Luckily, anyplace we'd go for a drink in Aerieville would be as casual as a family get-together. And there weren't a lot of choices.

My dad was in the office on the telephone when I passed through the lobby. I waved at him through the window and hurried outside. Bart was waiting on the side-walk, freshly showered and smelling slightly of menthol and pine-scented soap.

"Cuties' okay?" he asked.

"Yeah! That would be great." I pointed toward my orange car. "I'll meet ya there."

He nodded briefly and headed to a silver sedan. It was kind of odd to see him driving something other than his delivery van. Who knew what else I'd learn tonight?

I shot off a text to Deena, letting her know where we were going. I wanted to text Calvin too, but I didn't have time. I started up my car and drove the four blocks to Cuties' Pool Hall. We almost could have walked there.

It was surprisingly busy for a Monday night, though not even half-full. Some folks were watching football on the large screen behind the bar, while others were finishing up dinner in the attached restaurant. Bart led us to a corner booth in the pub side of the establishment.

Sliding into the seat across from him, I immediately felt a twinge of awkwardness.

Maybe he does *think this is a date.* In the dim lighting over the cozy table, it sure felt awful date-like.

"Are you hungry?" he asked. "I can ask for a menu."

"I could munch on something," I said. "Maybe I'll order an appetizer."

A waitress came by to take our drink orders—draft beers for both of us—and gave us menus. We spent the next few minutes studying our options. In the end, I decided on loaded potato skins, and Bart ordered a burger with a side of coleslaw. As soon as the waitress left, I sat back and grinned.

"Coleslaw? Who orders slaw with a burger?"

He looked at me with surprise. "I like it," he said, a touch defensively.

It was on the tip of my tongue to tease him about being old. (How old was he anyway, forty-five?) But I held back. I realized it might come across as flirty, even though I didn't mean to be. I was beginning to think I'd sent Bart the wrong signals with my friendliness.

"I like it too," I said. "And I bet it's pretty healthy. I just crave salty potatoes with beer."

He nodded without saying anything. Good ol' stoic Bart. Well, he'd invited me here, I thought. I'm gonna make him talk, darn it. It was time for some rapid-fire questions.

I leaned my forearms on the table and fixed him with an interested gaze. "Tell me about yourself, Bart. Where'd you grow up? Where do you live now? Do you have family around here?"

He took a swig of beer and averted his eyes. I just kept looking at him. Finally, he shrugged. "My life is kind of boring. I grew up in a tiny hamlet on the other side of the mountain. I've moved around some, but now I have a house and some acreage out in the country, 'bout twenty miles west of here."

"Do you have animals?"

"A couple of cats. I'm on the road too much to take care of more than that."

"What do you do for fun?"

A strange expression, something like wistfulness, passed over his face. Then it was gone, and he shrugged again. "I like to hunt and fish. I do some home brewing too, beer and cider mostly."

"Ohh," I said, knowingly. "You're a moonshiner!"

He cracked a hint of a smile—possibly the first one I'd ever seen on him. It made him look younger and even kind of cute.

I smiled back at him. "You ever been married, Bart?"

Just like that, his smile disappeared. Bart became stony-faced again, staring at his beer bottle like he might bore a hole through it with his eyes.

"I'm sorry," I said softly. "Sensitive subject?"

His jaw twitched. "My wife died. I don't want to talk about it."

"Oh, okay. I'm so sorry. No problem." I cringed at my faux pas. *Poor Bart!* Why did I have to press him like that? No wonder he rarely smiled. He was probably heartbroken.

For a moment, neither of us said anything. I wondered how long he'd been a widower. Was this a fresh pain? Or were the circumstances so terrible, he still couldn't talk about it no matter how much time had passed? Come to think of it, I was kind of surprised Felix had never mentioned it.

As we drank our beer, the absence of conversation stretched into awkward territory. When the waitress brought our food, I breathed a sigh of relief. It was a welcome distraction.

I used a fork to cut off a bite of cheesy potato and blew on it to cool it down. Bart offered me a taste of his coleslaw, which was a nice gesture, I thought. I declined and made small talk while we ate. I also gazed around the room. Where were Rocky and Deena?

Our booth was at the end of a line of tables, closest to the bar. On the other end of the long wooden counter, in the corner across from us, were a couple of dart boards. The center of the room held the main attraction: six pool tables situated in two rows of three. There were more booths on the wall adjacent to ours. At the end of those seats, in the opposite corner, were a foosball table and a pinball machine. Twisting in my seat, I finally spotted my brother chalking up a cue at the pool table behind the one nearest to our booth. Deena walked over to him and handed him a bottle of beer.

Speaking of ostensible dates. . . . If I didn't know any better, I'd think the two of them were on one. Then I noticed the way Deena watched Rocky as he geared up for a shot. There was definitely something like appreciation in her gaze. *Huh.* Well, Rocky was only four years younger than us, and he'd definitely been admired before by folks of all ages and genders. But Deena had never said anything to me about being interested in him. And they were so different from each other.

I started to turn back to Bart when I caught sight of a familiar trio enter the pub: April, Vince, and Isaiah. They strolled in from the adjacent restaurant, looked around, then claimed an empty pool table on the far side of the room. I could no longer see them from where I sat.

"Your brother is quite the protector, isn't he?" said Bart.

"What?" I gave him an innocent look, as if I had no idea what he was talking about.

"Twice now he's stopped someone from coming over here."

"Oh?" Now I really was surprised. "Like who?"

"Just townsfolk, I think. One was Nell Cusley. Rocky just held out his palm and shook his head no. That was enough to make her turn tail." Bart appeared to be amused.

"Well, I'm grateful to him, then. People want to gossip about the murder, and I'd rather not." I took another bite of my appetizer and took a peek at my phone. It wasn't that late yet, but I found myself thinking about Calvin again. I wondered if he'd want to come to Cuties' some time.

"People are terrible," Bart said with a scowl. "Always poking their noses where it doesn't belong."

"Yeah, sometimes. But it's natural to be curious. And it could be they wanted to offer moral support." I was starting to grow weary of Bart's dour mood. He also seemed to be discouraging any further questions.

We ate in silence for a minute. Bart finished off his beer and set it on the table with a tap. He waved the waitress over. I thought he was going to ask for the check, but instead he ordered a second beer. "You ready for another?" he asked me.

"Uh, no. I'm good." I looked over my shoulder again to make sure Rocky and Deena were still there. They were—and still apparently not paying any attention to me.

Just then April crossed the room, heading for the door. She held her cell phone to her ear and glowered. "Are you listening to me?" she said loudly. "I told you I have it covered!"

I pushed my plate away. "Would you excuse me for a minute? I'll be right back."

Bart nodded, as I slipped out of the booth and followed April. In between the pool hall and the restaurant was a narrow hallway leading to the restrooms. I exited the bar in time to see April push her way into the ladies' room. *Perfect.* I knew from past visits to Cuties' that the restroom had two parts: an outer room with a large mirror above a wide counter and a connecting inner room with three stalls and sinks. April was standing in front of the mirror, but her head was down as she continued her phone conversation. I proceeded directly into the other room and stood at a sink around the corner as I listened.

"Just because Lowry's gone doesn't mean the well is dry." April wasn't yelling anymore, but she still sounded intense. "I'm in charge now."

In charge of what? I craned my ears, so I wouldn't miss anything. After a pause, April raised her voice again. "Isaiah said what? That's not true. *I'm* the one you need to deal with now."

She fell silent, and it occurred to me her call must be over. Quickly, I switched the water on and washed my hands. When she didn't appear around the corner, I turned off the water, grabbed a paper towel, and walked into the adjacent room. April was redoing her braids and looking at herself thoughtfully in the mirror.

"Well, hi there!" I said brightly. "So, you decided to take my advice and give Cuties' a try?"

"Hey," she said. "Yeah. Fun place." She gave me a tight little smile.

I walked up to the mirror and pretended to fix my hair. I wanted to ask her so many questions, but I didn't know where to start.

She tied off her braid, then tilted her chin toward me. "Will you watch my bag?" She pointed to a pink leather hobo bag on the counter.

"Of course," I said.

April disappeared into the other room, and I was left staring at the open bag. *Oh, the temptation.* Would it hurt to take a tiny peek?

I glanced around the corner to ensure she was in one of the stalls. She was. It was now or never. Without moving the bag, I carefully lifted the flap to open it a bit wider and looked inside. Her cell phone was right on top, next to an oversized wallet and a striped makeup bag.

I sure would love to know who she was just talking to. If I could see the phone number, I could memorize it and call it later. For that matter, I was also extremely curious about her text messages—especially to Isaiah and Vince. What did they say to one another about the murder?

With my heart beating fast as a hummingbird, I grabbed the phone from April's purse and pressed a button on the side. The home screen flashed to life. The wallpaper image was a selfie of April making a duck face. I swiped the screen, and a keypad appeared. The phone was locked. *Dang it!*

For the heck of it, I pressed 1-2-3-4, which of course didn't work. Then I recklessly started pressing random buttons. The sound of a toilet flushing made me jump. Then the outer door opened, and I almost screamed. A middle-aged woman walked past me with barely a glance. *Jeesh.*

Catching my breath, I carefully replaced April's phone in her bag. By the time she rejoined me at the mirror, I was languidly applying lipstick from my own purse, just as calm as can be.

"Thanks," she said, shouldering her bag.

"Anytime. We girls gotta stick together, right?"

She gave me a look that almost made me laugh—that

of the cool teenager embarrassed for an adult who's trying too hard. Clearly, she didn't see me as a peer.

"Women," I amended. "We women gotta stick together."

"Mm-hmm." She started to leave. As she reached for the door handle, I called her back.

"April, wait a minute. Can I ask you something?" I couldn't resist the chance to question her.

Turning, she raised her eyebrows with a forced politeness that failed to cover her impatience. "Yes?"

"Could you tell me a little bit about Professor Lowry? I've been hearing different things, and I'd love to hear your perspective."

For a second, she narrowed her eyes in suspicion. Then she tossed her head, as if nothing could bother her. "He was brilliant. Top in his field. And he was an excellent teacher. He was involved in all kinds of important research projects, yet he still made time for his students outside the classroom."

"Outside the classroom? You mean . . . on a more personal level?" This was interesting. Was she going to confirm Calvin's assertion that Lowry had used some of his students as his personal "lackeys"?

She rolled her eyes, once again revealing what she thought of me. "That's not what I meant. He gave his best students opportunities to build their résumés and gain extra experience—like with special research projects. And the summer field trip."

I watched her closely as she spoke. For all her femininity and diminutive stature, she was certainly not shy. She was a confident young woman. There was also an edge about her, a note of defiance even. Maybe she felt the need to defend the professor against the accusations she must know Calvin had made about him. In a way, it was kind of admirable.

One thing, however, was noticeably absent from her demeanor: any hint of sadness or sorrow that he was gone.

I gave her a small smile. "I can tell you thought highly of him. I'm really sorry for your loss."

Something crossed her face briefly—I could have sworn it was a smirk.

"Thanks," she said shortly. Then she swept out of the room, as regally as a little queen.

By the time I returned to Bart, he was half-finished with his second beer. A fresh glass, filled to the top, sat in front of my place.

"I thought you'd got lost," he said.

"Sorry." I slipped into the booth and took a tiny sip of the beer. "I had to make a phone call and check on my dog." That was partly true. After April had left the powder room, I texted Calvin to let him know I'd be just a while longer. He'd replied that he and Gus were chilling out in front of the TV. That had tugged on my heartstrings a little. I almost told him to leave Gus in his apartment and come join us at Cuties'. But I resisted. I still had a mission to see out.

"I'm kidding," said Bart, with a smile. (His second one!) "Ladies always take a long time, right?"

Hmm. Was the beer loosening him up? I couldn't let this prospect go to waste. Lifting one shoulder in a coy shrug, I raised my glass. "A toast," I said.

Screwing his eyes in confusion, he held up his glass as well. "To what?"

"To flowers, of course! The source of your employment and mine."

We tapped glasses.

"To flowers," he echoed.

"How long you been driving for Pauly's Plants?"

He stuck out his lower lip in thought. "'Bout eighteen years. A long time."

"Wow, you must enjoy it. You get to see a lot of countryside, huh? How big is the region?"

"It covers Central and Eastern Tennessee, plus parts of Kentucky and North Carolina. I clock a lot of miles."

"Do you mostly deliver to flower shops in small towns?"

"Oh, no, I go to big cities too. Charlotte, Knoxville. Even as far north as Lexington."

"Is it true drivers in cities are the worst?" I didn't know if that was true, but I was curious to see his reaction.

He bared his teeth in a snarl. "Nothing makes me madder 'n bad drivers."

"Like Professor Lowry, right? Or was he pretty extreme?"

Bart gave me a strange look and took a gulp of his beer. "He was something else," he mumbled.

I quietly sighed. This was going nowhere. I tried to think of another approach, when Bart stood up and waved at the waitress. "I'll take a refill," he said to her. To me, he said, "I'll be back." Then he headed to the exit, and presumably to the restroom.

Rolling my eyes, I turned to try to get Deena's attention. That's when I saw Vince walking away from the bar. He caught my eye and came over, a bottle of beer in hand.

"You won't tell Professor Washington, will you?" he said, by way of greeting.

I shook my head. "You're over twenty-one, right?"

"That's right." He gave me a lazy smile. "I saw you over here with the delivery guy. You like to live on the edge, huh? Flirt with danger?"

"Danger? Bart doesn't seem dangerous to me."

He set his bottle on the table and leaned in close. "Don't think I don't know what you're doing."

I felt my eyes grow wide. "What am I doing?"

"You're playing detective. Tryin' to 'solve a mystery' like a regular Nancy Drew or something." He used air quotes as if solving a mystery were some kind of game.

I kept my tone light and playful. "It's a free country, isn't it?"

"That it is," he said.

Bart returned then, brushing past Vince as he resumed his seat. He glared at the younger guy until Vince picked up his bottle and tipped his head in farewell. "See you around," he said to me.

Bart eyed my still-full glass. "Don't you want anymore?"

I slid it across the table. "You can have it. I think the waitress forgot about you."

He took a swig of the beer and squinted in the direction Vince had sauntered. "Was that guy hitting on you?"

"Um," I said. *Was he?* It was hard to say.

"I bet a lot of guys hit on you," he said. "Like that pompous professor, Lowry."

The waitress came over then, as I tried to process what Bart had just said. Why did he think Lowry had hit on me? The only time I'd interacted with the professor was at the entrance to Flower House. Was Bart watching, and did he somehow misinterpret that exchange?

Bart motioned for the waitress to set the beer down next to the one I'd given him.

This is getting ridiculous. "Uh, Bart. You have a long drive ahead of you tonight, don't you?"

"Naw," he said, with a wave of his hand. "I don't drink and drive. I have a motel room here in town."

"Oh! Cool." That was a relief. I leaned forward, noting that Bart's eyes appeared bloodshot. "So, speaking of Lowry. Had you ever met him before?"

He frowned slightly. "No, I don't think so."

"Tell me something. That afternoon—before the cops came and everything—were you sitting in your truck the whole time? Did you notice people going in and out the back door of Flower House?"

He stared at me blankly. "Sure," he finally said. "I wasn't paying special attention, but I could see the door."

I tried to remember the timeline of events. "Did you see me and Cal leave the house with Gus?"

The corner of his mouth twitched. "Yeah. You started to come up to me and then didn't."

"I didn't know you saw me." I recalled he'd been looking at his phone. Maybe he'd caught a glimpse of me in his peripheral vision. "That was right after we'd discovered Lowry's body."

Bart didn't respond but continued to stare at me.

I swallowed. "Who came out of the house immediately before us? One of the students?"

Before answering, he took another swill of beer and licked his lips. Then he leaned forward and spoke in a hoarse slur. "I didn' tell the cops, but I *did* see somebody come out."

"Who?"

"That short older lady with the dyed hair 'n' the long dress. I think her name was Wanda."

Chapter 12

The night air felt cool and refreshing. I stood beside my car and texted Calvin to let him know I was on my way. Then I raised my face to the starry sky. *What an evening!*

A few seconds later, Rocky and Deena came jogging up the sidewalk from Cuties'.

"You okay, sis?" Evidently, Rocky was turning into our mom, the way he kept worrying over me.

"Why'd you leave so quickly?" asked Deena, slightly out of breath.

"Quickly? I spent, like, two hours with that guy. It felt anything but quick."

Deena peered at her phone in surprise. "Oh! It's ten o'clock. I didn't realize it was so late."

I suppressed a smile. *Time flies when you're having fun.*

"Did Bart do something to offend you?" asked Rocky. He looked like he was ready to go back in there and pull Bart out by his ear if I said yes.

"Besides drinking a bit too much and talking very little? No."

"So, you didn't learn anything?" said Deena. "Was this all for nothing?"

I hesitated, biting my lip. "No—I did learn a few things. For one, he told me he's a widower."

Deena's eyebrows popped up. "Oh, really? How—I mean, that's too bad. How did she die?"

"He didn't say." I met Deena's gaze and knew we were wondering the same thing. Were the circumstances of his wife's death in any way suspicious?

Rocky appeared puzzled. "I didn't know his wife died. Of course, I didn't even know he'd been married."

"He's not a big sharer, that's for sure," I said dryly. Glancing back at the pool hall, I narrowed my eyes. "I'm still trying to get a read on how trustworthy he is. I think I need to mull over everything he said."

After Bart had sprung his bombshell about seeing Wanda leave Flower House, he'd refused to say much else on the matter. When I'd pressed him as to why he hadn't mentioned it to the police, he said he didn't want to get "the old lady" in trouble.

"Besides," he'd said, "that Lowry guy was a jerk. Whoever did him in probably did the world a favor."

It was a callous thing to say and more than a little disturbing. Bart didn't seem to care that the police were focusing their investigation on an innocent man. I'd tried to tell Bart that the police needed a full picture of events and that, just because he'd seen Wanda, it didn't mean she was guilty. He'd only shrugged and turned his attention to the TV behind the bar.

After that, I'd told Bart I needed to leave and pick up my dog. He stood up and offered to walk me to my car.

"No need," I said, reaching into my purse. "I'll just pay you for my share of the food and drinks."

"No, no, no." He put his hand on my arm. "It's on me."

A sudden blush burned my cheeks. *Oh, man. He one-hundred-percent thinks this was a date.* I took a quick step backward, disengaging from his clasp. "Okay, thanks," I mumbled. "That's nice of you." On that awkward note, I hightailed it out of the bar.

Now, Deena and my brother both regarded me with concern.

"Are you okay to drive?" asked Rocky. "I can give you a ride."

I shook myself and smiled. "Oh, yeah," I assured him. "I barely had one drink this whole time. I'll fill you guys in tomorrow, okay?"

We said goodbye, and I got into my car and headed to Flower House. I was eager to see Calvin. And Gus, of course. But, more than anything, I wanted to talk with Calvin and get his take on everything that had happened today.

A few minutes later, I parked in the driveway and entered through the kitchen workroom. The light was on, and when I pushed through the door into the hallway, Calvin and Gus were just coming downstairs. The corgi was already leashed. Calvin handed the end to me.

"Here ya go. He's eaten, been outside twice, and chewed through another one of his toys. He should be ready for bed."

"Thanks." In that moment, I felt strangely like a divorced mother at a child-custody handoff. Calvin's wan, unsmiling face might have had something to do with the weird vibe. "Do you want to chat for a minute?" I asked. "We could sit in the . . . café." I'd pointed to the study, then moved my hand to point farther down the hall.

"I'm pretty tired," he said. "I'll just see you in the morning."

"Oh, okay. No problem."

Without another word, he turned and went back upstairs, letting the door click shut behind him.

Gus looked up at me, and I shook my head slowly. "I don't know either, buddy," I said softly. "I guess we'll just leave."

Although it was late, I showered as soon as I got home. Maybe it was all in my head, but there was a good chance I'd picked up an assortment of odors: sweaty health club, boozy pool hall, men's overpowering cologne, cigarette smoke. On second thought, it probably wasn't in my head so much as in my hair. As I let the water wash over me, I reflected on what a long, eventful day it had been. Yet, in spite of all my questioning, I'd only uncovered more questions than answers.

I breathed in the soothing fresh scent of my natural lavender body soap and shampoo and felt instantly better. After toweling off and slipping on a lightweight nightgown, I plugged in the diffuser in my room and added a serene blend of essential oils: lavender, frankincense, bergamot, and ylang-ylang. I would sleep well tonight.

Crawling into bed, I grabbed my phone to pull up some relaxing music. Then I paused. Having the phone in hand brought me back to my failed attempt to snoop on April's phone. I laughed out loud. *What was I thinking?* Gus perked up and gave me a disapproving look.

"Sorry," I whispered. "It was such a bumbling, foolish thing to do." *If only it had worked.*

I opened a search screen on my phone and typed in "April Finley, University of Tennessee."

Aha, I said to myself. "She really *is* active on social media."

There wasn't a lot of written text to peruse, but there

were a ton of pictures—at least from the last year or so. Not so much in earlier years. As I scrolled through her photos, I saw plenty of selfies and a bunch of memes, plus several of her with girlfriends. However, the most interesting images were the ones of April with Vince and Isaiah. I found only one with the three of them together, in a recent group photo. Prior to that, the pictures were of April and Vince together or April and Isaiah together, as if she'd been in a relationship with each of them at separate times.

A love triangle? *Ugh.*

From what I could tell, she and Vince were a couple last fall and early winter. By late winter and into spring, Vince had been replaced by Isaiah. There was even a Valentine's Day photo with a heart around April and Isaiah. However, by the start of summer, April was solo in all of her pictures again, and her relationship status was single.

Not that any of this mattered. There was nothing here to indicate any desire to "take Lowry's place." Wasn't that what April had said about Isaiah at Richard's B&B? Then he'd responded that it was *her* aim, rather than his. And in the phone call I'd overheard, April had said something about being "in charge now."

I yawned. This was all very curious but super frustrating. I had no way to find out any more and no idea if it was relevant anyway. Plus, I was starting to feel like a creepy voyeur.

I placed my phone on the bedside table, and it immediately buzzed. Frowning, I picked it back up. It was a text from Calvin: *You up?*

I replied, *Yes.* A moment later, my phone rang.

"What's up?" I said, upon answering. "Is everything okay?"

"Yeah. Sorry to bother you." His voice was low and husky. He sounded tired. "I just wanted to apologize for being rude earlier."

"You weren't rude," I protested. "If anything, *I* was rude for leaving Gus with you for so long."

He chuckled softly. "Okay, neither of us was rude. How was your evening? Did you get to talk to Bart?"

"Uh, yeah. You could say that." I told him about Bart asking me to join him for a drink.

"Oh. Wow. That's—that was convenient, huh?" He sounded less than thrilled, which, for some reason, made me smile.

"Yeah, in a way. I learned some more about him. But I wasn't able to definitively eliminate him as a suspect—or strengthen the case against him." *Unless you count the fact that his wife is deceased.* I felt bad even thinking it, poor guy. *Still* . . .

"That figures," said Calvin.

"Yeah. There was one thing he said, though, that might be significant." I shared what Bart had said about seeing Wanda come out of Flower House.

"Aw, man," said Calvin. "Really? Wanda?"

"I'm not sure what to make of it." In fact, the more I thought about it, the more I tended to question Bart's claim. Was he even telling the truth? "I think I'd better go pay a visit to Granny tomorrow."

"Sounds like a good idea."

We lapsed into silence, creating a natural point to say goodbye. Yet neither of us did. It felt as if we both wanted to prolong our connection.

"Well," Calvin said at last. "I should let you go."

"I'm glad you called," I said. *Did that sound silly?*

"Me too."

I smiled. "Good night, Calvin."

"Good night, Sierra."

As I hung up the phone, I felt a swirl of mixed emotions. Considering the events of the past couple of days, a fair amount of anxiety and doubt threatened to trouble my mind. On the other hand, there was also a healthy dose of relief after chatting with Calvin. I was glad there was no weirdness between us.

I decided to focus on the latter as I switched off the light and snuggled under the covers. It made for a more restful transition to sleep.

Chapter 13

Tuesday morning, Gus and I headed to Flower House for a quick stop before driving up to Granny's place. I planned to pop in the store just long enough to help open up and make sure Deena and Calvin would be okay on their own for a bit. However, when we arrived, I found a surprise out front: a UT van parked along the quiet street. For a split second, I had an unwelcome flashback to Saturday morning. Then I saw who was waiting on the front steps: Professor Sheila Washington.

With a slight twinge of dread, I parked behind the van and hurried up the sidewalk with Gus trotting at my side. To my relief, she greeted us with a friendly, if somewhat guarded, smile.

"Good morning," she said, rising from the steps. "The kids all slept in this morning, so I decided to take a little drive and ended up here. I hope you don't mind."

"Not at all! Come on in."

I unlocked the front door and flipped on the lights. As I unleashed Gus, freeing him to perform his routine sniffing inspection around the shop, Sheila stood in the foyer and gazed around.

"Would you like to have a seat in the café?" I asked. "It's not officially open yet, but I can make us some coffee or tea."

"Coffee would be great." She continued looking around, her eyes lingering on the hallway beyond the checkout counter.

Turning to her, I spoke gently. "Would you like to see where it happened?"

She rubbed a hand over her short hair before nodding. "I have to admit, I am a little curious."

"I don't blame you. Follow me." I gave her a quick tour of the shop, pointing out the powder room and orchid room and finishing in the kitchen. "There's the storeroom," I said, pointing to the closed door, still blocked with yellow tape. I moved to turn the knob, but she stopped me with a soft cry.

"Never mind! I'm good. No need to give myself a visual, destined to show up later in my nightmares."

I gave her a sympathetic smile. "I understand." I wished I hadn't seen it myself.

We retreated to the café, where I made coffee and small talk. We'd just sat down, when Deena came in and said hello before busying herself in the kitchen. At one point, I heard Calvin come downstairs and whistle for Gus. I assumed he wasn't too keen on facing his former colleague, even if they hadn't crossed paths very often.

Sheila seemed to be warming to me. She asked me how I came to be a florist, and I asked her about her decision to become a teacher. After sharing her background, she admitted she enjoyed working in the field more than in the classroom. "That's partly why I agreed to co-lead this trip."

"I'm so sorry," I murmured.

She nodded ruefully and took a sip of coffee.

Casting for a change of subject, I asked her if she saw the students when they came in last night. "I ran into them at Cuties'," I told her. "They seemed to be having a good time."

"That's good. I was already in bed when they got in." With a slight shrug, she added, "I've concluded that they don't need to be chaperoned twenty-four seven."

I smiled to show I agreed. "They *are* technically adults."

"That they are."

Recalling the scholarship tidbit she'd dropped, I wondered what else she might know about them. "They must be pretty serious students too," I ventured. "April mentioned something about working on outside projects with Professor Lowry."

"I suppose," she said noncommittally.

"I think she said only the best students were allowed to work on special projects with him?"

Sheila snorted, then quickly covered her mouth. "Sorry. Steve seemed to have his favorites, it's true. I'm not sure I'd call them the 'best' students, in terms of their grades. But they all had something else in common. An eagerness, I suppose. A determination to beat the odds they'd been handed."

"Ambition?" I added, thinking of April's mention of "being in charge."

"Yeah. Some of them have that."

"April seems to hold her own among the boys," I continued. "That's nice to see, especially in a field traditionally dominated by men."

Sheila looked thoughtful. "That girl is tougher than she looks. And . . ." She trailed off, as if trying to decide how much she should say.

"Maybe a little cunning?" I prompted. I had the impression April knew how to play up her innocent appearance to her advantage.

"Possibly." Sheila nodded. "She can come across as somewhat flighty, but she's a smart one. I once saw her take the lead in a group assignment, where she delegated all the tasks to the other group members. She did it in such a natural, almost cute way, that no one questioned her." She chuckled at the memory. "She's one to watch, I'll say that much."

I gathered she meant it as a compliment—April as a promising student with a bright future. But the student had a devious streak.

"For sure," I agreed. *One to watch indeed.*

It was still early when Sheila left and Gus and I hopped back into the car. And it was a beautiful day to get outside. A drive into the mountains always brought up feelings of nostalgia for me. This was the way we went "over the river and through the woods" every holiday growing up. Back then, it wasn't just "to Grandmother's house," but Grandpap's house too. With seven sets of aunts and uncles (my mom's siblings and in-laws) and oodles of cousins, Granny's homestead was the liveliest place I knew.

Over time, though, the numbers dwindled. While we'd still come out here for get-togethers now and then, it wasn't the same. A lot of times, like today, I'd make the fifteen-mile trek all by myself and find the place as quiet and peaceful as a nature preserve. Granny's homey farmhouse and verdant land were like an oasis of calm in the hustle-bustle of the modern world.

After parking near her house, I found Granny in her

large vegetable garden, stooped over a patch of leafy green bean plants. She stood up, hands on her lower back, as I approached.

"Well, howdy, Sierra. You shoulda told me you was comin'. I'da put the kettle on."

"Hi, Granny," I said cheerily. "I tried calling, but you didn't answer."

She pulled a cell phone from her apron pocket and squinted at it in the sunlight. "So, you did. I'm all a fuddle this mornin'."

I tied Gus to the clothesline pole, on a chain left over from dogs of yore, then got to work picking beans on the other end of the row.

"Can't believe I missed the signs," Granny said. "I shoulda known company was comin'. First I dropped a dishrag. Then I dropped a spoon."

"Or maybe you just have butter fingers," I teased. "After all, I'm not really company."

Granny chuckled. "If I do, it's Wanda's fault. She's got me all in a tither."

"Why? Did something happen?"

"Never mind," she said. "I'm glad you're here. You can help me snap these beans and get 'em canned."

"I'm happy to help. And anything else you need doing."

We finished cleaning out the row of beans and gathered a bucket of warm, ripe tomatoes. Then we sat on Granny's open-air back porch, she in a rocker and me on the swing, and snapped the beans.

I couldn't believe she was going to do this all by herself. Then again, Granny had been independent for a long time. In spite of my mom's constant pleas for her to sell the house and move to town, Granny steadfastly refused.

"What day is this anyway?" said Granny. "Tuesday? Shouldn't you be at the flower shop?"

"I can step out for a couple of hours," I said. "This is a slow month for florists anyway." That was true. With Mother's Day over and wedding season winding down, not to mention the fact that many folks grew flowers in their own backyards, we had far fewer orders this time of year. That was part of the reason we'd timed our café opening for the middle of summer. We figured we'd have more time to get it up and running, plus we could use the business. So much for that.

Granny glanced over at me. "Well, looky there. A yeller bee landed on your arm."

"Oh!" I flapped my arm and the bee flew off, though it still hovered nearby. "I know bees are good, but I don't want to be stung."

"It's not gonna sting you," said Granny. "That's a good luck bee. You're going to get good news soon."

I grinned in amusement. "That sure would be nice."

After a bit of chit chat, I tried to steer the conversation back to Wanda by asking how she was doing. "The police haven't been bothering her, have they? I don't know what they're doing with their investigation. They've been keeping me in the dark."

"It's not the law that's been pestering Wanda," Granny said soberly.

"What do you mean?"

She shook her head, apparently unwilling to say more. Granny's stubbornness was in fine form today.

"By the way," said Granny, "there hasn't been any trouble at Flower House, has there? Like last time?"

I knew what she meant. Following the last murder, there were some incidents that Granny attributed to the victim's ghost. She'd given me all kinds of tips and protections to put the spirit to rest.

"No, not this time." As soon as I said it, I remembered

the night of the storm: the power outage, the person out-side my window, and the rumpled flowers on my stoop. Did those count as "trouble"?

We finished with the beans and brought them inside to Granny's kitchen, where she already had all her can-ning equipment set out. We added the beans to two big pots on the stove, covered them with water, and mixed in vinegar, sugar, and salt.

"It's goin' to get hot in here," said Granny. "Let's sit in the living room while we wait for the pots to boil."

I brought Gus inside and gave him a bowl of water, while Granny poured us some iced tea. Settling down on her sofa, I noticed she had some photo albums laid out on a cloth-covered round table in the corner.

"Are you goin' through old pictures?" I asked.

"Yes, in a way."

I got up to take a look. The album on top seemed to be from the 1970s, when my mom was a little girl. But the opened pages featured a bunch of unfamiliar people, apparently friends and neighbors. There was one empty pocket with the photo missing.

"Ah," I said, suddenly putting two and two together. I turned to Granny and tapped on the album. "You're doing a working for someone. And since you said Wanda had you in a tither this morning, I'm betting it's for her. Am I right?"

Granny was known far and wide for her skills as a folk healer and herbalist. Sometimes this meant mak-ing tinctures and sachets filled with medicinal herbs and sundries. Other times it involved a little more superstition.

"Oh, alright." She stood up and joined me at the table. "You should've been a sleuth. Since you figured it out, I guess I ought to tell you."

"Is Wanda okay?"

"That's a loaded question," she said dryly. "Wanda thinks she's being haunted."

Oh, no. Did that mean she really did kill the professor? I held onto the edge of the table. "By who?"

"Her dead husband, Roy."

I breathed a sigh of relief. "That's good. I mean, that's odd, right? Didn't he die a long time ago?"

"Yes, he did. Had a heart attack ten years ago. Well, ten years next week. It happened the day before their wedding anniversary."

"Aw, that's sad."

"Even more so since they weren't exactly on speaking terms at the time. She thought they'd reconcile, but they never got the chance."

"Poor Wanda. But why does she think she's being haunted now?"

Granny sighed. "To tell the truth, I'm not entirely sure she is. She's been acting kind of confused lately. She says she's seen him and heard his voice. Maybe she has. Anyway, I'm going to try to help her."

I remembered how Wanda had seemed a little confused when Calvin and I encountered her on the sidewalk, shortly after we'd found the professor's body. Was she really coming from the park, as she'd said? Or had she just come out of the house a few minutes before we did, like Bart said?

"How are you going to help her?" I asked.

"I went to her house yesterday and made sure we had the basics covered—planted rue in her yard, hung dried basil over her doors and windows, and other such protections." Granny wandered into the kitchen to check on the green beans, then returned with a piece of meat for Gus.

"Wasn't that good enough for Wanda?" I asked. I still didn't understand what the problem was.

"Well, we're just not seeing eye to eye on this. I told her Roy probably wants to make peace. In that case, she should leave some offerings and honor his spirit. But she thinks he's angry at her. She just wants to make him go away."

"That's too bad." I glanced down at the photo album again.

Granny moved the albums over and picked up a picture from underneath. She handed it to me. "This is Wanda and Roy on their wedding day."

I studied the snapshot for a moment. Wanda was a pretty little thing with flowers in her hair. Her husband, Roy, was skinny and much taller—at least a head and a half taller than Wanda. I couldn't help wondering how she'd managed to clock him with a frying pan. He must've been sitting down or leaning over. Or maybe she just swung her arm up high.

Granny opened a different album and pulled out another photo. "Here's what he looked like when he was older," she said. "You can tell he was a drinker."

In the second photo, he was still tall and skinny, though he'd developed a pot belly. His cheeks and nose were ruddy, and, from his goofy grin, he almost looked drunk in the photo. But the thing that really caught my attention was his prominent white goatee: a feature that made him look remarkably like one Professor Steve Lowry.

I helped Granny fill her canning jars, adding a dollop of bacon grease to each one for flavor. Then I stayed back and watched while she handled the pressure-cooker part of the proceeding. I would have been intimidated to do it myself, but Granny was a pro. While the beans cooked,

Granny made up a platter of tomato mayo sandwiches and brought out a bowl of corn salad from the refrigerator. We went out to the back porch to eat.

After seeing the photo of Wanda's late husband, I hadn't known what to think. I'd told Granny about Roy's resemblance to the deceased professor, thinking maybe that was why she'd yelled at him in the first place. Granny didn't seem to think there was anything to it. She said she'd keep an eye on Wanda, and I wasn't to worry about it.

I couldn't help feeling Granny didn't want to ponder the implications any more than I did.

After lunch, I asked Granny if there were any more chores I could do for her. She was shaking her head no, when my cell phone rang. I took a peek at it and saw that it was an unfamiliar number. I was going to ignore it, but Granny said I should answer it.

"Remember the bee," she said. "It could be good news."

I shrugged. "Okay." But when I answered, I regretted that decision. It was Nell Cusley, the town gossip queen.

"Oh, Sierra, good," she said. "I finally reached you. I've been trying for days."

Rolling my eyes, I went back inside and paced around Granny's living room. "I'm sorry, Nell. Things have been kinda hectic lately."

"I know, I know. I heard all about it. But my niece Sue Ellen is getting married this weekend, and I want you to do the flowers."

You could've knocked me over with a daisy chain. "Oh? Well, that's real nice, but it's kind of short notice."

"I know. It's crazy. They were going to elope, but the family wants a wedding, so we're going to make it happen. The flowers are my gift to the bride and groom.

We'll need an arch trellis, a bridal bouquet, and three bridesmaids' bouquets. Plus all the corsages and bouton-nieres. The colors are peach and yellow. Oh, and Sue El-len's favorite flowers are buttercups, so we need to fit those in somehow."

As Nell chattered on, I grabbed a piece of paper and pencil from Granny's end table and jotted down some notes. Under normal circumstances, we'd be approached about a wedding months in advance—at a minimum. But I wasn't about to turn down the business. Not if I could help it. I would make this work if I had to go out and pick all the flowers myself.

Chapter 14

Before seeing me off, Granny supplied me with a special herb bag (a "protection sachet") filled with salt, basil, bay leaf, and cinnamon. I could have used it to flavor a nice soup, but I didn't dare question Granny's wisdom—not when she'd been right about the good news bee, not to mention the death-harbinger bird. I thanked her for everything and promised I'd keep it with me always. And I meant it. Maybe herb bags were like Dumbo's magic feather, just a symbol of the courage and power that come from within. But if it works, who cares?

By the time I reached Flower House, it was after two. The shop was quiet, but the lights were on. I found Calvin in the study updating our website. Deena was in the café lounging on the velvet couch with a magazine.

"Slow day?" I said, as I entered through the archway.

She set the magazine aside and swung her feet to the floor. "We had a couple online orders this morning. They've already been made and delivered."

"Well, get ready to get busy, because we have a big one: a wedding!"

"A wedding?" Deena's eyes lit up. Since working with

me over the past few months, we'd had only one wedding. Felix hadn't been known as a wedding florist. He could definitely do the job upon request, but he didn't market himself that way. He'd had no binders of photos to showcase his bridal designs. Deena wanted to change that. She'd had so much fun with the one wedding we'd done, she'd been eager for another.

I smiled. "Yep. It's for Nell Cusley's niece, and it's a rush job. The ceremony is this Saturday."

Calvin came up behind me, with Gus at his heels. "Did I hear you say we have less than a week to prepare for a wedding?"

I turned to him and nodded. "Isn't it exciting!"

"Shotgun wedding?" he said.

"Don't know, don't care. All I know is Nell wants the works: flower arch, aisle decorations, reception centerpieces, bouquets."

Deena's excited expression turned to worry. "This is going to be a huge challenge, isn't it? Did you tell Nell we charge a premium for rush orders?"

"Uh, no. I probably should've, but we really need the job. And if she's happy, she'll talk us up to everyone she meets."

"That's true," said Deena. "Free advertising!"

"That's the spirit."

We all three headed to the workroom to check on our inventory. I opened the large cooler and noted what peach and yellow flowers we had in stock, as well as any appropriate greenery and filler, such as baby's breath. Deena started a list of everything we would need.

"Where's the flower arch frame?" she asked.

"It's . . ." I trailed off, as I walked over to the storeroom, still blocked off with yellow tape. "In there."

"I don't understand why the cops haven't been back,"

said Deena. "Are they going to leave the crime scene tape there until the murder is solved?"

"Good question. I'm going to ask." I grabbed my cell phone from my purse and looked for the number for the Aerieville police station.

"Here," said Calvin, taking a card from his pocket. "Bradley asked me to call her if I decided to change my story."

"What?" I looked up at him to see if he was joking.

"Okay, maybe those weren't her exact words," he said. "But the sentiment was there."

Shaking my head, I took the card and punched in the number. A receptionist answered, and, when I asked for Deputy Chief Bradley, she said she wasn't available.

Thinking fast, I said, "This is Sierra Ravenswood from Flower House. There's something here in the shop I need to show a police officer. It's related to Professor Lowry's murder." I hung up with a smug smile. *We'll see if that doesn't get a cop here ASAP.*

In the meantime, I made a list of flowers I'd need to order from our wholesaler, starting with fully bloomed yellow ranunculus, aka buttercups. Normally, I'd place the order online, but this wasn't a normal situation. Sitting at the desk in the study, I dialed the number for Pauly's Plants. When an operator picked up, I explained that I was on a tight timetable and needed to base my order on the availability of flowers in a certain color scheme. She transferred me to Pauly himself.

A moment later, a booming voice came on the line. "Is that you Felix?"

"Uh, no. This is Sierra."

"Oh, sorry about that. When I heard it was the owner of Flower House, my mind automatically traveled to the past. I remember now. Felix retired, right?"

"That's right. And it's okay. I'm still getting used to it myself. How are you, Pauly?"

"Can't complain. Busy as usual. Wait—Flower House is in Aerieville. Didn't I see you on the news recently?"

I winced. *Here we go again.* Oh, well. I couldn't blame folks for their curiosity. I gamely gave Pauly the inside scoop. Then I said, "I'm surprised you didn't hear about it from your driver, Bart Hammerson."

"Oh, yeah. Bart. Not a big talker, that one."

"So, he's always been that way?" It suddenly occurred to me that I might gather a little information while I had Pauly on the line. "Even before his wife died?"

"Died? You mean left him?"

Chill bumps tingled along my arms. Bart had told me his wife died. Why would he lie about something like that?

"Um, maybe I got that wrong. I was thinking of the accident?" I phrased it as a question, hoping Pauly would take the bait. Rocky had told me Bart had been in a serious accident a few years ago.

"Oh, yeah, the accident. Terrible, terrible thing."

I couldn't believe this was working. I decided to press my luck. "I know Bart doesn't like to talk about it . . . for obvious reasons."

"Of course not. He felt terrible. Blamed himself."

"As would anyone," I murmured, hoping it sounded appropriate.

"I figure that's why his wife left him," Pauly continued.

"Because of the accident," I said, not really understanding at all.

"Well, the aftermath. With a paralyzed child, the strain was too much for their marriage to handle."

"The accident left their child paralyzed?" I exclaimed.

The news was like a blow to the gut, even if I didn't really know Bart or his family. How awful.

There was silence on the other end of the line. *Oops.* I'd forgotten I was already supposed to know this. "I mean, I knew it was bad," I said quickly. "But I'd forgotten how bad. This must be why Bart is so sensitive about reckless drivers."

"Drunk drivers, in particular," said Pauly. "Anyway, what can I help you with?"

I told Pauly what I was looking for, and he was kind enough to check his inventory while we were on the phone. After a brief discussion, I opted for yellow ranunculus and pink and yellow "sunset" dahlias. They were beautiful, romantic flowers with little fragrance—a plus if anyone in the wedding party suffered from allergies. Arranged with peach and pale pink roses from the hothouse, these would make up the focal flowers for the bridal bouquet, with loose greenery for an organic effect. I would base all the other arrangements on this design. For good measure, I also ordered some yellow and orange chrysanthemums for a pop of color, and green button chrysanthemums for contrast. Finally, I selected a bunch of hardy foliage for the base of the arch and the other decorations.

After Pauly confirmed he could provide the flowers in time, he said he just needed to find an available driver.

"Isn't Bart available?" I asked. "I actually just saw him yesterday."

"He has another run tomorrow, but I think he can get to you by Thursday. Will that work?"

"Yes, we'll make it work." That would essentially give us one day to make all the arrangements. I fanned myself with a piece of paper, as my nerves started to kick in. "The earlier Thursday the better."

I heard typing sounds on the other end of the line. "It can't be too early. He has a delivery to make to the college in Knoxville first. But I can tell him to bypass the florists between there and Aerieville and get to them on his way back."

"That would be great. Thank you." I was so focused on getting the wedding flowers in time, I almost missed what Pauly had said. As soon as it registered, I sat up straight. "Wait, did you say Bart makes a delivery to a college? Is it the University of Tennessee, by chance?"

"Sure is. I've been supplying UT for a few years now."

"For their gift shop? Or the hospital?" I couldn't understand why a university would order flowers from a wholesaler—unless they liked to have really pretty offices and common areas.

"It's for the science department," said Pauly. "Every semester, they need about a hundred perfect specimens, usually lilies. It's for dissection and other experiments."

"Oh. Interesting. Who knew?" I thanked Pauly again and hung up, lost in thought. *Who knew, indeed?*

Before I had a chance to ask Calvin about flower deliveries to the UT science department, there was a knock at the front door. It was a dark-haired uniformed officer, Patrolman Davy Wills. He was the officer who'd helped maintain order during the interrogations and spoke to Sheila when she first arrived. I sort of knew him in passing. He'd been in Rocky's class in high school.

He removed his hat, revealing a fresh buzz cut. "Hi, Sierra," he said. "I heard you have some information to share?"

"Yeah, a couple of things. Come on in."

I led Davy through the shop to the kitchen, where

Deena was washing out some flower buckets in the sink. Calvin had disappeared.

"Hello," said Deena, over her shoulder.

"I want to show you something outside," I said to Davy. "But, first, do you know when this tape can be removed? We really need to get in there." I pointed to the yellow tape across the storeroom door.

Officer Wills frowned. "Uh, we finished processing the scene the same day as the crime. I'm pretty sure forensics completed their work in there."

"What does that mean?" I asked.

"I'll double-check, but I'm pretty sure the tape can come down." He pulled a radio from his belt and walked into the hallway as he spoke into it.

Deena and I exchanged a look. A minute later, Davy came back and pulled the yellow tape from the wall. He wadded it up and tossed it in the garbage can.

"Okay, what else?" he said.

I put my hands on my hips. "You mean I didn't even need to close the shop?"

He looked slightly sheepish. "This isn't really my case, but I think it's okay if you want to open up. And I can pass along any information and comments you have." He pulled a notebook from his pocket and flipped to a clean page. "You wanted to show me something?"

I sighed. "Follow me." I grabbed my purse from the counter and led the way out the back door and around the corner. After being in the air-conditioned shop, even for a few minutes, the humidity outside seemed oppressive. I pushed my hair behind my ears and walked up to the juniper bush beneath the bathroom window. "There was part of a footprint there on Sunday morning." I pointed to the mud, which was now smooth following the subsequent rainfall.

"Oh-kay," said Davy, drawing the word out.

"Calvin took a picture of it. Also, I found this." I took the small *Made in the U.S.A.* sticker from my purse and handed it to the officer.

He scratched his head and frowned. "Where did you find it?"

I pointed to the bush. "In there." I explained how Professor Lowry had come in with a canteen, which somehow seemed to have disappeared. I also told him about the open bathroom window and my theory that the canteen might have been tossed into the bushes.

The expression on Davy's face morphed from deepening confusion to something like worry. "Oh, no," he muttered.

"What's the matter?" I asked.

He shook his head. "Uh, I have evidence bags in the trunk of my car. I'll be right back."

"I'll come with you," I said, tagging along. "Why did you say 'oh, no'?" I was a little miffed that the police hadn't bothered to come back to Flower House after my first call about the footprint, or to tell me anything about the investigation. Evidently, I was going to have to start being a squeakier wheel.

Davy didn't answer me. When we reached his patrol car, he opened the trunk and retrieved a small clear plastic evidence bag. He placed the sticker inside, then used a pen from his pocket to scrawl today's date on the bag.

"Speaking of evidence," I said, "did you get anything from the candlestick? Any fingerprints?"

"No. We think the offender wore gloves."

"Gloves?" This surprised me. I'd thought the killer might have wiped the candlestick down, but, now that I thought about it, that would take extra time. Still, who would be carrying gloves in the middle of summer? I said as much to Officer Wills.

Before he could answer, I noticed Flo Morrison emerge from the bakery next door. She looked our way and made a move as if she'd come over. Avoiding her eyes, I turned back toward Flower House.

"Uh, there's one more thing," I said. "Let's go back inside."

"Alright." He closed his trunk and followed me as I scurried up the walkway. Once inside, he waited patiently for me to continue.

I gestured to the café. "Can I get you something to drink? Tea or water?"

"No, thanks." He pulled out his notebook again.

"Right. Okay." I went into the café anyway and pulled out a chair from one of the small tables. "This is where Bart was sitting when the UT van pulled up, and again later after the students and professor came inside. But he wasn't in here by the time half the students left, and I didn't see where he went. I don't think he has an alibi for the time of the murder. Does he?"

Davy wiped his mouth with his hand, apparently trying to hide a smile. He snapped his notebook shut. "Sierra, I can't give you details on our investigation. Besides, like I said, I'm not the lead on the case."

"I know. But—oh, about the gloves! I didn't see any-one wearing gloves. It's not exactly glove weather."

"I didn't say anything about winter gloves," he said. "There are other kinds."

At the sound of footsteps, we both looked over to see Calvin come into the room. He was carrying a fern he'd repotted in the greenhouse. He stopped short when he saw us.

"There are gardening gloves, for example," said Davy, with a pointed glance at Calvin.

Calvin swallowed, then gave us a nod and placed the plant on an antique table in the corner of the room. He wasn't wearing gardening gloves, but it wasn't uncommon for him to do so.

"There are work gloves too," I said quickly. "I bet Bart had gloves in his truck."

Davy turned to me with raised eyebrows. "Do you have anything else to report, or are we done here?"

Calvin cleared his throat and addressed me. "I'll be in the greenhouse if you need me. Deena is in the garden, and Gus is in the office with the door closed."

"Thanks," I said. As soon as he left, I faced Officer Wills again. "I'm still concerned about that canteen. The investigators didn't find it, did they?"

He wrinkled his brow. "I don't think so. To tell you the truth, I'm concerned too."

"Why? Do you think the professor was under the influence?" I hesitated to repeat what Calvin had told me about Lowry appearing flushed and unusually relaxed. I didn't want to get Calvin in trouble for holding back information, even though he hadn't done so on purpose.

Davy rubbed his forehead and looked out the window. As if talking to himself, he said, "If we'd known there was a canteen, then the Deputy might've changed her mind and ordered an autopsy."

"Wait. There's not going to be an autopsy?"

Davy shook his head and scowled briefly. "The medical examiner ruled the cause of death blunt force trauma. So, Bradley thought there was no need to order an autopsy."

I didn't know much about police investigations, but

that sounded wrong to me. I thought all murders warranted an autopsy. "Well, it's not too late, is it?"

"I'm not sure." He looked at me and lowered his voice. "Look, you didn't hear this from me, okay? Deputy Chief Bradley is a good officer. But she's under a lot of pressure to solve this case as fast as possible."

"I get it," I said. But that didn't mean I liked it.

"So, if you have any other information you think might be relevant, please don't hold back."

I opened my mouth but no words came out. The only "information" I had so far was overheard snippets of conversation, hearsay, and conjecture. At last, I said, "There's one thing, but I don't know if it's relevant. I learned that Bart has made flower deliveries to the UT Science Department. I don't know if that means he ever met Lowry before, but it's possible."

Davy wrote down the info. "Anything else?"

I bit my lip. *Should I go on?* Oh, well, I had nothing to lose, while Calvin had plenty to lose if we couldn't help the police find the real killer. "I think there's something weird going on with the students. I've run into them a couple of times, and it seems like they're, um, not unhappy their professor is gone."

Davy looked dubious but made another note. "That it?"

I hesitated. *Was* that it? I felt like I was forgetting something, but the only thing I knew for sure I was holding back was the stuff about Wanda. And I didn't want to bring it up. It felt too much like gossip to mention her past or comment on her confusion. Besides, now that I knew Bart had lied to me about his wife, I wasn't sure if I could trust anything he'd told me—least of all his claim that he'd seen Wanda come out of the house but didn't want to tell the police.

"That's it," I said.

"Great." Davy shut his notebook and stuffed it into his pocket.

I walked him to the door. "Thanks, Davy. I mean, Officer Wills."

He grinned, as he stepped outside. "Say hi to Rocky for me."

"You bet."

I closed the door behind him and pondered the two-sided sign swaying on its hook. It currently said the shop was Closed. I flipped it over to Open. It was late in the day, but there was almost an hour left until our usual six p.m. closing time. There was no reason now we couldn't welcome potential walk-ins. That is, if anyone knew we were open for business.

I walked to the back of the shop and cracked the study door to check on Gus. He'd made himself comfortable on the upholstered chair in the corner and seemed content to remain there. He barely twitched an ear when I peeked at him. Smiling, I backed out and shut the door again. *Let sleeping dogs snooze.*

Deena was apparently still out back. On the kitchen counter was the list she'd started, of supplies we'd need for Sue Ellen's wedding. I picked it up, then moved to the storeroom.

Okay, Sierra, I said to myself. *You can do this.* I opened the door, flipped on the light, and stepped inside. Looking around, I shuddered involuntarily. It was eerie being in the exact spot where a man had been brutally killed. Something about the enclosed space made it so much worse than it already was. I wanted nothing more than to get out of there as soon as possible.

Where is the wedding arch? The metal trellis frame came in multiple segments that could be assembled in various sizes. After a cursory sweep of the room, I spotted the stacked metal pieces on the top shelf in the back. I overturned a wooden crate to use as a stool and climbed on top. Careful not to lose my balance, I reached for the topmost sections in the pile.

A faint creak sounded behind me, but I didn't look around. I figured Deena or Calvin must have come back inside. I was about to call for them to come and help me, when I heard another sound: the whoosh and click of the door closing.

"Hey!" I said, turning abruptly. I jumped off the crate and hurried to the door, only to find it wouldn't open.

Someone had locked me in the storeroom.

Chapter 15

I liked to think I was an even-keeled sort of person. I wasn't prone to making mountains out of molehills or freaking out for no good reason. But the second I realized I was trapped in a small, airless room—which happened to be the site of an unsolved murder—I couldn't stop the rush of panic if I'd wanted to. I screamed with all my might and pounded on the door with both fists.

"Help! Help! Let me out!"

No one came to let me out. But someone did hear me: little Gus. I could hear his frantic barks through two closed doors. He was stuck too.

I stopped yelling and rubbed the backs of my knuckles. With my heart hammering in my chest, I sucked in a breath and tried to think.

I'd left my phone in my purse, which I'd dropped on the counter in the kitchen. But that shouldn't matter. Somebody was sure to find me soon. The minute anyone entered Flower House, they'd hear me if I hollered again—and they'd for sure hear Gus's loud yelps. It was only a matter of time. After all, Deena wouldn't go home without coming inside to talk to me first, and Calvin lived here.

But who had closed the door on me? And barricaded it? I remembered that the storeroom door didn't actually have a lock.

Were we being robbed?

A fresh wave of panic surged like a storm tide. Only this time I didn't scream. I dug my nails into my palms and pressed my ear to the door. I couldn't hear anything other than Gus's muffled barks. It occurred to me that maybe it would be best if Calvin and Deena *didn't* come running in right away. Because what if an intruder—possibly a murderous, dangerous intruder—was still in here?

Then Gus's barks fell silent, and I started to fret about him too.

Just when my imagination threatened to run away with me, there was a scraping sound and the door burst open. Calvin stood in the doorway with an expression of astonishment and worry. Gus ran around him to jump on my legs.

"Sierra! What happened? Are you okay?"

"Oh, Calvin, thank goodness!" I tried to bypass Gus, as I stumbled out of the storeroom. At the same time, Calvin reached out to help, and I ended up smashing into his chest. He enveloped me in a tight hug. That turned out to be a good thing, since I was now shaking and felt mighty wobbly on my legs.

"Are you hurt?" said Calvin. He rubbed my arms, then pulled back to search my face. Gus danced excitedly around my feet, barking for attention.

"I'm okay." I reached down to pet Gus, then grabbed a hold of the back of the chair—which had apparently been wedged under the doorknob. My fear rapidly turned to anger. "Who shut the door on me?"

Calvin wrinkled his forehead. "I was hoping *you'd* know. I came inside and heard Gus barking like mad. As soon as I let him out, he came running in here and led me to you."

"Oh, good boy," I said, holding out my hand to Gus again. Then I looked around. "So, I guess they're long gone, huh? Is anything missing?"

My purse was right where I'd left it, apparently undisturbed. Calvin went to check the cash register and informed me that it was untouched as well. While he looked in the other rooms, I headed for the back door to step outside. But I stopped when I noticed the cooler door wasn't closed tightly. I was pretty sure it had been closed earlier.

Cautiously, I pulled the door open. I didn't know what I expected to find, but I was relieved to see nothing was amiss. Or was it? We always kept a small number of pre-arranged bouquets in this case (in addition to a few in the display cooler in the front of the shop), as well as several pails of single-stem cut flowers. If I wasn't mistaken, the containers seemed to have been pushed aside. Squatting down to examine the lowest shelf, I found the same thing. *Weird*.

I straightened the arrangements, then stood up and gazed around the kitchen again. My eyes fell upon a slightly open cabinet door above the oven. When I opened it wider, I found a cluster of clear glass vases. Nothing out of the ordinary there. But why was the door ajar in the first place? Was someone looking for something?

With Gus following my every move, I proceeded to take a gander inside all the other cabinets. Again, there didn't appear to be anything missing, and I couldn't be certain if anything had been moved.

Calvin returned to the kitchen. "By any chance, did you leave the cabinets open in the café?"

"No." I told him what I'd observed in the kitchen, then walked up front to see the café for myself.

Calvin followed closely behind me. "How long were you locked in the storeroom?"

"It felt like eternity, but it probably wasn't more than five minutes."

As I perused the kitchenette, Calvin walked to the front door. "Did you turn the sign over?" he called.

I joined him in the foyer. There was nothing to see in the café. "Yeah. Officer Wills said it would be okay. I also left the door unlocked."

"So, the person creeping around in here could have come in the front or the back," mused Calvin. "Though you probably would have heard the bell on the front door."

I frowned. "I suppose so, unless they opened the door slowly. If they came in the back, Deena should have seen them. She's out in the garden . . . isn't she?"

"She was earlier," said Calvin. "When I came out of the greenhouse, she wasn't there."

We looked at each other for a moment, and I sucked in a breath. *Deena!* Without a word, I bolted to the back door and ran outside.

"Deena!" I called. My eyes roamed the backyard and garden, as my overactive imagination conjured dire scenarios. *What if whoever locked me in the storeroom got to Deena first? Could she be lying somewhere, hurt? Could she have been kidnapped?*

Stuffing these scary thoughts, I ran up the driveway toward Oak Street. Deena's car was still parked next to the curb. Peering frantically up and down the sidewalk, I called her name again.

There was no traffic, nor any pedestrians in sight. The antique store across the street was dark. To the left, I noticed two cars parked in front of the historical society. I guessed that a volunteer had met someone there by appointment, probably a genealogist doing research. To the right, I saw one car parked next to Bread n' Butter and two bicycles leaning against a pole. Usually the bakery would be closed by now, but I could understand staying open as long as customers wanted to linger.

I was about to dash over to the bakery to ask if anyone had seen Deena, when I heard voices behind me. Looking over at the historical society again, I saw that two women had emerged from the building and were chatting on the porch. One of them I recognized as a girl we'd gone to high school with. The other one was Deena.

Oh, thank God! I slumped with relief. *She must have been next door the whole time.*

I debated whether to run over and join her or go inform Calvin first. Then I felt a tap on my shoulder. I gave a start and whirled around, emitting an involuntary squeak at the unexpected visitor: Isaiah Adams.

He flashed his dimples and blinked at me innocently. "Sorry if I scared you."

"I didn't hear you come up." I pressed my hand to my chest and tried to smile back. I was still jumpy from the worry over Deena—not to mention my experience in the storeroom.

"I wondered if I could see the orchids now," he said.

"The orchids? Sure." I nodded toward the bicycles. "Those must be Richard's bikes, huh?"

"Yeah. Vince is still in the bakery. He's not really interested in flowers. At least, not this kind."

There was a glint in his eye that made me feel I was missing out on a joke. What other kind of flowers were there?

Calvin came out of the front door with Gus. He seemed almost as surprised to see Isaiah as I was and gave me a questioning look. I pointed toward the historical society to show him where Deena was.

Good, he mouthed, relief showing in his face. Gus tugged at his leash to greet the newcomer.

Isaiah indulgently reached down to let Gus sniff his hand. To Calvin, he said, "Hello, professor."

"How's it going?" said Calvin. "Where are your cohorts?"

"Vince is having coffee next door, and April didn't want to stop."

So, April was around here someplace too. I met Calvin's eyes, then inclined my head toward the bicycles. "They rode here from Richard's B&B," I said. "Isaiah wants to see the orchids. Do you mind giving him a tour of the greenhouse?"

"Be happy to," said Calvin, handing me Gus's leash.

"Thanks, man," said Isaiah.

I walked with them around the side of the house, keeping a look out as we went. These college kids seemed nice enough, but I still didn't trust them. Especially since they had started seeming so nice only after their professor's untimely demise. In fact, other than the few people in my inner circle, I felt like I couldn't trust anyone right now.

"I always thought you got a raw deal," Isaiah was saying.

My ears perked up.

"Thanks," Calvin said.

"Yeah, that was wack. Professor Lowry really screwed you over."

I pulled up to Isaiah's side. "You knew about that?"

"About the article?" he said. "Yeah, I knew that wasn't Lowry's work. He stopped doing his own stuff a long time ago."

We reached the door to the greenhouse. Calvin, looking more like a teacher than ever, gave Isaiah a grim smile. "It doesn't matter anymore. What's done is done. And I'm still sorry Professor Lowry is gone."

Isaiah cocked his head curiously. "Really?"

"Of course," said Calvin. "No matter how big of a jerk he was, Lowry didn't deserve to die that way."

The younger guy twitched his shoulder in a slight shrug. "If you say so."

My inner alarm bells were ringing. It seemed callous to speak of the recently deceased in this way. I turned to Isaiah. "Was he a jerk to you too?"

Isaiah looked at me blankly. The twitch in his cheek was so faint, I almost missed it. "He could be cranky," he finally said. "He was not known as a warm and fuzzy teacher. Right, Prof?"

Calvin nodded. "Right." He opened the greenhouse. "Want to join us, Sierra?"

"Uh, no, thanks. I'll just take Gus for a quick walk." I'd learned so much recently I couldn't keep everything straight anymore. The best thing now was to clear my head.

Deena was still gabbing with her old friend, so I headed down the sidewalk in the other direction. As I passed Bread n' Butter, I peered in the window and saw Vince sitting at one of the tables. I picked up the pace and crossed my fingers, hoping he wouldn't chance to look outside and spot me. I felt slightly guilty about this. Part of me felt like I ought to go in there and strike up a conversation. Maybe I could get him to tell me more about Lowry and the other students. But I wasn't up to it right now. In truth, I was still a little spooked about being trapped in the storeroom.

When we reached Melody Gardens, I let Gus take the lead. We meandered along the narrow paths, him exploring with his nose and me admiring the midsummer lushness of the trees and flowers.

Soon we came to a wrought-iron bench beneath an old oak tree. I decided to rest a moment. As I sat down, I twisted to read the plaque on the back of the bench: *In loving memory of Georgina Maniford.* Of course, I'd seen it before. But it struck me anew how she and Felix must have planted many of the perennials in the little park. I was almost certain they'd started the gorgeous bed of celosias in the patch of sun across the path.

I knew from Granny Mae that young celosia leaves were mild, tasty, and chockful of vitamins and minerals, similar to spinach. Once they bloomed, however, the leaves became bitter and stringy. The problem was I could never bring myself to harvest them before flowering. The showy, feathery, jewel-toned flowers were the best part of growing celosias. Gazing at them now, I was tempted to go over and touch the fuzzy, otherworldly blooms.

Gus didn't want to stay in one place, so we walked on. The next flowers that caught my eye were a stand of delicate orange poppies along the border of the path. The petals were beginning to drop, but they were still pretty, bobbing in the breeze. I wasn't sure what variety of poppies these were, but I knew they weren't opium poppies—aka breadseed poppies, whose pods would be filled with delicious crunchy seeds at the end of the growing season.

Come to think of it, the red poppies Calvin had found on my porch steps might have been opium poppies—mostly likely grown innocently in someone's backyard. I'd have to ask my neighbors if one of their grandchildren had left me the little bouquet. I had to admit a thunderstorm was a strange time to do so, but maybe they'd left it for me beforehand and Calvin and I had missed it on our way inside. As I recalled, some poppies, such as wild California poppies, were edible and medicinal, while many others were dangerous for people and pets alike.

Gus led us off the path and into an area of grass and groundcover. There was no one around to tell us not to, and it was okay with me as long as we didn't step on any flowers. My mind continued to wander in the same directionless way. I recalled my idea to create an info card listing common edible flowers. We'd have to focus on the ones that were one hundred percent safe, such as roses and marigolds. I knew there were others, such as honeysuckle, that had edible flowers but highly toxic berries.

Another lesson I'd learned from Granny was that *how* you prepared some foraged plants made all the difference. For example, pokeweed could be cooked to make a delectable dish called poke sallet—*not* "salad," as the song said. If eaten raw, pokeweed leaves could be fatal.

Then again, some plants were extremely toxic from root to petal and seed to berry, such as the lovely scented but highly poisonous lily of the valley. Nature could sure be tricky and confusing.

Lost in these thoughts, I was startled when Gus gave an excited yap. He pulled me in the direction of a person quietly pulling weeds in a shady corner of the garden.

It was a woman, leaning over an overgrown clump of white hydrangeas. At the sound of our approach, she turned around—and I saw that it was Wanda Milford.

"Hello, there," she said with a smile.

I was so stunned to see her, I almost forgot my manners. I looked around, halfway expecting to see Granny here too.

"Hi, Wanda," I said, finding my voice. "What a surprise. What are you doing here?"

"Oh, just doing some yard work," she said, waving vaguely behind her.

I was so perplexed. I'd never known Wanda to do grounds work in the park. Yet, here she was, wearing gardening gloves and clutching a small trowel.

"Did you come down the mountain by yourself?" I asked.

"Mm-hmm." She leaned down to pat Gus, who was idly sniffing her shoes.

Tightening my hold on the leash, I took a step closer. "Why don't you come back to Flower House with me? Have a glass of tea or water."

She glanced distractedly at the sky. "That's nice of you, but I should probably get going. It's gettin' to be about suppertime, isn't it?"

Moving away from the hydrangeas, she reached for a willow shopping basket on the ground. This provided an opening for Gus, who made a beeline for a spot at the base of the bush—pulling me right along with him. Then I saw why. He was sniffing a sizable round hole in the dirt.

Had Wanda dug the hole? Was she trying to bury something?

She saw my curious look and laughed. "Maybe the doggie can help me," she volunteered. "I've been looking for something and having the darndest time. I'm probably looking in the wrong place." She pulled off her gloves and stuck them in her basket.

"What is it?" I asked.

As if she hadn't heard me, she draped the basket on her wrist and headed for the garden path. Shaking my head in bewilderment, I nudged Gus and followed her.

Suddenly, she turned to me with a sparkle in her eye. "Want to see something?"

"Uh, yeah," I said. "Sure." I was still trying to figure out if Wanda was in her right mind or if she was acting confused as Granny had said. So far, she seemed perfectly lucid, in spite of the odd circumstances and slightly strange way she was acting.

She walked over to the large oak tree next to the bench and circled it to the backside. "Here," she said, reaching up with her left hand to touch the bark.

I stood at her side and looked to the point she indicated. The first thing I noticed was that she had a red thread tied around her ring finger. Then I saw the carved initials: R.M. x W.S.

I couldn't help smiling. "Are you W.S.?" I asked.

She nodded. "Smith is my maiden name. R.M. is Roy Milford, my husband. This was our special place back when we were sweethearts, before we got married."

"That's sweet," I said, touched that the memento was still here after all these years. "What is it that you're looking for in the ground? Is it something you or Roy hid?"

Her face clouded. "Not hid, so much as lost. Roy gave me a promise ring here in this park, many moons ago. Sometime later, in a fit of anger, I threw it on the ground"—she waved her hand in the direction of the hydrangeas—"somewhere around here."

I furrowed my brow. "Oh. Well, how do you know somebody didn't already find it?"

"I know," she said with conviction, "because Roy told me so. That is, his ghost told me. And he won't rest until I find it."

Chapter 16

No matter how hard I tried, I couldn't convince Wanda to have a bite to eat with me or let me call Granny, or anyone else, to accompany her home. She insisted she was perfectly fine and wanted to get home before dark. In fact, she did seem as steady and feisty as ever, so I reluctantly bade her goodbye.

By the time I returned to Flower House, the two bicycles were gone from the bakery, and Deena and Calvin were sitting on the front steps waiting for me. Gus was so excited to see them, I let go of his leash and allowed him to run the rest of the way. He bounded up the steps as fast as his little legs would carry him. Calvin smiled, but Deena looked grim.

"Why didn't you come and get me?" she demanded. "I know you saw me at the historical society. I saw you look over and then go off the other way."

I opened my mouth to respond, but she didn't let me.

"And why didn't you call the police?" she continued. "Some creep sneaks in the shop and traps you in a closet—don't you think the cops should know about that?"

I felt my cheeks grow warm. "I wasn't hurt," I protested. "And nobody broke in. I'm not sure there was a crime to report."

"Are you kidding?" She was giving me a look that reminded me an awful lot of my mother. "Unlawful imprisonment is a crime. Trespassing in our private work area is a crime."

I knew she was right. "I'll call now," I said meekly, as I took out my phone. For the second time today, I dialed the number of the Aerieville police station. It took just a few minutes to report that there had been another incident at Flower House. The dispatcher informed me that an officer would be by shortly.

"Happy now?" I said to Deena.

"No," she said bluntly. "I'm worried." She picked at her fingers in a rare display of nervousness.

"I'm sorry," I began.

She raised a palm to stop my apology. "It's not your fault," she said. "It's mine."

Now it was my turn to gape at her. "How in the world is it your fault?"

She squeezed her eyes shut briefly, as if gearing up for a confession. Then she spoke in a rush. "I saw Bart's truck pull into the driveway, just as I was heading next door. I should have come back. I'm so sorry. I didn't think about you being alone inside. I had no idea he would—"

"Wait," I said, cutting her off. "First of all—Bart was here? But, secondly, of course you wouldn't have thought he'd do anything. He was a perfect gentleman with me yesterday—well, as much as he ever is."

Calvin made a sound that might have been a scoff. He covered it by clearing his throat. "What time did you see the truck, Deena? It must have been when I was in the greenhouse."

She shook her head. "I don't know. It was just a few minutes after I came outside, I think."

"Did you see him knock on the back door or come inside?" I asked.

"No." Deena winced regretfully. "I didn't even see him get out of his truck. I went inside at the historical society to see some artifacts Becki wanted to show me."

I pinched my lip in thought. I couldn't imagine why Bart would stop by without a delivery. In fact, I was kind of surprised he was still in town. Still, I wasn't completely convinced that he was the one who had locked me in the storeroom.

"Did Calvin tell you Vince and Isaiah were here too? And possibly April?"

"Yeah," Deena acknowledged. "I guess it could have been one of them."

I turned to Calvin. "How was the tour, by the way? Was Isaiah really interested in the orchids?"

"Evidently so. He asked intelligent questions and seemed to know a lot already."

"That's good, I guess."

"He was especially interested in rare and valuable orchids," Calvin went on. "Which we don't have here."

"Like the ghost orchid?" said Deena, with a hint of amusement. I figured she was remembering the book and movie about orchid poaching that had come out several years earlier.

Calvin nodded. "He mentioned that one among others." Gus nosed Calvin for attention. He ruffled the pup's fur before continuing. "I'll say one thing about the kid, he's clearly got ambition and drive. That much was clear. He even made a comment about looking out for himself and taking matters into his own hands."

"Really?" I said. "In what context?"

"He was talking about taking the initiative to bike over here. But I got the impression he was describing his philosophy with everything."

At that moment, a patrol car rolled up the street and stopped in front of Flower House. Once again, Officer Davy Wills got out and strode up the walkway. I was glad the bakery next door was dark, as was the Morrisons' cottage in back.

"Long time no see," I joked.

"This is getting to be a popular place," he said.

I invited him to have a seat on the porch, but he chose to stand as he took our statements. After explaining everything that had happened, we also told him about Bart's brief appearance, as well as the visit from Isaiah. Then I surprised everyone by describing my encounter with Wanda in the park.

Davy didn't seem to see the relevance of Wanda's presence in the neighborhood, but he dutifully wrote down what I told him. Of course, Calvin and Deena both knew.

"It's quite a coincidence," Deena mused. "Everyone who was here when the professor was killed, was also here when Sierra was locked in the storeroom."

"Maybe," said Davy. "Though we don't know that any of them were in the shop. And from what you've said, anyone could have entered through the front door without being seen. Is it possible someone was playing a practical joke?"

I glanced at Calvin, and he rolled his eyes. I'd been right that the police would want to blame this on a prank.

I knew better. Call it a hunch, but I felt certain the killer had returned to the scene of the crime. The question was, why? Or, more to the point, what had they been looking for?

After Davy left, I locked up and urged Deena to go home. She'd been here all day, and I was worried this place was starting to stress her out. I assured her I was fine and that I didn't blame her in the least for anything at all.

I made my rounds through the shop, changing out the water-and-flower-food solution in all the pails and trimming the stems of any flowers we'd had for a few days. Calvin helped, even though I told him he didn't have to. Secretly, though, I was glad to have his company.

That done, I printed out our most recent online orders and placed them on the worktable for tomorrow. Then I lingered in the workroom, rerolling loose ribbons and wiping down the already clean countertops. Though I usually didn't mind going home alone, I was having qualms tonight.

Calvin must have picked up on my reluctance to leave. "Hey," he said. "I was thinking about ordering a pizza. Want to join me?"

"Mmm! Yeah." I jumped on the offer. "I'm actually really hungry. Pizza sounds great."

We agreed on toppings—which wasn't hard since we both loved to load our pizzas with the works. When it arrived, Calvin suggested we take it up to his apartment. He had cold beer and soda in his fridge and said we might as well not dirty the plates in the café. That sounded fine to me. After what I'd been through, I opted for a beer.

It turned out to be a pleasant dinner in Calvin's small eat-in kitchen. The apartment's décor was pretty dated, since it had sat empty for more than a decade after Felix moved into a cabin in the woods, following Georgina's death. But it was clean and homey and featured a few of Calvin's personal touches, such as botanical wall art, some books on historical treasure hunting, and a collection of sparkly geodes.

Gus polished off his dog food and sat near our feet as we ate. I told Calvin about my Nashville days, and he asked if he'd ever get to hear me sing or play my guitar.

I sighed. "I haven't touched my guitar in ages. My life has taken an unexpected turn in a different direction."

"Mine too," he said, with a small smile.

"Not that this is a bad thing," I clarified. "I'm pretty happy with my life right now—other than the unfortunate death that occurred here. Aren't you?"

Calvin took a bite of his pizza and chewed thoughtfully, making me wait. When he finally swallowed, he looked me in the eyes. His gaze was tender and warm. My heartbeat quickened under his attention.

"Yeah," he said softly. "Before Saturday I was pretty content."

"Things will get back to normal soon," I said.

"I hope so."

He took a sip of beer and I followed suit. I was beginning to feel mellow and a little flirtatious. "Tell me about your childhood," I said. "You grew up on a farm in Iowa? Did you leave a lot of broken hearts back there when you moved to Tennessee?"

He laughed. "Yeah, a whole trail of them. It was devastating."

My cell phone jingled, so I reached for it and checked the incoming number. It was unfamiliar, which usually meant I'd ignore the call. Then again, the last unknown number had led to a wedding job. "Guess I'll see who this is," I said to Calvin, as I pressed Answer. "Hello?"

"Hi, Sierra," said a man's rough voice.

It took me a second to place it. "Bart?"

Calvin froze, holding a slice of pizza in midair.

"Are you home?" said Bart. "I'm in your neighborhood, and I wanted to stop by."

"Um. No, sorry. I'm not home right now." I shivered, struck with a sudden chill. *How does Bart know where I live? For that matter, how did he get my cell phone number?*

"Are you coming home soon?"

I swallowed, as my eyes slid to meet Calvin's. He was watching me closely.

"No," I said, making a snap decision. "I'm staying at a friend's house tonight. Was there something you wanted to tell me?"

There was a pause on the other end of the line. "Not really. I just wanted to apologize for yesterday."

"What about yesterday?" I asked.

"For drinking so much. I didn't mean to scare you off."

"You didn't scare me off," I said. Though, he was scaring me a little now. "And there's no need to apologize, but thank you anyway."

"Yeah."

I had the sense he wanted to say more. Could it be a confession? *I should keep him talking.* "Oh, I heard you stopped by Flower House this afternoon," I said. "I'm sorry I missed you. Did you come inside?"

"No. I chickened out."

"What do you mean?"

"Nothing. I was just going to say I was sorry, but I decided to call instead."

"Are you sure that's all?" I tried to keep my voice light and friendly. "You know, you can tell me anything." In my peripheral vision I saw Calvin's eyebrows shoot up. Maybe I'd sounded a little more like Mae West than I'd intended to.

Bart cleared his throat. "Likewise. You can tell me anything too."

I frowned. *What would I have to tell him?* "Thank you," I said uncertainly. "So, are you staying in Aerieville again tonight? Don't you have deliveries to make tomorrow?"

"Yeah, no. I'm going home tonight. Unless you want to meet somewhere for a drink?"

Not again. Bart was obviously interested in more than a platonic friendship with me. And I most certainly was not. "Sorry. I'm pretty tired. And, like I said, I'm with a friend. I'll see you Thursday, though."

"Right. Special delivery."

"Good night, Bart."

I hung up, set my phone on the table, and gave Calvin an embarrassed grin. "That was kind of weird, huh?"

"Is it weird that a guy would ask you out? No."

"It's just weird because Bart has been acting weird." I told Calvin about my conversation with Pauly earlier today, including the fact that Bart had lied about his wife having passed away.

"Maybe his *ex*-wife died," Calvin suggested.

"I don't think so. Pauly seemed to know Bart's wife had left him following a car accident." Now that I thought about it, maybe Bart was just shy and out of practice with women. Still, that didn't entirely explain his odd behavior. "Get this—Pauly also said Bart made deliveries to the UT science department. For flower experiments or something?"

Calvin nodded. "Flowers are needed for classes every semester, from Botany 101 to Plant Physiology. The deliveries usually happen early in the morning. I don't think I ever encountered the delivery person when I was there."

"Would Professor Lowry have accepted the deliveries?"

Calvin looked doubtful. "Lowry wouldn't usually be in the science building that early."

Hmm. I toyed with the label on my beer bottle, as I contemplated my impression of Bart. Maybe he hadn't lied about never having met Lowry after all. But his behavior, on the whole, was still pretty sketchy. And it really bugged me that he was supposedly in my neighborhood and thought he'd just stop by my house. The idea gave me the creeps, especially after what had happened this afternoon.

Calvin regarded me with interest. "So, you're staying at a friend's house tonight?"

Oh, right. He'd heard me lie to Bart about that. I laughed nervously. "I was just saying that to—"

"You can stay here," he interrupted. He'd said it mildly, as if it were no big deal.

"Oh! Well . . ." I trailed off, not sure what to say. In truth, the idea was appealing for more than one reason.

"You can have my bedroom. I'll sleep on the couch."

I smiled. "Thank you. I *am* feeling uncommonly nervous tonight. I'll stay, but on one condition."

"Yeah?"

"I get the couch."

Chapter 17

It took me a moment to remember where I was. Gus was sprawled on my feet, and my head rested on a soft pillow, but the high plaster ceiling above me, with a square mid-century light fixture, was not at all familiar.

The smell of coffee drifted to my nose, and I heard the quiet clinking of dishes. *Oh, yeah.* This was Calvin's apartment. I felt a slow smile spread across my face, as I recalled our lovely evening. We'd stayed up late talking. Besides some serious discussion about the murder, and a little joking around, we'd had some nice getting-to-know-you conversation. I'd thoroughly enjoyed myself.

And his couch was surprisingly comfortable. Luckily, I kept an overnight bag in my car for times when I visited my folks for dinner and decided to stay the night. So, I was able to brush my teeth and change into clean clothes. Moving quietly, I slipped into the bathroom to freshen up, get dressed, and comb my hair. We may have grown a little closer, but that didn't mean I was ready to let Calvin see my bed head.

When I joined him in the kitchen, he was adding salt and pepper to a skillet of fried potatoes and onions.

Another steaming pan held scrambled eggs with cheddar cheese. On the table were bowls of sliced Ruby Red
grapefruit and a platter of toasted sourdough bread next
to a jar of rose petal jam. My mouth watered at the sight
of it all.

"Wow! This is way better than the bowl of cereal I
usually have." I poured myself some coffee into a mug
he'd set out. I had to grin when I saw what it said—"I
think you're dandy"—above a picture of a dandelion. Calvin's mug was equally punny, featuring a picture of a
cactus under the words "Looking sharp."

He flashed a shy half smile. "I wasn't sure what you'd
like, so I kind of made everything I had."

"It looks and smells delicious."

Gus thought so too. He eagerly pranced around the
kitchen hoping for a taste.

We chatted comfortably over breakfast but, unfortunately, couldn't dawdle long. Gus needed to go out, and
there was work to do. After cleaning up together, we went
downstairs and opened the shop. Calvin offered to take
Gus with him to the greenhouse for a while, while I arranged flowers. I walked outside with them and stashed
my overnight bag back in the Fiat. As I was returning to
the house, Deena pulled in. I waited for her beside the
driveway.

"You're just getting here too?" she said, checking her
watch.

"Uh, not exactly."

She raised an eyebrow. "Wait a minute. You have that
look again."

"What look?" I pressed my lips together in an effort not to smile, but it was useless. Deena saw right
through me.

"The look you get when you're thinking about Calvin as a prospective boyfriend." She was grinning now too. "Did you make it official?"

"Official? No. Not really." Come to think of it, with all our talking last night, we'd never once discussed the nature of our relationship. In fact, other than the palpable chemistry between us, we might have been a couple of friends having a sleepover. He hadn't even kissed me goodnight.

Deena and I went inside and gathered our floral supplies for the morning's orders. As we filled vases with water and flower food and stripped leaves from flower stems, I gave her all the details—starting with the call from Bart and ending with Calvin's feast of a breakfast.

"One thing's clear," said Deena. "No, make that two things."

"Do tell." At this point, I was yearning for some clarity. My mind was as tangled as a briar patch.

"First, Bart is more suspicious than ever and probably guilty. But we already knew that. Second, Calvin has it bad for you."

I laid out two types of greenery: glossy myrtle, with small fragrant leaves, and hardy salal, with shiny lemon-shaped leaves. Selecting the myrtle (an ancient symbol of love), I shot Deena an inquisitive look. "What makes you say that? About Calvin, I mean."

"Oh, only everything." Tapping her fingers, she ticked off the reasons in turn. "He offers you a place to stay; he spends hours with you just hanging out; and he goes overboard trying to impress you with breakfast. *And*, most importantly, he was respectful of you last night and didn't try to take advantage of the situation. So he's a really good guy, and he must really like you."

There I went, smiling again. I handed Deena the order I was working on and asked if she'd gather some of the flowers. She went up front and returned shortly with half a dozen stems of stargazer lilies. I interspersed them with blush and crimson roses and finished off the bouquet with a couple of pink snapdragons and a few sprigs of baby's breath. The result was a dreamy, romantic concoction that smelled as sweet as it looked.

"Someone has romance on the brain," said Deena, handing me a pink ribbon.

"I'm just making what the customer asked for," I said—even though the order only requested "something nice with lilies for under $100."

I placed the bouquet in the cooler and got started on the next order, a cheerful daisy bouquet. This was what I loved most about working with flowers: no matter what the variety, they were always uplifting.

The front door jingled. Deena opened her eyes wide in mock wonder. "Do we actually have a walk-in?" she said.

"Let's find out!" Setting the daisies aside, I headed up front, with Deena right behind me. We found Nell Cusley gazing around the shop as if she were trying to memorize every flower. She was a plump, motherly woman, with short hair and fair skin prone to redness. I'd always found her overt nosiness and gossip habit irritating, but I knew she meant well. And now that she was a customer, I was inclined to be forgiving.

"Hi, Nell," I said warmly.

"Hello, girls." She barely looked our way. Instead, she gravitated to the café, swiveling her neck to take in every inch of it. "I like what you've done to the place. It's very rich-looking. Luxurious. But inviting too."

"Thank you." I walked around her and gestured to the

tables and sofa. "Why don't you come on in and have a seat. Can I get you something to drink? Herbal tea or iced tea?"

"I'll take ice water, if you have it."

"Of course."

"I'll get it," offered Deena.

I excused myself to grab my notebook, a wedding flower catalog, and contract form from the office. When I came out, I found Nell opening the door to the orchid room.

"Everything's so pretty," she said. After a quick sweep with her eyes, she backed out of the orchid room and turned to face the closed kitchen door. "Is that where you found the dead body? In there?"

I drew a slow breath and tried to smile. "It was in the storeroom, actually. We're going to remodel and get rid of that room altogether."

Deena came out of the kitchen with a tray holding a tall glass of water and a plate of the pansy cookies she'd made at my house the other night. She glanced at me in puzzlement. "Did you say 'we're getting rid of a room'?"

"Yes, the storeroom. I just decided. We can ask Richard to remove the door." Before opening his Bed and Breakfast, Richard had been a part-time handyman.

"Sounds good to me," said Deena.

Nell followed our exchange with wide-eyed interest. "You mean Richard Wales? I heard he quit his job at the bank rather suddenly last spring. I suppose it was to work on his mother's house?"

I pretended not to hear her, as I led the way back to the café. Gesturing for her to sit on the sofa, I pulled up a chair and opened my notebook. "So, Sue Ellen is getting married! Let's talk flowers."

For the next half hour, Deena and I plied Nell with

questions about the wedding and shared our ideas about the floral design. She was enthusiastic about our choices. I was a little concerned about Nell's budget, considering all the extras she said she wanted. But she didn't bat an eye when I told her the price. When Nell signed the contract, Deena treated me to a little dance of joy. I was trying not to laugh, when Calvin and Gus came inside.

After saying hello to Nell, Calvin turned to me. "I need to make a run out to Ranker's Garden Center," he said. "Do you have any deliveries you'd like me to make on the way?"

"Yes, that would be great. Can you wait about five minutes? We're just wrapping things up here."

Nell handed me a check for the deposit, then finished off her water and hoisted herself to her feet. "I'll see you all on Saturday. What did you say, about two hours before the ceremony?"

"Right. We don't want the flowers to wilt, so we shouldn't show up too early. Two hours should give us plenty of time."

Before I could say anything else, the front door jingled open again. I was already standing, so I excused myself and headed out of the café to welcome the newcomer. It turned out there were three visitors: Deputy Chief Renee Bradley, Officer Dakin, and another officer I didn't recognize. For some reason, the sight of them made my stomach drop.

Nell sidled up next to me and saw them too. "Morning, Deputy," she said. "How's Chief Walden? Any news on when he'll return to the force?"

"Good morning," said Bradley. Ignoring Nell's question, she addressed me. "Is Calvin Foxheart here?"

Calvin and Deena both came out of the café, with Gus scurrying around their legs. "I'm right here," said Calvin.

His voice was quiet and calm. In contrast, Gus let out a sharp bark that made us all jump. The corgi tried to run up to the police officers, but I called him back. For once, he actually listened. Still, he emitted a low, restrained growl.

Bradley took a step toward Calvin and held up an official-looking piece of paper. For one terrible second, I thought she was going to arrest him. What she said next wasn't much better.

"This is a search warrant. Could you please show us to your apartment?"

The cops spent more than two hours combing through Calvin's apartment. He stayed up there with them, while Deena and I waited on pins and needles below. I had a heck of a time getting Nell to leave. She wanted to stay and play twenty questions, guessing what the police might be looking for. She was deaf to every hint I dropped, but I couldn't be more forceful. The last thing I wanted to do was offend her. It was bad enough that Nell had witnessed this embarrassment and would be blabbing it all over town.

And here I was hoping she'd be spreading the word about our floral arrangements instead.

Finally, Nell received a phone call from a waitress at her diner, saying she was needed in the kitchen. As soon as she left, I locked the door behind her and flipped the sign over to Closed.

"Should I go ahead and make these deliveries?" asked Deena. "I could pick up some sandwiches on the way back."

"Yeah, might as well," I said.

We finished up the morning's orders and packed them

into Deena's car. Five minutes after she left, the cops finally came downstairs. To my surprise, they were empty-handed. I'd thought for sure they'd cart out as much as they could carry, from Calvin's laptop to the clothes he'd been wearing on Saturday. Then again, I had no idea what they were looking for.

Deputy Chief Bradley nodded at me as I unlocked the door for her. The other two officers avoided looking at me. Once they were gone, I let Gus out of the study. He ran straight for the open door to Calvin's apartment and bounded up the stairs. I decided to follow him.

The door upstairs was open too. I tapped on it before entering and found Calvin sitting on his couch with his head resting on the cushion and his eyes closed. He looked up when Gus jumped on his lap.

"Are you okay?" I asked.

"Terrific," he said glumly.

"It looked like they weren't carrying anything when they left."

"That's because they didn't find anything."

"What were they looking for, anyway?"

He waved his hand listlessly toward a paper on an end table. I picked it up and saw that it was a copy of the search warrant. There were only three items listed: gloves, a canteen, and Steve Lowry's university identification card.

I felt a surge of guilt about the canteen. If I hadn't mentioned it to Officer Wills, the cops wouldn't even know it was missing. The gloves I could understand; though, it seemed strange to me that they would search only Calvin's apartment and not the entire property. On the other hand, I supposed they'd had their chance to search the shop on the day of the murder. Also, I seemed to recall hearing someplace that search warrants were supposed to be narrowly focused.

The university ID, however, was a surprise to me. "I wonder how they knew the professor's ID was missing."

"I asked the same question," Calvin said. "Bradley told me the dean had asked her about it. It's a key card that allows access to all school buildings." He sat up and placed his hands on his knees, as if he was thinking about standing but couldn't muster the energy. "Evidently, there was an empty space in his wallet where they think the ID was usually kept."

Pacing across Calvin's living room, I glanced out the window and thought about what he said. The killer had taken the time to remove the professor's wallet, pull out the ID, and return the wallet to the dead man's pocket? It would be difficult to do something requiring that level of dexterity in something as bulky as gardening gloves. The killer must have worn something tighter, like surgical gloves.

I returned to Calvin's side and sat next to him on the edge of the couch. "Well, hey," I said cheerfully. "It's good that they didn't find anything. They ought to leave you alone now." I couldn't understand why he seemed so down.

He shook his head, evidently not convinced. "Chief Bradley is chatty and pleasant for a reason. She was trying to put me at ease, hoping I'd slip up and say something incriminating."

I wanted to challenge Calvin's assumption and reassure him that he could be wrong—but I didn't know that for sure. And he didn't seem very amenable to my optimism anyway. With a sigh, he pushed himself to his feet and gathered his wallet—and its loose contents—from the coffee table. I realized the police must have rifled through everything.

"I'll go ahead and run those errands now," he said.

I stood up too. "Deena took the deliveries already. Don't you want to wait and have some lunch?"

"Nah. I'll grab something while I'm out."

Saying little else, Calvin left, and Gus and I went downstairs. Deena returned with sandwiches. I brought her up to speed while we ate in the café.

"You don't suppose . . ." She trailed off and took a sip of her iced tea.

"Suppose what?" I asked.

She gave me an apologetic look. "I was wondering if the police might know something about Calvin that we don't."

"Deena!" *How could she say that?* I trusted Calvin. It troubled me to hear her voice her doubts.

"Never mind." She finished her sandwich and cleaned off the table. "By the way, I called Richard. He's going to stop over and look at the storeroom door sometime this afternoon."

"Good. Thanks." I chewed my last bite of food, even though I barely tasted it. This business with Calvin had me worried.

Fortunately, I had a pleasant diversion in work. After lunch, we made a detailed checklist for the wedding and cleared off a countertop to hold all the non-plant supplies we would need. This included everything from ten centerpiece vases, a dozen corsage and boutonniere pins, and a flower-girl basket to reams of floral wire, tape, and ribbons. Since we were a sustainable, foam-free florist, we also needed plenty of chicken wire and floral water tubes for hydration. Even though it was a modest-sized wedding, the flowers would be plentiful.

In the middle of these preparations, we had two walk-in customers in a row, followed shortly by Richard. His buoyant energy was a welcome ray of sunshine.

"This place is a vision!" he gushed, wandering around the café. "And it smells heavenly. I just want to curl up in here with a steamy novel and sip cappuccino all day."

"How about rose tea?" suggested Deena.

"Even better."

I held up a container of shortbread pansy cookies. "You have to try one of these. Deena made them."

With an expression of delight, he examined the delicate purple petals pressed on top of the cookie. Then he took a bite. "Mmm! Deena, I knew you were a woman of many talents, but this is sorcery."

Grinning, she gave a little curtsy. "Thank you, sir. I've learned it's fun to be crafty."

"She's amazing," I agreed. "And speaking of multi-talented people—come and see the job we have for you, Richard."

We went to the kitchen and gathered at the entrance to the storeroom. Richard scanned the interior and wrinkled his nose but refrained from commenting. He turned to the door and gave it a small thump.

"Solid," he said. "This is probably original to the house. You sure you want to remove it?"

"Positive." I told him about my harrowing experience being trapped in the little room. Even though it had only lasted for a few minutes, it had made a big impact.

"That's horrible!" he said, shuddering. "How distressing that must have been."

Deena ran a finger over one of the shelves just inside the storeroom. "We need to repurpose this room somehow. Clear out the negativity." She laughed shortly. "Listen to me. I sound like Sierra now."

"You're welcome," I said wryly.

"I'll give it some thought," said Richard. "What's on the other side of the far wall?"

"Nothing," I said. "It's an exterior wall."

He gazed thoughtfully around the room, as if he were imagining the possibilities. Then he frowned and turned to me. "I can't get over the fact that somebody trapped you in here. Who do you think it was?"

I withdrew into the kitchen and sat on a stool. "I don't know, but I have some ideas."

Richard looked from me to Deena. She pursed her lips. "It turns out all of the murder suspects were in the vicinity at the time."

"Huh," said Richard. He picked up a rose petal from the worktable and felt its velvety softness.

"What are you thinking?" I asked. I sensed he had something on his mind.

"Um, I don't know. It might be nothing."

"Come on, Richard," said Deena. "If you have info to share, then spill it."

"Well, I did overhear something. Some arguing. April and Isaiah have been sniping at each other lately. Then she was in the boys' room last night, and there were raised voices."

"What were they saying?" I asked.

He shook his head. "I couldn't make out their words very clearly. However, I did hear them say 'Lowry' a time or two."

"To be a fly on that wall," Deena murmured, echoing my sentiments exactly.

Richard met my eyes. "You might have been right in the first place, Sierra. There may be something off about these visitors. Perhaps they're not quite as adorable as I'd thought."

Chapter 18

Calvin still hadn't returned by the time Deena and I closed the shop. I planned to head straight for my folks' house for dinner. Dumbbells closed early on Wednesdays, so it was the one day I could count on a home-cooked meal. I asked Deena if she'd like to join me—I was sure Mom wouldn't mind.

She paused in the middle of wrapping a bouquet she'd made for herself. "That's a tempting offer. I'd love to actually. But I promised my mom I'd help her tonight. She's making final preparations for the Lee family reunion next month." She looked genuinely disappointed.

"Another time then." I had a feeling Deena's regret wasn't solely on account of my mom's cooking. I'd have to ask her about that another time.

My parents lived in a two-story brick house in a quiet cul-de-sac. The plot of woods behind the backyard was the site of endless adventures for Rocky and me when we were kids. When my mom shooed me out of the kitchen, telling me to relax before dinner, I decided to take Gus for a walk through the trees, revisiting some of the well-worn trails of my youth.

At first it was a lovely little stroll. I'd always drawn energy and comfort from the nearness of trees. But as the shadows lengthened, and the crickets chirped a lonely evening song, my skin began to prickle. Suddenly, I became aware of how isolated I was. With the leaves at their fullest and no one else around, I might as well have been in the middle of a dense, dark forest.

I shouldn't let myself become complacent, I realized. Especially considering there was still a murderer on the loose.

Urging Gus along, we returned to the house at a fast clip. Once we were safely inside, I resolved to set my fears aside, but stay wary. I fed Gus, then checked my phone, hoping for a message from Calvin. There was none. I thought about sending him a text, but I wasn't sure what to say. I tucked my phone back in my purse and decided I'd forget about him for a while.

Sitting at the kitchen table, with Rocky across from me and Mom and Dad at the two heads (and all three wearing matching Dumbbells sweatshirts), I unfolded my napkin and admired the delicious-looking feast. The table was laden with platters: garlic and lemon baked salmon, tangy three-bean salad, roasted baby red potatoes, and farm-fresh sweet corn. I took a bite and was savoring the flavors when my mom had to go and bring me back down to earth.

"I heard the police searched Calvin's apartment today." She slathered butter on her corn but her eyes were on me.

I set down my fork. "Where'd you hear that?" As if it mattered.

"Charlene mentioned it," she said, referring to an aerobics instructor at the gym. "She'd heard it at Nell's Diner."

Dad narrowed his eyebrows, as he sliced into his salmon. "Does Calvin have a lawyer? He should hire one, if he doesn't."

"I think he does. At least, he mentioned speaking to one."

"I don't suppose the police found anything," said Mom. "Did they?"

I stabbed into a potato a little more aggressively than necessary. "No. They didn't find anything."

"I wonder if they received a lead or a tip. Is it true Calvin had a history with the professor?"

And that was pretty much how the whole supper went—my parents grilling me about the case and me trying to defend Calvin. Rocky attempted to change the subject a couple of times, to no avail. My parents kept circling back to the murder. I knew they were just worried. That's why I didn't dare mention the storeroom incident. If I did, they'd probably pressure me to board up the shop for good and join them in the family business.

Somehow I still managed to enjoy the food. After dinner, I volunteered to clean up and load the dishwasher. "Rocky will help. Won't you, Rock?"

"Sure," he said, good-naturedly.

We put away the leftovers and condiments, then stood side by side at the sink. He rinsed the dishes and handed them to me to place in the dishwasher. I wanted to ask him about his personal life—and, in particular, if he was interested in Deena. But he spoke first.

"So, Bart asked about you yesterday. At Dumbbells."

"He did? What did he say?"

"Not much. He just said, 'How's Sierra?' He's not a big talker."

For a second, under the clink of the dishes, I thought Rocky had said *stalker* instead of *talker*. I glanced toward the window and the darkness beyond. "He called me last night," I said quietly. "He's starting to weird me out."

Rocky squeezed the water from his dish rag. "Do I need to have a talk with him?"

Normally, I would've laughed at the proposition. Now, I said, "I don't know." Bart hadn't really done or said anything overtly inappropriate. It was more a feeling I had. Well, that and the fact that he hadn't been entirely truthful to me. "Do you know anything about Bart's wife? Like, whether she died or left him?"

Rocky shook his head. "I didn't even know he was married."

I heard my phone ping from my purse, where I'd left it hanging on the pantry doorknob. I dried off my hands to check it.

"It's not Bart, is it?" said Rocky.

"No. It's a text from Calvin." I frowned as I read it. "He said he won't be in to work tomorrow."

"He hasn't been arrested, has he?" There wasn't a single hint of humor in Rocky's voice.

"No. He said he needs to take care of a few things. He's going to Knoxville."

I stared at my phone, as a million thoughts floated through my head. Was Calvin fleeing from the law? *No.* That didn't make sense. If he were, he wouldn't tell me where he was going. Come to think of it, I wasn't sure if he was even allowed to leave town. I assumed the police couldn't restrict his movements without a court order, but appearances mattered. Taking off didn't exactly smack of innocence. It would probably be a quick trip.

Rocky watched me with a mixture of curiosity and concern. "That sounds kinda vague. What kind of 'things'?"

My mind whirred. It had to relate to Professor Lowry's murder. Considering the missing key card and the professor's strange behavior—not to mention the unusual attitude of the three student suspects—the answer to the mystery must lie at the university.

Calvin probably realized this. In order to clear his name, he'd need to uncover what was really going on with the professor. *He must be heading to Knoxville to do just that.* It was what I would do. In fact, now that I thought about it, it was definitely what I *wanted* to do.

I looked over at my brother, still standing at the sink. "Rocky, can you do me a huge favor?"

"Yeah, if I can."

"Will you keep Gus tomorrow? I need to take care of a few things."

I texted Calvin, asking if we could talk, but he didn't reply. Then I tried calling him several times over the course of the evening. When he failed to pick up, I ended up sending him one last text before I went to bed: *I'm coming with you. Don't leave without me.*

The next morning, I arose extra early. I dropped off Gus with Rocky, then swung through Coffee Art Café for two coffees and a couple of banana-nut muffins. When I arrived at Flower House, Calvin was just exiting the back door. His eyes flickered with guilt when he saw me.

I handed him a coffee and the paper bag, then I patted my purse. "I have my road-trip playlist all queued up on my phone. The coffee's hot, and breakfast is in the bag. Do you want to drive, or should I?"

I grinned impishly, as I waited for his answer. He was tough to read, but he seemed conflicted. At last, he relented, a small smile tugging at the corners of his lips. "I'll drive."

It was a clear, sunny morning, and already shaping

up to be a scorcher. Calvin's car was a functional beater he'd recently picked up on the cheap at a used-car lot. At least the a/c worked. As we set off on the two-hour drive to Knoxville, we fell into a light friendly banter, as if we hadn't a care in the world.

"Where's the little guy?" he asked, flipping his visor up as we headed west. "I thought you were turning into one of those people who takes their dog with them everywhere."

"Ha. As if you're not a dog lover too." Using a paper napkin, I handed Calvin a muffin, then took a bite of my own.

"I am," he conceded. "I wouldn't let a dog sleep in my bed, though." He knew from our past conversations that Gus regularly slept at my feet.

"Oh, really? You'd turn Gus away? Reject his furry snuggles? Somehow I doubt it."

He shrugged. "I'm just saying. It's important to have boundaries."

"Right." I smirked knowingly. I'd seen Calvin and Gus napping in a chair together on more than one occasion. He loved the pup as much as I did.

I told him Gus was with Rocky. I also mentioned I'd asked Deena to hold down the fort at Flower House. I wasn't sure what time we'd return, but I assumed I'd miss the drop-off from Bart. Which was fine with me.

Taking a careful sip of coffee, I shoved aside thoughts of Bart. "If anyone asks, Deena will say we're out delivering flowers. I figured we probably shouldn't advertise this little excursion. Don't you think?"

"Yeah," said Calvin shortly. His jaw twitched, and I felt a kick of sympathy. He had to be thinking about the seriousness of his predicament.

"So, what's the game plan?" I asked. "Are we going to break into Lowry's office? Hack into his computer?"

Calvin raised his eyebrows. "Not if we don't want to get arrested. Jeesh. Am I going to have to leave you in the car?"

I playfully swatted his arm. "I'd like to see you try."

He grinned briefly, then concentrated on the road in silence. I studied his profile, from his earnest blue eyes to his chiseled jawline and soft lips.

"Are we going to talk to people?" I guessed.

"One person in particular," he said. "One of Lowry's Lackeys who didn't come on the trip. His name is Benji. I've been trying to get a hold of him, but he won't return my messages."

"Ah. Are you sure he's in Knoxville? Maybe he went home for the summer."

"He's there. I asked a teacher I know to check for me."

"Cool." I still liked the idea of snooping in Lowry's office, but I'd wait and bring it up again later.

The closer we got to Knoxville, the more withdrawn Calvin became. His tension was almost palpable. I longed to reach out and rub his shoulder, to loosen him up and distract him from his worries. But I held back. I didn't want to risk any awkwardness between us. Instead, I put on my tunes and filled the car with happy, thumping funk music. It was impossible to feel too low beneath a soundtrack of James Brown's soulful shrieks.

When we arrived in the city, I turned down the radio and looked out the window. Knoxville wasn't as big as Nashville, but it was still a thriving, picturesque city—the largest in Eastern Tennessee—with plenty to see and do. I wished we had more time to spend here. The prospect of taking in the sights with Calvin, maybe catching a show or dining on some excellent Southern BBQ, was mighty appealing. Alas, it wasn't to be. At least not today.

Calvin headed straight for the university. When we reached the campus, he turned into a visitor parking lot and found an empty space.

"I've been thinking," he said, cutting the engine.

"Yes?"

"I need to find Benji's address. The only way I know how to do that is to access the student directory . . . which means we may have to sneak into Lowry's office after all."

"Yay!" I clapped my hands together like a little kid.

"To be more precise, I think *you're* gonna have to do it. I can't let anyone see me."

"Yay?" I repeated, much less enthusiastically.

He grabbed a baseball cap from the back seat and donned a pair of dark sunglasses. Then he led the way to the science building.

Although the second session of summer school was in full swing, we didn't encounter very many people on our way. Calvin pulled out a university key card to access a back door of the modern redbrick building. "I kind of forgot to turn this in when I left," he said under his breath. "And Lowry was too preoccupied to remember."

I grinned at his cheekiness. "Lucky for us."

We slipped up to the third floor and hovered outside an administrative office. Removing his sunglasses, Calvin peeked through a window, then ducked to the side. "This is going to be tricky."

"Where's Lowry's office?" I whispered.

He pointed to the left. "Down that hall. But we'll need a key—which is in the admin assistant's desk."

I peered in the window too. Besides the admin assistant, who perched officiously behind her desk, there were at least two other people in the office. My mind conjured various diversions, each more outrageous than the next. I was just looking around for a fire alarm I could pull, when the jingling of keys announced the entrance of a maintenance man. He was short and stocky with a shock of salt-and-pepper hair, and he wore a blue-gray work shirt with matching pants. As he walked by us, Calvin quickly leaned close to whisper in my ear—and effectively hide his face.

"Dang, that was close," he murmured, his breath tickling my neck. "I know that guy. He would have recognized me for sure."

With Calvin's close proximity, I could smell his spicy sandalwood aftershave. It was so nice, I was tempted to lower my lids and breathe it in. Instead, I kept my eyes trained on the maintenance guy. He headed down the hallway toward Lowry's office.

"I have an idea," I said softly.

Calvin looked over his shoulder, then straightened. "What is it?"

"Instead of getting the key from the office, why not get one from the janitor?"

Calvin's face cleared with relief. "That's a great idea. I bet Terry could be persuaded to help us out."

"You mean like with a bribe?" I'd never known anyone to offer or accept a bribe in real life, and I had no idea what it would take. I tried to remember how much cash I had in my purse. It probably wasn't much more than twenty dollars.

"Not necessarily. Some fast talking might do the trick. Come on."

We rushed over to the hallway and chased after Terry, the maintenance man. He rounded a corner at the end of the corridor, so we sped up. By the time we reached the next hall, we saw him enter a glass door marked Aquaponics.

"We need a private place to talk to him," said Calvin. "That's as good a place as any."

The aquaponics lab was dimly lit, with purplish LED grow lights over several rows of green leafy plants. Beneath or near the plants, aquarium pumps bubbled and splashed, while goldfish and koi darted silently through the water. I paused in front of one of the fish tanks, mesmerized.

From somewhere within the lab, there was the sound of a trash can scraping along the floor, and then the click of a door opening.

"There he is," said Calvin softly. "The labs on this floor are interconnected. I think he went into the next one."

I followed Calvin deeper within the room. When we reached the door to the adjoining lab, Calvin started to pull it open, then froze. "There's someone coming, and it's not Terry. It's . . . Bart!"

Casting about for a place to hide, I spotted a closet at the back of the room. "In here!" I said, tugging on Calvin's shirttail.

We darted into the closet and pulled the door shut most of the way. I peeked out through the narrow slit. Sure enough, Bart Hammerson entered the aquaponics lab, swinging an empty plastic shipping container. He sauntered by, seemingly in no rush, and idly gazed at the nearby fish tanks.

What is he doing? He'd obviously completed his flower delivery and now seemed to be wandering around.

"Is he still there?" Calvin whispered close to my ear.

"Yeah," I breathed. Now that the initial shock of seeing Bart was wearing off, my attention shifted to Calvin's nearness once again. Standing together in the pitch blackness reminded me of the night the power went out after our dinner at my house.

At that moment, Bart shuffled near the closet, causing my heart to skip a beat. Biting my lip, I willed him to keep moving. Thankfully, he did. A few seconds later, another door opened and Bart crossed into the lab on the other side of the aquaponics room.

Breathing a sigh of relief, I reached for Calvin's hand in the darkness. "I think he's gone," I whispered.

"Good," he said, squeezing my hand. When neither of us made a move to leave, he said, "Déjà vu, eh?"

"I was just thinking that!" Instinctively, I turned toward him. "Cal?"

"Yeah?"

I didn't know what I was going to say. Maybe I'd make a declaration of my feelings, or maybe I'd crack a joke. All I knew was I really wanted to kiss him. Then I was distracted by something that caught my eye at the rear of the closet.

"What's that light?" I said.

"Huh?" He turned and saw what I'd noticed: a thin, barely perceptible crack of light. It appeared to outline a narrow door.

Moving farther into the closet, Calvin pulled out his phone and directed its light to the back wall. Under the glow, the outline disappeared. It was only in the darkness that we could see the slim light.

"Weird," he muttered. "There doesn't seem to be a doorknob."

"What's on the other side of this room?" I asked.

"Nothing that I know of. This doesn't make sense."

I fumbled in my purse and grasped hold of a metal fingernail file. "Let me try something," I said, squeezing up next to him.

He lowered his phone so I could see the line of light again. I forced the file into the tiny crack and worked it back and forth, trying to pry the door open. It didn't seem to be working. I was about to give up, when my fingers touched a metal protrusion along the edge of the doorway. It felt like a keyhole. I stuck the file in the opening and turned it. The door clicked open.

"You did it!" whispered Calvin. "Holy cow."

The door swung toward us, letting in a bright shaft of fluorescent light. Cautiously, we peered through the doorway into what appeared to be a small, old laboratory. It was empty of any occupants, so we stepped inside and looked around.

"Don't touch anything," Calvin murmured.

I nodded, as my eyes took in the small room. It was a compact space, painted white, with a center island, a stainless-steel sink, and plain cabinets above and below counters along each side wall. The island and counter-tops held a few pieces of equipment, including a micro-scope, a Bunsen burner, a high-speed blender, and a hot plate supporting a large stainless kettle. On one of the counters was a row of empty sixteen-ounce glass jars and a funnel. There was also a box of latex gloves.

"A secret lab?" I said. "What is this, a drug operation?"

"I don't know," said Calvin. "It's not a meth lab, I don't think. Not that I've ever seen one."

He was right. This room seemed far too clean to be an illegal meth lab. There were no chemical odors, tubing, or any of the household products used to make methamphetamine. Nor were there any vials, powdery residue, or plastic baggies that might indicate a cocaine or heroin operation.

Walking slowly around the island, I tried to imagine what it was we'd stumbled upon. I was dying to look in the cabinets, so I plucked a single glove from the box on the counter. Using my gloved hand, I pulled open one cabinet at a time. The top cabinets contained glass bottles and more jars, as well as some dusty test tubes, flasks, and beakers. The bottom cabinets held bulky black garbage bags. Kneeling on the floor, I pulled open one of the bags.

Calvin came up behind me. "Be careful," he cautioned.

Through the opening of the bag came a familiar nutty, earthy scent. Gingerly, I placed my gloved hand inside and let the contents slip through my fingers. Cupping my palm, I scooped up a small handful and brought it out to the light, revealing a clump of tiny black seeds. Poppy seeds.

Calvin whistled. "That's a lot of poppy seeds. You could make, what, a million muffins?"

"Or something else." My eyes flitted from the pot on the hot plate to the funnel and jars.

"What are you thinking?" said Calvin. "Not opium. Opium comes from the milky fluid in poppy pods. Not the seeds."

"True. But the unwashed seeds contain alkaloids. Even the washed, processed seeds used in cooking can result in a positive drug test."

"Yeah, I've heard that," said Calvin. "I assume these are unwashed."

"I do too." I knew from Granny that parts of the opium poppy plant, including the seeds, could be brewed into a tea for medicinal purposes. I also knew they could be abused.

"What are you thinking?" Calvin repeated.

"I'm thinking I know what was in Professor Lowry's canteen."

Chapter 19

A hidden door to a secret lab. It sounded like something from a fantasy game or a mystery movie. Certainly not real life. Yet here it was. As the implications sank in, Calvin and I had the simultaneous impulse to get the heck out of there. Leaving the light on, we exited the way we came and shut the narrow door behind us.

Back in the dark closet, I removed the latex glove I'd snagged and stuffed it in my purse. We were about to push our way out of the closet, when we heard a noise on the other side. We stood stock-still, listening. Had Bart returned?

Then the door swung open. A flashlight beam lit up our surprised faces.

"What are you doing in there?" boomed an astonished voice. It was Terry, the maintenance man.

Calvin grabbed ahold of my hand and stepped out of the closet, pulling me with him. "Just having a little fun," he said with a laugh. "Sorry, man."

"Professor Foxheart?"

"Hi, Terry," said Calvin. "How ya been?"

"Uh, not bad." He squinted his eyes, bewildered. "I thought you left."

"I did. Just back for a visit." Calvin lifted our clasped hands. "I was showing my girlfriend around. This is Sierra."

"Hi," I said, feeling as off-kilter as Terry looked toward me.

"Hi," said Terry, scratching his head.

Calvin adopted a more serious demeanor. "I guess you heard about Professor Lowry."

Terry nodded. "Yeah. I was sorry to hear it. What happened?"

"Don't know, exactly. Hey, do you know if his office has been cleaned out yet?"

"I don't think so. The dean said to leave it alone."

"Good idea. It's just that . . . well, it's not a big deal. But there was a book of mine that I left in there. My name's in it, but I'm afraid it will get lost whenever the office is cleaned up. Do you suppose I could take a quick look?"

I watched Calvin with fascination. It was amazing how easily he lied. In fact, I almost believed him myself. Maybe he *had* left a book in Lowry's office. Then again, he'd told a few fibs the first time I met him. The guy should have been an actor. Yet, in spite of all that, I realized I still trusted him.

Terry hesitated, then shrugged. "I guess it would be okay."

We followed him out of the lab and down the hall to Lowry's office. Calvin's eyes darted about, but we didn't encounter anyone else. Outside the professor's door, Terry pulled out his key ring and fitted a key in the lock.

"Thanks, man." Calvin put his hand on the small of my back and gently pushed me into the office. "I think we'll close the door, so we don't draw any attention. This will just take a minute."

"Oh, okay," said Terry. "Sure."

Calvin flipped on the light and closed the door. Then he went straight to the computer. While he booted it up and logged on, I looked around. It was a typical professor's office, with walls of books and stacks of paper. Two guest chairs faced the simple desk in the center of the room. Although a high window let in a fair amount of natural light, there were only two plants: a succulent and a potted cactus. I randomly pulled out a couple of books and opened the covers, at least making a pretense of looking for "Calvin's book." In truth, my mind was still reeling about all the poppy seeds we'd found.

Where had they come from? Who was responsible for the secret lab? I felt sure Lowry and his students must have something to do with it. After all, he was the head of the Botany Department. And if he'd become addicted to poppy tea, that could explain his careless behavior the past few months. It could also explain the urgency with which he'd wanted to be alone in the bathroom with his canteen, and his relaxed appearance when he came out.

I closed the plant book in my hands and returned it to the shelf. The answer wasn't in here. Sitting in one of the visitor chairs, I thumbed through some of the papers on the desk. They included student essays from the past semester, multiple copies of the itinerary for the summer field trip, and some junk mail. Nothing about a bulk poppy tea enterprise.

I looked at Calvin, who was typing rapidly on the keyboard. "Is there anything interesting on the computer?"

He made a face. "Not so far. I knew the password to log in—he gave it to me way back when I was a grad assistant and never changed it. Unfortunately, I don't know the password to access his emails."

"What about the student directory?"

"It should be in here somewhere."

I checked the time, confirming what my empty stomach was telling me. It was almost noon. I stood up again and walked around to join Calvin on the other side of the desk. There was only one drawer. Nudging him to move over, I pulled it open. It contained only pens, paper clips, and similar desk items.

Calvin sat up straight. "Bingo! I found Benji's address. Now I need something to write on."

I grabbed one of the trip itinerary sheets and handed it to him. "Write on the back of this. No one will miss it."

A minute later, Calvin shut off the computer and the light, and we slipped out of the office. Terry was gone. Wasting no time, we hurried down the hall, hopped on an elevator, and left the building.

"Should we pick up some lunch?" I asked, when we reached the car. "Or should we track down Benji first?"

"Let's go by his house. I'll offer to buy him lunch."

"Ooh, good idea."

At least, it would have been a good idea if Benji were home. When we knocked on the door of his unit, in a row of identical shabby-looking student apartments, no one answered. After waiting a few minutes, we decided to grab some takeout Chinese food from a nearby restaurant and come right back. Once we returned to the apartment complex, we parked in one of the angled parking spaces facing Benji's front door. We tucked into our lunch with one eye out the window.

"I feel like we're on a stakeout," I said, around a mouthful of fried rice.

"More like an ambush," said Calvin. "Based on his

avoidance of my calls, I have a feeling Benji doesn't want to talk to me."

"So, what's the plan here?"

He shot me a sheepish glance. "Um, I don't really have one."

"What? No plan?"

"I thought I'd rely on my good looks and charm?"

I snorted. "And then what?"

"I don't know. I figured when I could talk to him, face-to-face, I'd convince him to open up. I'll just ask him to tell me whatever it is he's been holding back."

I raised a doubtful eyebrow. I supposed it could work. After all, Calvin *could* be persuasive. He'd gotten Terry to let us in Lowry's office. Still, this was too important to leave to chance. The kid could easily blow us off, and then what? It was already growing late, and I needed to return to Aerieville. We had only one shot.

"How about if I talk to him first?" I suggested.

"You? But he doesn't know you."

"Exactly. He'll have no reason to run away when he sees me."

"But what will you say? You—" Calvin broke off, his eyes directed at the sidewalk. "Oh man. Here he comes."

"Wait here," I said, setting my takeout container on the dash. "Just give me a minute." I hopped out of the car and moved toward the sidewalk.

The boy heading my way was thin and scruffy-looking, with ripped jeans, shaggy brown hair, and long sideburns. He carried a backpack over one shoulder and had earbuds in his ears. I had to wave at him to get his attention. Startled, he removed the earbuds.

"Are you Benji?" I said with a smile.

"Yeah?" he said uncertainly.

"My name is Sierra. I was wondering if I could talk to you for a minute. It's about some of your classmates."

He edged toward his apartment, giving me a look that said, *Whatever you're selling, I don't want it.*

I decided to take a chance. "It's about the poppy seeds."

The color drained from his face, but he played it cool. "What poppy seeds?"

"The ones in the lab. I know all about it. And pretty soon so will everyone else."

Benji bit a fingernail. "I don't know what you're talking about."

"Come on, Benji," I said, taking a step closer to him. "The jig is up. But if you answer my questions, I'll leave your name out of the report."

He frowned. "You're a reporter?"

"I'm conducting an investigation," I said, which was essentially true.

Benji removed his backpack and dropped it at his feet. Then he slumped his shoulders. "What do you want to know?"

I motioned for him to sit at a faded picnic table in the shade, and I sat across from him. Taking a deep breath, I tried to exude a confidence I didn't really feel.

"What did Professor Lowry have his students doing for him?" I asked, as if I knew for sure that there was something. "Were they making poppy tea to sell it? How did that work?"

"Lowry was a fiend," Benji said bitterly. "A shark. A criminal."

I was momentarily stunned. I'd guessed right?

A car door opened, and we turned to see Calvin step onto the sidewalk. He sauntered toward us with his hands in his pockets.

Benji widened his eyes. "Professor Foxheart?"

"It's okay," I assured Benji. "He's cool. He works for me."

Calvin shot me an incredulous look, which I couldn't help returning with a smug smile.

"Go on, Benji," I said. "Why was Lowry a shark and a criminal?"

Benji shook his head. "I don't even know where to start. He had all these schemes he was involved in, and he used students to do the dirty work."

"What kind of schemes?"

"Like selling grades, for one."

That was unexpected. Calvin seemed surprised too. "You mean he made students pay for better grades?"

"Yeah. If a student was failing, he'd try to find out if they were willing to pay for a better grade. He also purposely graded some students harder and pressured them to give him money. If they couldn't pay, he taught them how to hack into the school's computer system and sell tests to other students. That was a different scheme."

Calvin and I exchanged another look. Lowry was even more corrupt than we had imagined.

Now that Benji had agreed to talk, he didn't hold back. He seemed relieved to unburden all his knowledge. "Lowry was devious," he continued. "He preyed on students barely hanging on, in terms of grades and finances. Once they were involved, they couldn't report him without implicating themselves."

"Were these students the ones known as Lowry's Leaders?" I asked.

"That's a lame name," Benji said. "But, yeah. Basically, Lowry targeted vulnerable students. When he found some who had no problem breaking the rules, he'd make them his soldiers, so to speak."

I knew this must include Vince, Isaiah, and April. I didn't even need to ask.

"Was this a recent thing?" asked Calvin. "He never approached me about any schemes like that when I was a student."

"He probably thought you were too ethical," said Benji. "Or he knew you didn't need the money."

I recalled Professor Washington talking about the scholarship recipients, and how many were poor and had come from rough backgrounds. I wondered if that made them extra vulnerable to their respected professor's ill influence. It really was despicable.

"He must have been extremely careful," said Calvin, apparently still in disbelief that all this had been going on under his nose.

I thought again about the secret lab. "What about the poppy seeds? It would take a lot of poppies to produce that many seeds, possibly over multiple seasons. That must have been going on for a while."

Benji nodded. "There's an experimental farm behind campus. It includes a huge field of prairie grass and wildflowers. Lowry sectioned off a piece in the middle to grow poppies. It's pretty well hidden."

"Why poppy tea?" I asked. It seemed like an odd choice. If he wanted to make money, why not just grow and sell marijuana?

"I think he fell into it by accident. He started drinking it himself. Then he got the idea to market it to students as a way to get high without getting caught or in trouble. And even though it's not hard to make, he knew most people wouldn't bother. They'd rather take something that was already prepared. He was like a what-do-you-call-it. A snake oil salesman."

"So weird," I murmured.

"And dangerous too," said Benji. "I heard of a kid dying after drinking too much of that stuff. That's when I decided I had to get out."

"Good for you," said Calvin. "That was brave of you."

"Yeah, well, I finally wised up," said Benji, without a trace of pride. "I realized Lowry was in it too deep to rat anyone else out. He'd only expose himself."

"Maybe he realized it too," I mused. "Maybe part of his odd behavior was paranoia."

"I don't know about that," said Benji. "But I do know one thing: I'm not at all surprised that somebody killed him."

We thanked Benji profusely and promised not to reveal his involvement with any of Lowry's schemes. Back in the car, I told Calvin I was going to text Deena. "I feel bad for being gone so long," I said.

"Actually, I have one more stop to make." Calvin backed his car out of the parking space, and cranked up the air-conditioning. "It won't take long."

"Oh?" I figured he was going to say he needed to gas up his car. I was eager to hit the road, not only because I had work to do at Flower House, but also because I was looking forward to the drive. It was the perfect opportunity to talk things over and analyze the astounding discoveries we'd made.

Calvin didn't say anything more. Instead, he drove slowly down side streets and through residential neighborhoods, bypassing at least one gas station along the way.

"Where are we going?" I asked.

A moment later, he pulled over in front of a small Tudor-style home and cut the engine. "Right here."

"And 'here' is?" I couldn't understand why he was being so vague.

"It's my old place. I left a few things here I want to pick up."

What? "You still have a house in Knoxville?" Would the surprises today never stop?

"Not really. My ex . . . roommate lets me keep some stuff here. I'll be right back."

Taking his keys with him, he strode up to the house and let himself in.

He still has keys to his old house? I didn't know why this bothered me so much, but it did. I knew he had family in Iowa and some contacts here in Knoxville, but he'd never mentioned he still had some of his possessions here. And who was the so-called ex-roommate?

The longer he took, the more I stewed. *Just when I thought I was getting to know the real Calvin, I find out he's been holding back on me.* It also felt like a slight to be left in the car, like a child.

Checking my watch, I decided I'd give him five more minutes. Then I was going to go after him. I'd offer to help. Yeah, that'd be a good excuse.

The five minutes were about to elapse when I heard the buzz of a small motor. Through the rear windshield I saw a powder blue Vespa speed up the street. It turned into the driveway next to the Tudor. As I watched, a trim-looking woman in leather pants climbed off. She removed her helmet and tossed her hair: long golden tresses that gleamed in the sunlight. With barely a glance toward Calvin's beater, she walked up to the front door and went straight inside without knocking.

So this was the ex-roommate. Or had he meant to say "ex-girlfriend"?

By the time Calvin finally emerged from the house fifteen minutes later, I'd transitioned from angry-hot to angry-cold. I was in no mood to chat with him about the case or anything else. I didn't even ask him what was in the box he stowed in the trunk.

Instead, I put on some music—classical this time. We passed the drive without speaking much at all, each absorbed in our own private thoughts.

Chapter 20

When we arrived at Flower House, we found Deena elbow deep in fresh-cut wedding flowers. She'd unpacked the delivery from Bart and had been busy trimming all the flowers and placing them in fresh water to rejuvenate them after transport.

"Wow!" I said, looking around the workroom. It looked like a fairytale floral explosion. "I need to get a picture of this. It gives new meaning to the name *Flower House*."

Calvin took his cardboard box upstairs, saying he'd be right back to help. Deena appeared more frazzled than I'd ever seen her—which was to say she still looked nearly flawless. Her forehead was slightly dewy, and a few strands of her glossy hair had slipped from her long ponytail, framing her slightly tense face.

"I knew we'd never had an order this big," said Deena. "But I didn't fully realize how much space this was going to take. The last wedding we did was just bouquets, corsages, and small centerpieces. By comparison, this one feels like we're prepping for a royal wedding."

I picked up a bucket of dahlias and inspected the

petals. They were a little tired-looking, but I knew they'd open up by tomorrow. "I'm so sorry I left you alone to do this. I can take over now, if you need a break."

"I'm fine. But I don't know where we're going to put everything. I think we'll need both coolers."

I realized she was right. I opened the cooler in the workroom and began removing bouquets. "We'll donate these to the nursing home," I said. "That will free up some room."

Calvin came in then and saw what I was doing. "Do you need me to make some deliveries?"

"Yes, please." I packaged the bouquets for delivery and told him where to go.

As soon as he left, Deena gave me a curious look. "How was the trip? Did you learn anything?"

"Yeah. A *lot*." I moved a bucket from a stool and sat down. "I learned that Calvin apparently lived with a woman, still has a key and some belongings at her place, and didn't say a word about it to me!" My mind returned to the night I'd spent at his place. We'd talked for hours, about all aspects of our lives. He could easily have shared this bit of information.

Deena stared at me with arched eyebrows. "Okay. Wow. That's big. And, not to minimize that bombshell, but did you find out anything about Professor Lowry?"

I waved my hand. "Yes, that too. He was involved in all kinds of illegal schemes."

I filled Deena in, while we finished cleaning and organizing the flowers. By the time we'd completed both tasks, I'd told her everything. She was duly impressed— and as elated as I'd felt back in Knoxville. But my excitement had worn off. Because, in spite of everything we'd learned, we still had no way of knowing who struck the professor with the candlestick.

"What are you going to do with all this intel?" asked Deena. "Go to the police?" She swept the floor, while I cleaned off the worktable.

"Yes, definitely. At first, I wasn't sure how exactly to do that, but I think I know now."

"Anonymously?" she guessed.

"Yep. I think I'll type up a letter describing everything the student, Benji, told us. I'll include detailed directions on finding the secret lab and the hidden poppy field. And I'll send the letter to both the Aerieville Police and the Knoxville Police. Maybe the UT dean as well."

Deena held open the door for me, so I could fit through with the bin of leaves and stems. She walked with me as I carried it to the compost pile behind the garden.

"Then what?" she asked.

"Then, I assume the police will investigate and confirm what a louse the professor was."

Deena shielded her eyes from the late day sun. "Maybe then people will rethink Calvin's claims about his research paper," she said. "If it comes out how dishonest Lowry was, they might believe he stole Calvin's work after all."

I didn't respond, but I might have rolled my eyes a little.

"What? Don't you want Calvin to be vindicated at the university?"

Deena watched, as I dumped over the bin and shook out all the debris. Then I grabbed the pitchfork we'd left leaning on the fence and turned the compost pile. It released a faint rotten odor, which meant we hadn't been aerating it often enough.

The foul smell matched my mood. Of course, deep down, I wanted Calvin to have his name cleared at the university. That would be amazing. He should absolutely get credit for his research, if at all possible.

But then what? Would he go back to his old job—and his old life—in Knoxville? Right now I was so irritated (and, okay, hurt) by his attitude toward me that I wasn't sure I cared. So what if he did leave?

I returned the pitchfork to where I'd found it and brushed off my hands. "It's all well and good for the truth to come out about Lowry," I finally said. "But it doesn't get us any closer to solving the murder."

Deena regarded me thoughtfully. "Doesn't it?"

"I mean, sure, it provides potential motives. All three of the students might have had reason to want him gone. But which one did it? Maybe all three were in on it together. Or two of them. Or just one." I started back for the house, my thoughts spinning like the pinwheel in the garden. "Then, there's Bart. It was so odd to see him wandering around—and so close to the secret lab. It makes me wonder if he knew what was going on in there."

"You're right," said Deena. "They're all more suspect than ever."

"I just wish I could spy on the students somehow."

Deena laughed. "Listen to you. That trek to Knoxville gave you a taste for secret agent life. All that hiding in closets and infiltrating the professor's criminal enterprise. Look out, James Bond."

I smiled. "I'm not gonna lie. It *was* a little thrilling." I wasn't compelled to add that having Calvin at my side might have had something to do with that.

We paused at the back door, and Deena smoothed the front of her blouse. "Maybe if we hang out more with Richard we'll overhear something like he did."

I looked at her, moved by her interest and readiness

to get a little sneaky. And just like that, my optimism kicked in again. "You know what? You may be on to something. Do you have plans this evening? We should go over to Richard's right now. We'll call ahead and ask if we can bring a pizza or something."

She grinned at me. "I'm in, partner. Let's do it."

Sometimes things work out so perfectly it makes me wonder if a higher power is at play. Maybe it was serendipity or maybe it was fate. (Though, I often said I didn't believe in fate.) Either way, the stars were aligned tonight. Richard welcomed our offer to bring pizza to the B&B. Sheila and Isaiah had decided to visit Aerieville's used bookstore and, after that, Augie's Steakhouse. Neither of those destinations appealed to April and Vince, who stayed behind. Richard felt obligated to provide them with supper, and he didn't know what it was going to be.

With two of the guests out of the way, that would make it easier to focus on the remaining two.

On our way to Richard's, Deena and I stopped at our favorite Italian restaurant (the only authentic one in town) to pick up a couple of pizzas. While waiting for our order, I checked in with Rocky. He assured me all was well with Gus. After that brief call, I almost phoned Calvin too. *Darn it.* The guy had gotten under my skin. I couldn't seem to go ten minutes without his image popping into my brain.

Well, if he wanted to talk to me, he knew my number. I was done inserting myself into his life. Besides, I had more important matters to focus on: like finding a way to get April and Vince to talk.

As we sat around Richard's dining room table munching on pizza, one thing became abundantly clear. April's phone was a potential goldmine. She stared at it almost nonstop, madly texting as if her life depended on it. What I wouldn't give to know who she was conversing with and about what.

In between casual conversation with Richard and Deena about the upcoming wedding, and polite small talk with Vince, I was secretly obsessing over how I might get my hands on April's phone. But with every imagined scenario, I kept bumping up against the bigger problem: how to get past her password protection.

"I hope it cools off for you guys tomorrow," said Richard, evidently falling back on weather talk. "Hiking in the boiling heat is not my idea of fun."

"You're going on another hike?" asked Deena, addressing Vince and April.

Vince shrugged and April nodded. She pulled her eyes from her phone long enough to say, "Isaiah is insisting on it. He says we have to go on at least one hike in the national park. Even though our trip was canceled, he says I *have* to see his favorite trail. I guess it leads to one of the tallest peaks or something."

"It's a challenging hike," said Vince. "But it's exhilarating. You can never feel more alive than when you're standing at the top of a mountain you've just scaled."

Deena smiled. "In some places, you can take a sky tram to the top. If you ask me, that's plenty exhilarating enough."

"Here, here," said Richard.

I took a sip of sparkling water and wiped my mouth. "Do you need to get permission to leave town?" I was genuinely curious about that. The whole reason they were still at the B&B was because the police had asked them not to leave. Legally speaking, they could probably leave anytime they wanted. But I recalled Sheila mentioning that the university wanted them to cooperate with the investigation.

"Sheila said it would be okay," said April. "Because it's not overnight."

"Plus, we've exhausted everything there is to do in Aerieville," added Vince.

"You poor kids," said Richard, without sarcasm. "I know this isn't how you wanted to spend any part of your summer break."

"You've been great," said April, giving him a sweet smile. "We like staying here."

"That's kind of you to say. And, hey, the county fair starts this weekend!"

"Sounds fun," April said politely.

"It can be," said Richard. "Anyone ready for another slice?"

Vince raised a finger. I accepted another small piece too, but I waited to take a bite. I needed to redirect the conversation before we got too far off topic.

"I can't imagine y'all will have to stay here much longer," I said. "I'm sure the police are getting closer to solving this thing."

"That's not what I heard," said Richard.

Deena and I both looked at him in surprise. "Where'd you hear that?" I asked.

He shook his head. "A little birdy told me, but forget I said it. I need to work on my optimism."

I turned to April and Vince. "Say, I have a question for you two."

"Shoot," said Vince.

"That day—Saturday morning—when you all were waiting next to the greenhouse—did you happen to see Calvin and me exit the back door of the flower shop? With my dog, Gus?"

"Oh, that was such a cute doggie!" said April, setting her phone down for a moment.

"I saw you walk by," said Vince.

"Did you see anyone else leave that door any time before us?" I still didn't know whether or not to believe Bart's claim that he'd seen Wanda leave the house. I wondered if the students could corroborate his story.

"Yeah," said Vince. "I saw somebody. That delivery guy, Bart."

Deena lightly slapped the table. If I could read her mind, I was sure she was thinking, *I knew it!* She'd always suspected Bart.

"I didn't see him," said April. There was a hint of defiance in her voice, as if she was challenging Vince's assertion.

"That's because you were hypnotized by your phone," said Vince. "An asteroid could fall in front of you, and you wouldn't notice it."

"Ha ha," she said, picking up her phone again.

As we finished our pizza, Richard announced that he had a special treat for dessert. "Fondue!"

"What's fondue?" asked April.

"It's hot chocolate sauce for dipping, with strawberries and other fruit."

"Then why didn't you just say that?" asked Vince.

Richard rolled his eyes with pretended impatience. "Young people," he said drolly.

"It sounds delicious," said Deena.

I murmured in agreement, but my attention was elsewhere. I'd been watching April with her phone, and I'd observed something very interesting. The screen stayed open for about thirty seconds after she stopped typing and swiping. It was only after the thirty-second mark that the screensaver appeared, requiring her to enter her password again. From my vantage, it was impossible to see what she typed in for the password. But if I could get a hold of her phone within thirty seconds of her last click, I wouldn't need the password at all.

"I think I'll skip dessert," said Vince, patting his rock-hard torso. "I need to do something active. Anyone up for a game of ping-pong?"

"Not me," said April. "I want to try the fondue."

Deena looked to me for my lead. It was as if she sensed I was cooking up a plan.

"Maybe later," I said to Vince. "Deena and I both *love* chocolate. We gotta have some of this dessert."

"Thanks for speaking for me," said Deena dryly. "But it's true."

I winked at her, then turned to our host. "Richard, why don't you go play a round with Vince. Is it called a *round*? A *match*?"

Richard opened his mouth, as if to protest, but thought better of it—probably because of the sharp kick I gave him under the table.

"Of course, I will. I want all my guests to have a good time here."

"Are you sure, man?" asked Vince. "I can wait."

"Totally sure. Let me just get the fondue ready for the others. Maybe I'll convince you to try a taste after our match."

Everything seemed to be coming together perfectly. *Serendipity.* Now I just needed to communicate with Deena.

"Dee, could you come out to the car with me for a quick minute? We should bring in that . . . flower thing before we forget."

"Uh, right. Good thinking."

As soon as I closed the front door behind us, I spoke

quickly. "Here's the deal. I need five minutes alone with April's phone. I'm gonna spill chocolate on her lap. The *second* that happens, you need to whisk her off to the kitchen to treat the stain. Keep her in there for as long as you can. Okay?"

She looked a little wary but gamely nodded. "You got it."

We returned to the table as Richard was setting up the fondue pot. He'd also brought out an assortment of fresh fruit and set out small bowls and plates in front of each seat. "It's all ready," he said. "Enjoy." He and Vince left through the kitchen and out the back door toward the garage.

It was now or never. Deena stood at the head of the table, waiting for me to make a move. April was in the chair across from me, filling her plate with strawberries and sliced melon.

"This is so cute," she giggled. "It would be perfect for a date night."

"Yeah," I said, standing up. "Perfect." I picked up a small bowl and ladled myself a serving of hot chocolate sauce.

My heart thudded in my chest. *How hot is this anyway?* I didn't want to burn the girl.

Deena cleared her throat, and I shot her a look. Her eyes were bright. I felt her willing me to get on with it.

Time passed in slow motion. Crossing my fingers for luck, I dipped the ladle deeply into the fondue pot. Then, in one swift motion, I jerked my hand up and screamed, sending a splash of chocolate sauce directly onto April's shirtfront—and splattering onto the table and her plate as well.

"Oh my gosh!" I exclaimed. "I'm so sorry! I thought I saw something. Something touched me. I don't know what happened." I babbled incoherently, as Deena rushed over and grabbed April's arm.

As for April, she screamed in shock and dropped an f-bomb—which, coming from her delicate rosebud lips, was almost as startling as my outrageous performance.

"Go!" I urged. "Go clean that off right now before the stain sets." My window of opportunity was closing rapidly. I'd already lost a few precious seconds during my hesitation.

"Come on," said Deena, pulling April to the kitchen. "I know what to do."

I ran around to the other side of the table. The instant the kitchen door swung shut, I grabbed the phone and touched the screen to keep it from closing. Droplets of chocolate sauce dotted the phone case like teardrops. I hastily grabbed a napkin to wipe it off.

Okay, okay, okay, I said to myself. "What can I see?"

Chapter 21

I realized right away that I was never going to have enough time to fully explore April's phone. There were a million and one ways she could be communicating with people: emails, texts, instant messages, social media direct messages, chat apps. I'd even heard of apps that didn't save the user's message exchanges. The words would disappear shortly after they were sent, like some kind of fading invisible ink.

Yet, things had worked out for me so far. I wouldn't give up. With no time to waste, I went straight to April's text messages and skimmed as fast as I could.

I saw immediately that the most recent communications were with people I'd never heard of. Some were inane notes with friends back home. But some were another sort altogether. From what I could tell in my hasty review, most of these senders fell into one of two categories: customers and people who worked for April. Messages to the latter consisted of instructions about making and delivering "T." *Has to be poppy tea!* More important (based on her prolific usage of all caps) were directions on how to transfer payments to her.

In her messages to the customers, April made promises about how good the "T" was and connected them with one of her workers. She also repeatedly warned these folks that they'd better deal with her alone—and definitely not "Iza," who "only cares about himself."

Iza?

I wished I could capture the messages somehow—forward them to myself or take pictures of them. Of course, that was impossible. I'd just have to commit them to memory. On the other hand, I didn't need to remember them verbatim to understand the gist. It was obvious to me that April was trying to take Professor Lowry's place. She wanted to be the Poppy Tea Queen.

Still, I hadn't found the smoking gun I was looking for. I needed to find out what she was thinking immediately after Lowry's murder. Scanning through her contacts, I found the messages with Vince and Isaiah. *Which to open first?* Time was running out. I had to choose one. My finger hovered between the two names and finally clicked on Vince. Then I had to scroll up (through a hundred exchanges!) to find the messages from last Saturday.

Finally, I reached the right time frame—and found the payoff. I could hardly believe what I read.

> **April:** *OMG he did it. I can't believe he did it. Why didn't he wait?*
>
> **Vince:** *He probably saw his opportunity. Or got tired of you trying to talk him out of it.*
>
> **April:** *Weren't you trying to talk him out of it too? I thought we agreed. We all wanted out, but this wasn't the way.*
>
> **Vince:** *He did what he thought he had to.*

April: *I guess. Now that L is gone, somebody will have to step up. You know?*

Vince: *I'm done. You can battle it out with Iza.*

"*Iza*" had to be a nickname for Isaiah. This was the second mention of him in April's texts. I rapidly scrolled back in time, stopping on Friday, the day before the trip. The name "Iza" jumped out at me again.

April: *Iza is starting to worry me. I don't think he's joking about you know what.*

Vince: *I'll talk to him.*

April: *Seriously. He says he knows the perfect spot. A lookout point overlooking a cliff or something. He has it all planned out.*

Vince: *I said I'll talk to him.*

I was so enthralled with the text exchange between April and Vince that I almost forgot where I was. I nearly jumped out of my skin when the kitchen door burst open.

"Wait up!" Deena yelled, a hair late and a smidge too loud.

"I need to change," April grumbled. Her shirt was soaking wet.

With my back to them both, I used a napkin to wipe off the device again—and in the same motion shut all the messages. She paused at the table, evidently looking for her phone. I held it out to her.

"I'm so sorry, April. Some chocolate got on your phone, but I think it's okay."

She took it from me and curled her lip. "Thanks," she snapped, before stalking out of the room.

Deena looked sapped. She fell into a chair and blotted her blouse, which was almost as wet as April's shirt. "Oh, my goodness, Sierra. That has to be the craziest thing you've ever done. Was it even worth it?"

I was feeling a little dazed myself. I'd just seen a ton of incriminating messages in a very short time. I still needed to process it all. I also needed to figure out what to do next. For now, though, I needed to call the mission a success.

I dipped my finger in the small bowl I'd filled and licked the chocolate from my finger.

"Yes, ma'am. It was definitely worth it."

Before discussing anything, my first priority was chocolate removal. Deena and I gave the dining room a thorough cleaning, effectively erasing all evidence of our fondue flimflam. We tidied the kitchen and did the dishes too. Richard came through the back door as we were breaking down the pizza boxes.

"What a nice surprise! Y'all didn't need to do this."

I exchanged a guilty glance with Deena. "We wanted to. But there's plenty of fruit and chocolate left, if you want us to get it back out."

"Mm . . . yes. I think I will heat up some of that sauce for myself. You ladies have a seat and tell me the latest scoop. Anymore strange shenanigans at Flower House?"

I pulled out a chair from the small kitchen table, while Deena perused Richard's countertop wine rack. "Mind if we open one of these?" she asked.

"Please do." He brought out three wine glasses and handed Deena a corkscrew, before making himself a plate of fruit. He heated a bowl of chocolate sauce in the microwave.

I tapped my glass nervously on the table. "Where's Vince?" I was dying to share what I'd learned, but I definitely didn't want to be overheard.

Richard left the fondue and fruit on the counter and indicated we should help ourselves. "Vince went to his room. He said they plan to get an early start tomorrow."

Deena selected a sweet red dessert wine and filled our glasses. I arose from the table to make my own plate of fruit and chocolate, and Deena followed suit. After all, we didn't have a chance to enjoy any before.

As soon as we all gathered at the table, I spoke in a low voice. Deena and Richard both leaned in to hear me. "You guys, I think I know who killed Professor Lowry."

"Ooh, juicy," said Richard. He apparently didn't think I was being serious. "Do tell."

"You found proof on April's phone?" asked Deena.

"Wait, what?" said Richard.

"Yeah." I took a sip of wine, then told Richard I'd had an opportunity to sneak a peek into April's text messages.

He cocked his head. "There's so much I want to ask right now, but maybe we better stick to the important stuff. You really know who the murderer is?"

Nodding, I said the name in a whisper. "*Isaiah.*"

"No way," said Richard.

"Are you sure?" asked Deena. "Did he confess? What exactly did you see?"

I told them about both snippets of conversation between April and Vince. "I had to read between the lines a little, but it absolutely sounded like Isaiah had a plan to push Lowry off the mountain. April and Vince were trying to talk him out of it."

Deena and Richard both looked horrified. "That's dark," said Richard.

"I know. Then, right after the murder, April said she couldn't believe he did it. Or something like that." The exact wording of the messages was fading from my mind already. "It sounded like they both believed Isaiah had done it."

Deena frowned. "So, were they just speculating? Maybe Isaiah was joking about offing the professor. And, when somebody actually did it, they simply assumed it was him. For all we know, it still could have been Bart."

"Or maybe it was one of them," said Richard.

"You mean April or Vince?" I asked.

"Sure, why not? Either of them could have been lying to the other when they said Isaiah must have done it. If the professor was as horrible as you say, it sounds like they all had a motive."

"Actually, he was even worse." I told Richard what I'd discovered at the university. "And April is definitely trying to take over as kingpin. I saw some text messages that confirmed it."

Richard covered his mouth to stifle a snicker. "I know this isn't funny, but really? Little April a drug lord?"

Deena appeared skeptical too. "Well, *poppy tea* is the drug, which seems about right."

I dragged a strawberry through chocolate sauce and considered what they'd said. It was true: this whole situation sounded like something out of *Alice in Wonderland*—if Alice wanted to become the Queen of Hearts and take charge of the Mad Hatter's tea party.

I shook off the reverie and bit into a strawberry. "I know this is absurd," I said, "but these students are not the innocent kids they seem to be. They got themselves mixed up in some dangerous business."

As I thought about it, I recalled April's intensity every time she was on her phone. And from what Richard told us earlier, she'd been arguing with Isaiah. Their rivalry seemed to be real.

Then I remembered something else. What was it Calvin had said Isaiah told him in the greenhouse? It was something about watching out for himself and having the drive to take matters into his own hands.

Richard looked worried. "Are you saying they're still dangerous?"

"I don't know. I mean, if Isaiah decided it was okay to murder once, who's to say he wouldn't do it again?" I glanced at the kitchen window, ensuring it was closed. It felt risky to be talking like this when the students were so nearby. Presumably, Isaiah would return with Sheila anytime.

"If Isaiah did it, I don't know if April and Vince are necessarily dangerous," Deena said doubtfully. "But they could probably be arrested as accomplices. They didn't go to the authorities before the trip, when they knew what he was planning, or afterward."

"Jeesh," muttered Richard. "It's like *Lord of the Flies.* Do those people have no morals?"

I fell silent and pushed my plate away. I needed to go to the police with what I'd learned. That much was clear. But I began to wonder if there wasn't an even more pressing issue. If Isaiah's original plan was to push Lowry over a precipice—and he was now urging April, his rival, to go on the same hike . . . could that mean April was in danger?

It was an unbelievable idea. Yet, once it arose in my mind, I couldn't let go of it.

"Richard, do you know exactly where they're going tomorrow?"

He shook his head. "They didn't say. Somewhere in the Smokies."

"No problem," Deena said sarcastically. "There are only, what, three-hundred-plus trails?"

"Covering nearly a thousand miles," Richard added.

"Isaiah has been on this trip a couple of times," I said. "He apparently knows the trails pretty well." *Including the "perfect spot" to push someone off the side.*

Suddenly, I recalled the trip itinerary I'd seen in Professor Lowry's office. I'd handed a copy to Calvin to write down Benji's address. I wondered if he still had the paper with him. I reached for my phone, thinking I'd call and ask. Then I stopped myself and scowled. I'd almost forgotten. I was mad at him.

"What's wrong?" asked Deena. "Are you going to call the police now?"

I laughed shortly. "Uh, yeah. That's a better idea than I had. As if I have time for a hike in the Smokies tomorrow. I've got wedding flowers to arrange."

Richard raised an eyebrow. "A hike? You didn't think *you* were going to follow them into the mountains? You may be spunky, but I know you're not stupid."

"Gee, thanks." I made a face at him and grabbed my phone. But then I paused, uncertain who to call. "I'm not sure who's in the station at this hour. Should I call 9-1-1?"

Deena tapped her manicured nails on the table. "How would that play out? An officer arrives here and you accuse Isaiah of murder—with no evidence to back it up?"

"That's a good point," said Richard. "The only proof, if it can be called that, is on April's phone. If she gets suspicious, she'll delete those messages faster than you can say *poppy tea*."

Biting my lip, I pushed my chair back and stood up. I felt so helpless. I had to do something, so I took my plate and glass to the sink and rinsed them out. Then I turned to my friends. "We *have* to stop that hike tomorrow. I'll go to the police . . . somehow. Maybe I'll add the new info in the anonymous letter I plan to write. But I'm afraid I won't be able to get the cops to do anything before the students leave tomorrow morning. What can we do?"

Deena gave me a look of helpless regret. We'd already carried out one harebrained scheme tonight. Neither of us could come up with another one.

Richard, on the other hand, had a devious glint in his eye. Nodding to himself, he snapped his fingers. "I've got it."

Deena and I spoke in unison. "What?"

Smiling, he stood up and corked the wine bottle. "You don't have to worry. I'll take care of it. The three musketeers won't be going on a hike tomorrow."

"How?" Deena and I again spoke at the same time.

"You two spend too much time together," Richard joked. "Now, stop speaking in stereo and get yourselves home. It's late. I'll talk to you tomorrow."

No matter how much we begged and cajoled, Richard wouldn't tell us his plan. I had no choice but to let go of my fear and have a little faith.

On our way out, we passed through the living room— and were startled to see Isaiah and Vince. It was so unexpected, Deena gasped and I clapped my hand over my mouth. They were sprawled in the armchairs, each watching something on his own phone. I wondered how long they'd been there.

They barely looked up as we walked by. When we reached the foyer, my skin prickled and I looked back at them. It felt for all the world like someone had been watching me.

Then again, it was probably just my imagination.

Chapter 22

Rocky met me at the curb with Gus. Mom and Dad were early risers, so we both thought it best that we not risk waking them up. When I stepped out of the car, Gus was so excited to see me, he practically jumped into my arms.

Laughing, I caught my balance and leaned down to ruffle his ears. "I'm happy to see you too, buddy."

"He had a good day, I swear," said Rocky. "He was treated like a celebrity everywhere we went."

"That's my little prince."

Rocky opened the back door of my car and stowed Gus's travel bag on the back seat. "How's Deena," he said casually.

I tried not to smile too wide. "She's great. Why do you ask?"

"Why? No reason."

"Come on, Rock. Do you like her? Want me to put in a good word for you?"

"You don't have to do that." Grinning, he flexed his biceps. "My attributes speak for themselves."

I yawned loudly, partly to annoy him and partly because I was really tired.

He dropped his arms. "Seriously, though, I do like Dee. She's smart and interesting. Pretty too. But I don't want to make things awkward or anything, since she's your friend."

"We're all adults," I said sensibly. "There shouldn't be any awkwardness."

"In that case, how about a double date? My buddy, Craig, has been asking about you."

"Craig? The P.E. teacher, Coach Craig?" I only knew of him because Rocky had mentioned him before. I could barely picture the man.

"That's the one. He's a good guy. I wouldn't set you up with a jerk."

"That's a relief." Stifling another yawn, I opened my car and urged Gus inside. "I'll get back to you on that."

"Okay. Drive safe, sis."

"I will. Good night, Rocky."

The drive home was quiet—all the better for reflecting on recent events. I had a lot to sort out. While I seemed to have found a lot of answers, there were still so many gaps in what I knew.

In particular, there was one new question on top of all the others: What would Calvin think if I went on a date with Rocky's friend, Craig?

I parked on the street and made my way carefully up the path to my house. The dollhouse was cloaked in darkness. With my purse over my shoulder, Gus's leash in one hand, and his bag in the other, it was a bit of a juggling act. At the front door, I had to set down the bag and use the light from my phone to fit my key in the lock. I was so focused on my task, I was only vaguely aware that Gus was sniffing something on the stoop.

"What is that, Gus?" Once I got the door open, I

flipped on the porch light. "Come inside, buddy." As I coaxed him into the house, I glanced down—and was surprised to see a small bouquet of red poppies. Frowning, I picked them up and took them inside.

They were similar to the other bunch of flowers left outside my door, except that these hadn't been rained on. Tied loosely with a red string, they were floppy and a little sad-looking. There was no note.

"Who left these?"

Gus had lost interest. He wandered into the kitchen to examine his food bowl, on the off chance he'd find a bedtime snack. Following behind him, I set the flowers on the counter and refreshed his water dish.

"That's all you're getting for now. I'm sure you were well fed today." Spoiled with dog treats was more like it.

Rummaging through a cabinet, I found an old glass soda bottle. I rinsed it off, filled it partway with tap water, and propped the poppies in the bottle.

For a moment, I stared at the droopy red blossoms. I was mystified. Previously, I'd thought one of my neighbors' grandchildren had gifted me a handful of flowers, like a belated May basket surprise. I didn't think so anymore. Considering what I'd learned about Professor Lowry and his favored students, the choice of flowers was too much of a coincidence.

Could they be a message of some sort? I tried to recall what poppies symbolized. Red poppies were associated with Memorial Day, of course, as a token of remembrance for soldiers who'd lost their lives in World War I. (This started after a poem brought attention to a former battlefield, muddy and barren until a field of beautiful poppies sprang forth from the ground.)

Besides that, the poppy was also associated with

Morpheus, the Greek god of dreams and sleep. I assumed
that was because of its narcotic properties. Perhaps that
was also why L. Frank Baum had chosen poppies as the
cause of Dorothy's poisoned slumber in *The Wonderful
Wizard of Oz*. In the movie version, this scene had fright-
ened me as a child. The Wicked Witch almost succeeded
in diverting the girl from her quest . . . until Glinda the
Good Witch made it snow.

My eyelids grew heavy. All these sleepy thoughts
were making me drowsy—and no closer to figuring out
who had left the flowers or why.

I headed to bed, fully expecting to sleep as soundly
as Toto in a field of poppies. However, it turned out
to be a restless night. I kept waking up, feeling disori-
ented and panicky, without knowing why. My dreams
were murky. In one, I was lost, trapped in a university
science building, which looked more like a nineteenth-
century psychiatric hospital. Naturally, someone was
chasing me.

In another dream, I was arguing with Deena. It
seemed we were decorating a church for a wedding—
hers and Rocky's! Only she wanted to call it off at the
last minute. That dream was more distressing than the
other one.

Finally, somewhere in the wee hours, I dropped into
a deep sleep and stayed there for the rest of the night.

In spite of the rough night, I made myself get up early.
It was going to be a busy day. Over breakfast, I slugged
coffee and typed up the letter I'd been planning—Re: Illegal Activities of Professor Steve Lowry. In it, I described
everything I'd learned, with particular focus on the poppy

tea operation. I printed three copies, then looked up the mailing addresses for the police headquarters in both Knoxville and Aerieville, as well as that of the university dean.

Reading over the letter, I was satisfied I'd accurately laid out all the necessary details, without divulging my sources. However, after stuffing the envelopes, I left them unsealed. I realized I ought to show Calvin the letter, before dashing it off on my own. After all, he could have other plans.

Thinking about Calvin made me feel grumbly again. I took my breakfast dishes to the sink and shook off my irritation. It was time to get to work. I had flowers to prepare for tomorrow's wedding. Everything else would have to wait.

The grass was still dewy when Gus and I arrived at Flower House. After parking in the driveway behind Calvin's car, I let Gus sniff around the garden for a minute. When we approached the back door, I stopped in my tracks at what I saw on the doorstep.

"You've got to be kidding me."

It was another bouquet of red poppies, tied with a red string. I picked them up and turned them over in my hands. They appeared to be freshly cut. I knew they weren't here yesterday when I'd left with Deena. And they looked too fresh to have been here when Calvin returned from making deliveries yesterday evening. Had someone dropped these off in the middle of the night, or right after leaving the ones at my house? Or were they placed here just this morning?

Looking around, I saw the light on in the bakery next door. Maybe Bill or Flo had seen something. I didn't relish talking to them, but I headed over there anyway. Since

Bread n' Butter wasn't open yet, I figured I'd tap on the door. However, I was distracted from my purpose by the sight of a familiar car on the street. It was Wanda's SUV.

Is Wanda at the park again?

Still clutching the poppies, I let Gus lead me down the sidewalk toward Melody Gardens. Could Wanda have been leaving the bouquets? I recalled noticing a red string around her finger the other day, similar to the strings that bound the flowers. Red string was a common element in folk workings. Granny had told me there was power in the color, likely stemming from its associations with the blood of Christ. Or anyone's blood, for that matter. It was our life force. I didn't know if Wanda shared all of Granny's superstitions, but she probably held a few of them. At least, I knew she believed in ghosts and omens.

On that note, another strange thought crossed my mind, and not for the first time. If Professor Lowry strongly resembled Wanda's husband Roy—and she started seeing an apparition right after Lowry died— could it be *Lowry's* ghost appearing to her?

Goose bumps prickled along my arms. I wasn't sure where I stood on the subject of ghosts. I'd never seen one myself, but I liked to keep an open mind.

Gus seemed to know where he was going. When we reached the park, he guided me directly to the secluded grove where we'd encountered Wanda before. Sure enough, there she was again. She was a little more disheveled this time, with mud on her knees, leaves in her hair, and a scowl on her face. Her expression of disgust seemed to be aimed at a circle of holes in the ground around the hydrangea bush.

I approached cautiously and spoke in a gentle tone, so as not to startle her. "Good morning, Wanda."

She looked up and sighed. "Hello, dear."

"Are you still looking for your ring?"

She removed her gardening gloves and tossed them to the ground. "Not anymore. It's hopeless."

To my dismay, her lower lip trembled. I rushed to her side. "Come sit with me a minute. Let's chat."

She allowed me to usher her to the bench beneath the oak tree. As soon as we were seated, I held up the poppies. "Do these look familiar to you?"

She narrowed her eyebrows, as if she couldn't understand why I'd ask such a thing. "They're poppies."

"Yes, they are. Did you pick them and leave them by my door?"

Now she looked at me like I might have a screw loose. "No," she said, drawing out the word. "Why should I do such a thing?"

Good question. "Well, somebody did. And since you were in the neighborhood . . ." I trailed off, realizing now that I'd been mistaken.

Wanda shook her head. "Wasn't me. I don't have poppies in my yard. Besides, the season is pretty much over here." She motioned toward the orange poppies along the path, whose petals were now faded and fallen.

"That's true," I admitted. *Then, where did these poppies come from?*

Wanda smiled. "You must have an admirer, dear. Perhaps it's that handsome blue-eyed boy who works with you at Flower House."

I felt my eyebrows shoot up to my bangs. *That* statement was rational enough.

"It wasn't Calvin."

"Are you sure?"

I nodded, suddenly feeling glum. "Positive."

Wanda's face became serious. "Can I give you some advice?"

"Sure."

"If you like this young man—or anyone else for that matter—find a way to work out your differences. Talk it out. And, whatever you do, don't hold onto petty grievances for no good reason. Take it from me, life's too short for that."

As she spoke, her eyes veered up to the waving branches of the old oak tree. My heart went out to her. Granny had said that Wanda and Roy were on the outs when he passed away—the day before their wedding anniversary. How sad that she'd never had a chance to patch things up with him, and that she'd been carrying that regret ever since.

"That's good advice," I said quietly. "I'll remember it."

"I wish Roy knew I forgave him," she said, as if speaking to herself. "His drinking problem was a sickness. I know that now."

"Maybe he does know," I murmured.

"He'd know if I wore his ring. If I could ever find it."

I glanced toward the cluster of holes she'd dug around the hydrangeas. "You threw it toward the bush?" I asked.

"I thought I did. I was standing near this tree, where he'd carved our initials. I was hopping mad at the time. In a fit, I closed my eyes tight and threw it over my shoulder, somewhere behind me."

I looked from the tree to the bush, not following her logic. The ring could have landed anywhere.

She saw my confusion and laughed a little. "Okay, you got me. The truth is, Roy told me to look there. He came to me in a dream."

I opened my mouth, about to ask how she knew it was really him. Then I thought better of it. "He told you to dig beneath the hydrangea bush?"

"Not exactly, but close. He kept saying 'hydra.'" She

looked at me and shrugged. "It's always windy in the dream. I can't make out anything else."

"Hydra?" I repeated. "Like the mythical water monster?"

"I don't know about that," she said dismissively. "Hydra, like *hydrangea*."

I stood up and walked with Gus to the oak tree. As he sniffed the groundcover, I gazed around this little corner of the park.

Why "hydra"? It was only part of the plant's name. Granny had once told me that *hydrangea* meant "water barrel," since that's how the flowers were shaped. *Hydra* meant "water."

The instant I thought it, my eyes fell upon the bubbling fountain on the other side of a line of boxwood shrubs. Wanda would have had to have made a pretty wild throw to send the ring that far, but it wasn't outside the realm of possibility.

She got up from the bench and joined me near the tree. "You look like you've had an inspiration," she said.

"Tell me something, Wanda. What did Roy do for a living?"

"He was a machinist. Worked for the TVA. Why?"

"I was just thinking, could he have meant hydra as in water? Like *hydro*?"

Wanda's eyes lit up. "You might be on to something!"

Together, we made our way quickly to the fountain. The electric pump couldn't have been more than a few years old, but parts of the rocky feature were much older.

"This used to be a goldfish pond," said Wanda.

I handed her Gus's leash and kneeled down to get a better look. The bottom of the fountain was carpeted in pennies, with a smattering of nickels and dimes—for the bigger wishes, I supposed. What were the odds that a ring flung in here eons ago would still be here? Probably not too good.

Undaunted, I grabbed a stick and scraped coins away from the edge. In the process, I swirled dirt and muck, making it even more difficult to see through the water. I sat back and stared at the fountain for a moment. Above the little reservoir, water trickled from a jumble of large rocks like a mini-waterfall. Several crevices between the rocks were certainly large enough to hide a ring.

Wanda must have been thinking the same thing. She produced a penlight and handed it to me.

Inching closer to the rocks, I leaned over and shined the light into every crack and cranny. I didn't see a thing, not even a spider. I was about to call it quits, when I passed the light across the largest crevice a second time—and caught a glimpse of a tiny round object. It might have been a pebble, or it might have been a coin. Then again, it might've been something else.

With mounting excitement, I removed my shoes and socks and rolled up my pant legs. "It's probably nothing," I said, not wanting to get Wanda's hopes up.

I stepped into the pond and walked gingerly across the slimy, cold coins. Gus barked enthusiastically. No doubt he wanted to help, or at least join in the game. Wanda held him back, as I grasped the largest rock for support and reached two fingers into the shadowy crevice. Making contact with the small object, I carefully eased it out of the hole.

It *was* a ring! The gold was dull and tarnished, but the round diamond still held a hint of sparkle.

"That's it!" whooped Wanda. "You found it!"

The leash slipped from her hand, as Gus ran up to the edge of the fountain. His stubby tail wagged furiously. It

was clear he longed to join me in the water, but he didn't
have the nerve.

"Stay back, Gus," I cautioned. "I'm coming out."

Grinning widely, I turned on a dime (literally)—and
slipped, landing smack dab on my rear end with a big
splash.

Chapter 23

I was too pleased to care about my wet jeans—or the growing bruise on my backside. The gratitude in Wanda's expression, not to mention the tears in her eyes, were enough to keep me warm through a thousand winters.

She gathered her things from the ground where she'd left them, and we exited the park together. Outside Bread n' Butter, we parted with a hug. She went into the bakery for a cup of coffee, and I headed for my car. Once more I was glad I kept a change of clothes in my just-in-case overnight bag.

Deena was in the kitchen setting out corsage pins and ribbons, as if readying for an assembly line. "There you are," she said when I came in the back door. "Did you take Gus for a walk?"

"Yes, I did. And we had quite an adventure. I'll tell you about it in a minute."

I took Gus to the office and rewarded him with a dog treat and a chew toy. Then I changed in the bathroom and freshened up. When I rejoined Deena in the kitchen, she asked me about my adventure.

"We ran into Wanda again," I said. "And hopefully managed to put her husband's spirit to rest."

She tilted her head at that. "Seriously?"

I laughed. "Well, I guess that remains to be seen." I started to lay out flowers on the table, then paused. "Where's Calvin? Have you seen him yet?"

"Briefly. He's in the greenhouse."

"I think I'll go out there now." I grabbed a clean bucket from the floor and filled it with water and floral solution. "I'll get the roses we need."

"Okay," she said agreeably. "Get ready for the silent treatment, though. Calvin seemed a little down."

"Thanks for the warning."

I found him in the rose side of the greenhouse. He was pouring liquid fertilizer into the soil around some of the plants. He looked up as I approached him.

"I'm about done here, if you need help with wedding prep."

"Yeah, that would be great." I picked up a pair of gloves and gardening shears from a workbench and headed to the next row over. After slipping on the gloves, I examined the blooms on a bush of light peach Tiffany roses. They would be perfect for the bridal bouquet.

However, before I made the first snip, I heard Wanda's voice in my head. *Talk it out.* Far be it from me to ignore the wise woman. After all, I did tell her I'd take her advice. Placing the bucket and shears on the floor, I looked over toward Calvin.

In truth, my anger at him had already begun to fade. And finding Wanda's ring had left me in an exceptionally tender mood. At this point, I was ready to let bygones be bygones. I would make peace with Calvin's past, present, and future, whatever that might entail.

I walked to the end of the row and saw that he was putting away the fertilizer. With his eyes on his feet, he trudged my way.

"Hey," I said brightly. "I have something to show you." He looked up in surprise.

"It's in the shop, though," I continued. "In my purse. It's an anonymous letter I wrote, to send to the police."

"About Lowry?"

"Yeah. The truth needs to come out about him, don't you think?"

"For sure. Thanks for doing that."

We locked eyes for an instant, then he looked away. I wished I could read his thoughts. Probably, he was feeling discouraged, considering he was still a murder suspect. I couldn't fault him for that.

"If—" I began, stopping when he spoke at the same time.

"I—" He broke off, one corner of his mouth curving in a faint half smile. "You go first."

"I was only going to say that if you want to talk, I'm a good listener."

His smile broadened, before dropping into an expression of remorse. "And I was going to say I owe you an apology. I'm sorry for being weird yesterday." He paused, running his fingers through his hair. "And for not being completely forthright with you."

"That's okay," I said automatically. I was eager to forgive him and set things right between us. "But thank you. That means a lot."

"I, uh, wasn't in a great place emotionally before I came to Aerieville. Besides losing my job and my reputation, I'd broken up with my girlfriend."

"Your roommate?" I guessed.

He nodded. "We'd already grown apart a long time

ago. The stress of the Lowry situation only made things worse. She thought I should've been more assertive and—well, whatever. It doesn't matter now."

As he talked, he moved down the row to the peach-colored roses and picked up the bucket of water. I took the shears and began gathering the flowers, while he held the bucket. He didn't seem inclined to elaborate about his ex-girlfriend, and I was okay with that. This was a start.

I snipped a rose and handed it to him. "On the bright side, your reputation may soon be restored. When it comes out how dishonest Lowry was, it will be more believable that he stole your research."

"Yeah," Calvin acknowledged. "It might help a little, especially if there's a thorough search of his papers." He didn't seem overly cheered by the prospect.

"They might even let you have your old job back." I'd tried to sound encouraging, but it still pained me to say it. Perhaps he could tell.

"Are you tryin' to get rid of me?" he joked.

"No! Of course not. I . . . rather like having you around."

His mouth twitched, as if he was holding back a smile. "I rather like being around."

"Good." I looked down to snip another rose. For some reason, I felt a blush warm my cheeks. Careful not to prick myself on a thorn, I concentrated on the task at hand. Soon the bucket was full.

"Want me to go grab another one?" asked Calvin.

"No, thanks. Let's start with these and see how far we get."

"Aye aye, cap'n."

Grinning like a loon, I led the way out of the green-house. It was good to have goofy Calvin back again.

For the rest of the morning, Deena, Calvin, and I

trimmed, stripped, and de-thorned roses; arranged bouquets and centerpieces; and made all the corsages and boutonnieres. By the time we broke for lunch, my fingers were sore from so much ribbon-wrapping. I felt good about our progress, though. We worked efficiently together and, fortunately (under the circumstances), didn't have a lot of interruptions. There were only two walk-in customers, one who ordered a dozen red roses and one who wanted a potted orchid—both of which were quick and easy to provide.

After lunch, Calvin took Gus for a walk, while Deena and I got to work on the aisle decorations: pew bows of satin ribbon and tulle, which we would later embellish with a cluster of roses and baby's breath. The arch, on the other hand, would have to be put together at the church. She watched me create the first bow, since she'd never done it before. As I attached the frothy tulle to the folded ribbon, I recalled part of my dream from the night before.

"So," I said casually. "I was talking to Rocky yesterday."

"Oh?" she said, without looking up.

"About you."

That got her attention. "Why me?"

"Because Rocky likes you." I felt like a teenager talking like this, but I didn't care. Matters of the heart could make anyone feel young again. "He thinks you're—and I quote—'smart, interesting, and pretty.'"

She stood back, with her hands on her hips. "He really said that?"

I nodded, grinning. "I don't mean to put you on the spot. It's cool if you don't feel the same way."

"Oh! Well," she said. "Actually, I wouldn't mind getting to know him better. I think he's smart, interesting, and pretty, too." She smiled cheekily, then took on a thoughtful expression.

Part of me wanted to issue a warning about not breaking my brother's heart, but I held back. No one needed pressure like that.

"He mentioned going on a double date," I said.

At that moment, Calvin and Gus came in the back door. "Just passing through," he said. "I'll keep Gus out of here."

"Thanks," I said.

"Double date?" said Deena. "With who?"

"He's trying to set me up with a friend of his." I fluffed the bow and held it up for inspection.

Calvin froze, with his hand on the hall door. "Did I miss something?"

"We're talking about Rocky," Deena told him. To me, she said, "A double date sounds fun. Where would we go?"

Before I could answer, my cell phone rang.

"Maybe it's Rocky," said Deena.

I snickered at her eagerness and resisted an eye roll. Grabbing my phone from the counter, I looked at the display. "It's Richard!"

With Deena and Calvin watching, I perched on a stool to answer the call. "Hey, Richard. I've been hoping to hear from you."

"Hi, Sierra." In place of his usual zest, there was a serious note in his voice.

"What's wrong?" I asked, immediately on alert. "Did your guests go on their hike after all?"

"No. The hike was canceled, like I said it would be. But I have some potentially bad news."

"Bad news?" I glanced up at Deena and Calvin. Their faces mirrored my own worry. Calvin let up on Gus's leash, so the pup could hurry to my side. I used my free hand to pet the top of his head.

"There was a police officer here this morning, asking questions," said Richard. "That's what kept them from the day trip they had planned. I was hovering nearby, so I got to hear much of what they said."

My mind jumped ahead, already anticipating what was to come. "What did they say?"

Richard sighed. "Well, they apparently decided to throw Calvin under the bus. In spite of whatever they said before, they're all now in agreement that they saw him arguing with the professor. They also claim they saw you and Calvin exit Flower House right after Lowry was killed."

"Just Calvin and me, and no one else?" So much for trying to place the blame on Bart.

"No one else. I hate to say it, Sierra, but they're pointing fingers at you too. They all said they believe Calvin killed Lowry, and that you were in on it."

Of course, they'd say that. I squeezed my eyes shut, as if I could make this problem disappear. I'd carried on this morning as if everything were peaches and cream. Between helping Wanda, making up with Calvin, and playing cupid for Deena, I'd acted as if there wasn't a murder investigation hanging over Flower House like an ominous cloud. Well, I wouldn't do it anymore.

I opened my eyes. "Thanks for the heads-up, Richard."

"What are you going to do now?"

"I'm not sure, but I'll figure something out." In fact, my wheels were turning already.

After the call from Richard, I remembered the letter I'd written. I showed it to Calvin, and he agreed we should send it right away. He offered to deliver a copy directly to the Aerieville Police Station before dropping the other two envelopes in the mail.

"I don't care if anyone sees me," he said, opening the kitchen door. "It doesn't matter if the cops associate me with the letter. The evidence at UT ought to speak for itself."

"We'll hold down the fort here." Under the circumstances, it almost felt like he was undertaking a risky covert mission across enemy lines. I had to resist the urge to give him a good-luck kiss. Instead, he had to settle for Gus, who got to go along for the ride.

As soon as they left, Deena and I finished the pew bows and made sure everything was organized for our final preparations in the morning. All the while, my mind never left the new accusations Richard had relayed. I wondered what prompted the change. And would it even matter? Would the police give any credence to the students' contradictory statements? I said as much to Deena.

Like the good friend she was, she gave me a reassuring answer. "I wouldn't think so. It seems suspicious to me that they changed their tune at this late stage."

"Totally suspicious!" I agreed. "And why now? Do you think April figured out I snooped in her phone?"

Deena pursed her lips, considering. "Maybe. Or maybe they're just tired of being here and want to go home."

Whatever the reason, I couldn't shake the feeling that time was running out.

We completed our work in the kitchen and headed to the orchid room, Deena with a feather duster and me with a spray bottle. As I misted the plants' roots and leaves, my thoughts returned again to the day of the murder.

From what I'd observed that afternoon, Vince, Isaiah, and April—whom I'd dubbed the rebel, the preppy, and Blondie—had stood apart from their classmates. They weren't in a fun-loving, excited mood. They didn't even seem very chummy with one another. I remembered April trying to get the attention of both guys, who seemed to be ignoring her—until Vince apparently went into the bathroom with her. Did they go in there to discuss Isaiah's plan to kill the professor and how they might stop him? Or were they plotting to make it happen sooner?

Something tickled my arm and I jerked it away. It was Deena with the feather duster.

"Earth to Sierra. What were you doing, building a mind palace à la Sherlock Holmes?"

I wrinkled my nose playfully. "Ha. In a way, actually. And I think I might have a plan." An idea pieced itself together, as I spoke. "It involves talking to Vince alone."

"Alone, alone? Is that safe?"

"Well, I don't need to be alone," I amended. "I just need him to be alone."

Deena nodded. "Gotcha."

I loved it that she knew what I meant. "I'll call Richard right now and see what I can arrange."

While I called Richard, Deena finished dusting the shelves in the orchid room and moved on to the front of the shop. A few minutes later, I rejoined her near the cash register.

"Okay, here's the plan. Richard is going to tell Vince to meet me at Cuties' at six o'clock. He'll let him know the invitation is for Vince only."

"And Vince will assume he's meeting you alone?" asked Deena.

"Probably. When he arrives, he'll find that he's meeting with the two of us, but I don't think it will matter."

Deena looked at her watch. "It's nearly five now. Want to go soon and have a drink and a bite?"

"Yeah. Let me just see where Calvin is first."

Before I could send Calvin a text, he and Gus came through the front door.

"Mission accomplished," he said. "And no one said a word to me when I left the letter in a tray for the chief."

"Good." I told him my plan to meet Vince and asked if he'd keep Gus a while longer.

He hesitated before answering. "I'd rather go with you."

I smiled to myself. *Another time.* "Vince will probably be more inclined to talk without you there."

"Don't worry," said Deena. "I'll be there to chaperone."

Calvin looked at me as if he wanted to say something more but changed his mind. In the end, he patted me on the back and muttered, "Good luck."

Chapter 24

Cuties' was always more crowded on Friday nights, and tonight was no exception. Even though it was relatively early, Deena and I had to sit at the bar until a table became available. We each ordered a glass of Pinot Grigio (further validating Richard's theory that we were becoming the same person) and swiveled in our stools to watch the other patrons play pool. I kept one eye on the door for Vince.

"Tell me again what the strategy is here," said Deena. "Are we trying to sweet-talk him, or intimidate him, or what?"

Her uncertainty was understandable. I wasn't entirely sure myself what I expected to happen. "I guess it depends on how he reacts," I said. "I'm gonna tell him I know everything—about the poppy tea operation, about Isaiah and April, everything."

"And hope he'll turn on his friends?" asked Deena.

"Basically, yes. I'm hoping he'll be mature and reasonable—and want to protect his own neck."

It seemed like a solid plan, but I was still nervous. For all I knew, Vince could be the mastermind of the whole thing. After all, he had a criminal record . . . and a slick way about him. If my notion was wrong, I could make things worse rather than better.

I finished my wine and contemplated ordering another. Then I checked the time. It was six twenty.

"He's late," I said.

"Maybe he's in the restaurant," said Deena. "Should we look?"

I shook my head. "Richard told him we'd be in the bar. He should be here."

A waitress came over to let us know that our table was ready. We followed her to a booth near the door and ordered a not-so-light dinner of portobello burgers and French fries (seasoned for me, sweet potato for Deena). As the evening wore on, it became apparent Vince was a no-show.

Feeling kind of pouty, I drew a circle in my ketchup with a French fry. "I can't believe he stood me up. I guess I don't have the appeal I thought I did."

"I wouldn't take it personally," said Deena. "Something must have come up. Otherwise, he would've jumped at the opportunity to flaunt his abs for you again."

"Aw, you're sweet." I fluttered my eyelashes and bit into the fry. I didn't really think Vince was interested in me in that way, but I *had* thought he'd be tempted by my invitation. Wouldn't he want to know why I'd asked to see him?

I checked my phone (again) to see if Richard had called or texted. He hadn't.

"Why don't you just check in with Richard?" asked Deena.

"Yeah, I might as well."

I sent a quick text. A few seconds later, Richard sent a reply.

"Huh," I said, after reading the message. "He said Vince left an hour ago. He thought he was coming to Cuties'."

Deena sat up in her chair and looked around the pool room. "Well, he's not here."

"I can't imagine where else he'd go. Some other bar?"

We finished our dinner and paid the check. Then we took a quick walk through the restaurant to make sure we hadn't missed him. Among the couples and families enjoying an evening out were some friends of Deena's parents. While she said hello, I asked the hostess if she'd seen anyone fitting Vince's description. She assured me she hadn't.

In the parking lot, we stood for a moment beside our cars. By this time, it was eight-thirty and growing dark, even more so under thickening clouds. As we talked, we were treated with a light show in the sky, thanks to flashes of heat lightning in the distance.

"So much for *that* idea," I said. "Long shot or not."

"What now?"

I sighed. "I suppose we should call it a night. Tomorrow's going to be a big day."

"We could stop by Richard's after the wedding," Deena suggested. She gave me a sly grin. "You can try to take up smoking again and catch Vince alone that way."

I rolled my eyes and laughed. "Right. Because that was so successful the first time."

We said goodbye and went our separate ways. As I headed back to Flower House to pick up Gus, I considered Dee's idea to try to talk to Vince at the B&B. It made sense, absent any other plan. One thing was for sure, I wasn't ready to give up.

The problem was I needed to speak with Vince away from Isaiah and April—yet, without being completely alone with him. I didn't exactly trust the guy. He was like Captain Jack Sparrow or Count Dracula: seductively charming and not bad to look at—but with blazing red flags waving all around him.

I was about four blocks from Flower House when I became aware of a van behind me. Thanks to my meandering daydreams, I wasn't sure how long it had been on my tail. In the darkness, I couldn't see the driver or the color of the vehicle. When I turned onto Oak Street, it turned too. Someone was following me.

My heart thrummed in my chest. Was it Vince in the school van? Had he been waiting for me to leave Deena, so he could catch me alone? If so, why?

Instead of pulling into the unlit driveway, I rolled to a stop on the street in front of Flower House. The van parked right behind me, its bright headlights flooding the interior of my Fiat. With the motor still running, I dug my phone out of my purse. My fingers trembled as I searched for Calvin's name in my contacts. I was about to press Call when there was a rap on my driver's side window.

I yelped in surprise and dropped my phone. Then I saw the face in the window and gasped. It was Bart. I stared at him, paralyzed. *What should I do?*

He squinted at me with an inscrutable expression. Was it anger? Confusion? Concern? Finally, he spoke. "Are you okay?"

I blinked, then nodded. "Yep. I'm good."

He continued to stand there, waiting, apparently. I reached down and retrieved my phone from the floor. My shock at seeing him was short-lived. Now I was more curious than anything else. *What was he doing here?*

I lowered the window partway. I figured I could always hit the gas pedal if he tried anything funny.

"What's up?" I asked. "You startled me."

"I'm sorry. I saw your car and thought maybe we could talk."

There was something in his eyes that tugged at me, an earnestness, maybe. Or loneliness. He didn't seem threatening. He never had, really—at least not to me. Still, I wasn't ready to leave the safety of my car.

"Sure, we can talk. What's on your mind?"

A crease of consternation formed between his eyebrows. I got the impression I was making something difficult for him. He shifted from foot to foot. "I wanted to let you know that you can talk to me. Or tell me . . . anything. I'm here for you."

He's here for me? What was he talking about?

Lightning flashed, and a peal of thunder rang through sky. The sound took me back to the night of the big storm and the figure outside my window. That night had also marked the first appearance of red poppies on my doorstep.

And just like that, as swift as that bolt of lightning, I finally put two and two together. It had to have been Bart leaving me the flowers. After all, he had ready access to almost any variety of flower, regardless of the season. I also recalled what Wanda had said—that I must have a secret admirer.

My face grew warm with the realization. What a fool I was not to figure it out sooner! All my efforts to be friendly to the man must have been misconstrued. He must've thought I was flirting with him, or at least signaling encouragement.

Still, I felt there must be more to it than that. Gently, so as not to embarrass him, I went ahead and asked. "Bart, why have you been leaving me poppies?"

To my surprise, he broke into a lopsided grin. "You figured out it was me."

Before I could respond, fat drops of rain splattered on

the windshield—and on Bart's head. I cut the engine and opened my car door. He stepped back to let me out.

"Come on," I said. "Let's talk on the porch."

I darted up the brick path and took shelter under the porch roof. Bart came along more slowly. At the top of the steps, he pulled out a handkerchief to wipe the rain from his face.

I turned to him and crossed my arms. "Okay, mister. I have some questions for you, and I'd like straight answers. First of all, why poppies? And secondly, why all the secrecy?"

He looked me square in the eyes. "I can trust you, right?"

"Yeah, sure. Of course."

"Okay, well. I was leaving you clues. The professor was growing illegal poppies at the university."

I nodded. *Tell me something I don't know.* "You said you'd never met him before Saturday. Are you saying you *did* know him?"

Now he looked away. "Not by name. But I'd seen him there before, at the college, when I was making deliveries."

"And you saw him doing something with poppies?"

"Yeah. I'm not sure what he was up to exactly, but I know he didn't want anyone to find out. I, uh, came across it by accident."

Wandering around, no doubt. I couldn't help wondering if Bart had been stealing things from the science department—maybe something to do with his home-brewing operation. That would explain why he felt he couldn't come out and tell anyone what he'd discovered.

"I think Lowry was involved with drugs somehow," Bart continued. "Making it, selling it, using it. That could be why he ended up dead."

It "could be"? I studied Bart, trying to figure out why

he sounded so coy. His habit of using the fewest words possible had led to one misunderstanding after another. I was determined to get the truth out of him, if I had to stand here all night.

"Let's talk about the day of the murder," I said. "Did you really see Wanda coming out of the back door?"

"I think you know the answer to that."

"Um, I think the answer is no."

"Correct."

"Then why did you lie?" By now, I thought I knew why. It was for the same reason he'd brought up Lowry's involvement with drugs: to detract from the truth. Throwing caution to the wind, I came right out with it. "Did *you* kill Lowry?"

His reaction was so stark, it was almost comical. "Me? What—why would you say that?"

"What else am I supposed to think? You've been acting secretive and telling lies. Which reminds me—why did you tell me your wife had died? Are you really just divorced?"

In an instant, his expression hardened. I thought he might turn heel and leave, but he only narrowed his eyes. When he spoke again, his voice was thick and stilted.

"She's dead to me, that's why. I don't like to talk about the divorce."

"I'm sorry," I said. "I—I heard about your child too. I'm *so* sorry."

He met my eyes and held them for a moment. I had the impression he was struggling with a decision, perhaps whether or not to open up to me. I waited. After a moment, his urge to share won out.

"When the accident happened," he began quietly, "I was behind the wheel. It was a drunk driver who swerved into our lane, but I didn't react as fast as I should have.

I was distracted, messing with the radio." Twisting his fingers, he looked away. "Right afterward, my wife and I . . . we agreed to say that *she* was driving. Otherwise, I would have lost my job as a delivery driver."

"But that wouldn't be fair, if it was a drunk driver . . ." I trailed off, realizing that was beside the point. He'd just told me he was partly responsible.

"I guess I never got over the guilt," he admitted. "And my marriage suffered for it."

I reached out and lightly touched his arm. *Poor guy. What a burden to live with.* "I can understand why you get so angry at careless drivers. It's a very personal issue for you."

"Yeah," he agreed.

"So, about Lowry," I said, gently returning to the matter at hand. "His attitude, after the way he drove the college van, that really set you off, didn't it?"

Bart glanced up at me and frowned.

"You went after him pretty hard that day, about running you off the road. Did you follow him in the shop to confront him again?"

"What? No!" He looked at me as if I'd slapped him.

"You didn't hit him with the candlestick?"

"Of course not! And, besides, I have an alibi! I was on the phone with my boss during the time he was killed."

My jaw dropped at that. He had an alibi? *Darn the Aerieville Police!* Why couldn't they keep me in the loop? No wonder they hadn't seemed interested in Bart.

"Oh," I said, slightly embarrassed but still confused. "I didn't know that. So, why'd you try to blame Wanda, then?"

His eyes shifted to the side, as he mumbled his answer. "I thought I was helping you."

"What do you mean?"

"I was trying to help you. I thought *you* did it."

I took a step back. "Wait. You thought *I* killed Lowry?" This was turning into a comedy of errors. I wasn't sure which was more disturbing, the fact that he believed I was capable of murder or the fact that he was willing to help me get away with it.

He didn't respond. From the looks of it, he seemed to realize he'd been wrong and was now trying to adjust to an entirely new perspective. That's what I was doing. *Bart had thought I was a murderer.* I recalled what he'd said to me at Cuties'—something about thinking Lowry had made a pass at me.

I shook my head. All this time, Bart thought I had wacked the professor. Yet, because of his feelings for me, he trusted that I must have had a good reason. He clearly also felt protective of me, and he wanted me to know my secret was safe with him.

It made sense now. I'd been friendly to Bart—purposely extra friendly—at a time when he most needed a friend. His loneliness probably led him to crave an even more intimate connection, one he thought we were forging together in some kind of an us-against-the-world alliance. And I'd just burst his bubble.

The front door clicked open, making us both turn our heads. Calvin stepped onto the porch.

"Hope I'm not interrupting anything." There was a twinge of a challenge in his tone, and a swagger in his posture, as he stood next to me and faced Bart.

The delivery man looked from Calvin to me. "I should go."

I nodded. It was probably for the best.

He started toward the steps, then paused, reaching into his jacket. To my surprise, he pulled out a rumpled little bunch of red poppies. He laid them on the edge of a pedestal plant stand. "That's the last one," he said, in his old gruff manner.

Ducking his head in the rain, he strode to his van and took off.

I stood at the front window in Calvin's apartment and watched the rain fall. My eyes roamed from the dimly lit street to the shadows beneath the trees. I was feeling bad about the whole situation with Bart. Now that I knew a little more of his backstory, I felt even more sorry for him than I had before.

Calvin handed me a cup of hot tea. "I'm sorry I didn't come down sooner. I kind of fell asleep in the chair with Gus."

I accepted the tea with a smile. "He has that effect on people."

He ran his fingers through his already tousled hair. "The thunder woke me up. Then I happened to see your car out front. I was wondering what took you so long to come up."

"It's just as well you didn't come outside sooner," I said. "Bart is pretty skittish. You probably would have scared him away."

"And that would be a bad thing?"

"This time, anyway. He cleared up a few things for me." I moved to the couch and told Calvin everything I'd learned from Bart.

Calvin appeared skeptical. "If he lied before, how do you know he's telling the truth now?"

"I'm sure the cops confirmed his alibi. And everything else he said matched what I already knew."

"Fair enough. Then we're back to the lackeys, huh? It had to be them."

"One or more of them," I agreed. Unfortunately, proving it was the ever-present problem.

For a moment, we didn't say anything. Calvin scratched Gus's ears, and I sipped my tea. This predicament was driving me crazy. I longed to change the subject and return to the flirty, carefree banter Calvin and I had shared on several recent occasions. But that wasn't possible, not with the unsolved murder hanging over our heads like a twenty-ton elephant.

The ringing of my cell phone pierced the cozy silence. Given the lateness of the hour, I immediately assumed it was something urgent. Then I saw it was my dad and my heart nearly stopped. I hastily answered the call.

"Hello? Dad?"

"You're still up," he said, with a trace of judgment in his voice. He probably couldn't help it.

"Yes, what's up? Is Mom okay? Is Granny?"

"Everybody's fine. I'm calling to give you a heads-up. I spoke with Walt a little while ago."

I knew who he meant: Walt Walden, Dad's old friend and Aerieville's usual Chief of Police, when he wasn't out on medical leave.

"Oh? How's he doing? Is he back on the force?"

"He's better. He's not officially back yet, but he's still privy to police information."

Uh-oh. I didn't like where this conversation was going.

"You need to call a lawyer, Sierra. You're going to be brought in for questioning very soon. Most likely tomorrow."

Chapter 25

The rain let up sometime overnight. I was cheered by the bright sunlight streaming through my bedroom window. It was a lovely day for a wedding.

The ceremony was scheduled for three o'clock, which meant we'd decorate the church and drop off the bouquets and corsages between noon and one. We didn't want to arrive too early and risk the flowers wilting, even a tiny bit. From there, we would leave to decorate the reception room at the church hall next door. When the wedding guests transitioned to the reception, we'd return to the church to retrieve our flower arch. The other decorations would stay for Nell to do with as she pleased.

Though we still had at least an hour of work at the shop, to complete the bows and pack up our vehicles, I wasn't in a rush. I allowed myself to sleep in and take my time getting ready. I wanted to dress up a little, not because I had to, but because I felt like it. After my shower, I blow-dried my short hair and applied a touch of natural makeup. Then I slipped on a cute short dress (in poppy red!) and silver ballet flats. I finished off the look with an embroidered cross-body purse with a bold flower design. I was determined to bring the fun today, come what may.

It wasn't that I was ignoring my dad's advice. He'd given me the name of a lawyer he knew, and I put her number in my phone. However, I didn't feel the need to make the call unless (or until) I heard from the police myself. After all, who knew if they would even contact me? Anything could happen. The cops could get busy with other cases. Or they could catch the actual murderer. Now *there* was a novel idea.

I dropped off Gus with Rocky and arrived at Flower House in good spirits. As Deena, Calvin, and I got busy with our big job, I could almost forget the terrible accusations that had been hurled in my direction.

Almost.

Not quite.

I might have been a little jumpy.

As I filled the flower-girl basket with fresh rose petals, I bounced from foot to foot. As I stuck floral tubes of water onto the ends of freshly cut stems for the pew bows, I managed to stab my own hand a time or two. And when the front door jingled open, I nearly fainted from fright—until I saw that it was Nell, stopping in to check on us on her way to the church.

I plastered on a smile and assured her all was well. And I pretty much kept telling myself that as we loaded the car, traveled to the church (a five-minute drive, natch), and adorned the center aisle.

Assembling the arch at the entrance to the aisle took all three of us—especially with my divided attention. In the midst of weaving greenery and blossoms through the metal arbor, I couldn't stop glancing out the open front doors. At any moment, I expected to see a man or woman in blue, badge out and handcuffs gleaming.

Regardless of my nerves, our efforts were rewarded. The flowers were gorgeous, and we received tons of compliments.

As I pinned Nell's corsage onto her dress, she gushed at the wonderful job we'd done. "I'll tell everybody I know: Flower House is *the* place to go for wedding flowers."

"Thanks, Nell. I appreciate that."

The door to the vestibule swung open, giving me yet another mini-panic attack. The thought of being approached by the law in front of Nell was almost worse than the thought of being arrested at all.

It was only Deena, thank goodness. She held up her camera. "I got lots of great shots for our website."

"Wonderful," said Nell. "I can't wait to see them."

The afternoon passed quickly. After decorating the reception room, with centerpieces on each guest table and garland across the head table, Calvin and I headed back to the church. Deena stayed behind to take more pictures.

Guests were trickling out of the church and across the lawn. The bride and groom stood in a receiving line at the bottom of the church steps. They'd had their professional photos taken prior to the ceremony but still mugged for anyone and everyone with a phone camera. I paused on the fringe of the lawn to admire the young couple.

"They look so happy," I said, with a sigh.

Calvin touched his chin and tilted his head. "They look a little shell-shocked, if you ask me."

"Hey," I said playfully, elbowing him in the side. "Where's your sense of romance? Don't you think they look sweet, all fresh-faced and dolled up? They're like a princess and prince."

He eyed me for a second, before saying, "Actually, you resemble a princess more than she does."

I narrowed my eyes, in mock annoyance. I knew he was teasing me. Yet, I also detected a hint of appreciation in the look he gave me. I couldn't keep a grin from forming on my lips. Honestly, Calvin looked more like a prince than the groom too—*my* kind of prince, with his sparkling blue eyes and laid-back style. He was particularly cute today, in dark blue jeans and a crisp white T-shirt beneath a lightweight blazer.

"You look nice. I like your dress," Calvin added more seriously.

"Thanks." I was somewhat surprised at his change of tone. Perhaps he was remembering all the friction and misunderstandings of the past few days. Being candid was always better.

We continued up the walkway toward a side door into the church. We'd gone only a few steps when I caught sight of a police car rounding a corner at the end of the block. It turned into the church parking lot.

"Oh no," I said under my breath. "Couldn't they have waited just a little bit longer?"

Calvin saw it too and grabbed my hand. "Come on!"

Together, we ran the rest of the way, slipping into the church undetected. The building wasn't entirely empty. A few stragglers chatted in the pews or waited for a turn in the restroom.

"What are we going to do?" I whispered. "It's going to take several minutes to take apart the flower arch. If the police come in the main entrance, they'll see us for sure." If the cops wanted to bring me in for questioning, I would of course cooperate—but I didn't want it to happen here, at our first big wedding job. Besides, if I could buy just a little more time, maybe I could ferret out the real culprit. Call it a hunch, but I felt certain I was getting closer to the truth.

Calvin walked around the vestibule, opening doors and peeking inside. I thought he was looking for a hiding place, until he said, "What if we move the arch out of the way and come back for it later?"

"Good idea!"

The structure was unwieldy but not too heavy. Between the two of us, we managed to lean it over and haul it into a lounge area near the restrooms. We lost only a few petals and leaves along the way. I found a piece of paper and wrote "Property of Flower House. Hold for pick-up," and stuck it on the front of the arch.

We returned to the side door and peeked outside. The challenge now was getting to our cars without being spotted. The coast was clear on the sidewalk, but when we neared the parking lot, we saw the police car, double-parked behind the first row of spaces. Two officers, including Dakin, were sauntering toward the lawn. We ducked behind an evergreen.

"Maybe I should go ahead and talk to them," I said, with zero enthusiasm. Nell was nowhere in sight, but the bridal party was still in front of the church posing for pictures. The police were bound to attract attention.

Calvin threw his arm in front of me. "Wait a minute. Look."

As we watched, Deena marched up to the police officers. She had an air of authority about her, which came as much from her confident pose as her appearance. Lovely as always, she looked exceptionally polished today, with her long sleek ponytail and tailored white pantsuit. We couldn't hear her words, but we could see her wide smile and animated gestures.

A moment later, the officers tipped their hats at her

and returned to their car. She waited until they drove away, before spinning on her heels and rushing toward the church. I stepped out from behind the tree and hollered.

"Deena! Over here!"

She halted and looked our way. Jogging over, she fluttered her hand to her chest. "Oh, Sierra, thank goodness! The police were just here."

"I know. We saw them—and you. What did you say?"

"I asked if I could help them, and they said they were looking for you. I told them you'd finished your work here and had probably gone back to Flower House. Was that okay? I didn't know what else to say." She wrung her hands and glanced at the bridal party. "I didn't want to lie, but I really didn't know where you were, and I figured if you had stuck around, you'd be better off with them out of the way."

I touched her arm. "You did great. That was perfect."

"Yeah," agreed Calvin. "There was no reason for the cops to come here anyway. It's not like they couldn't just call Sierra or find her at home."

"That's true." I pulled my phone from my purse and confirmed that I had no missed calls.

"Now what?" said Deena. "They'll be waiting at Flower House."

Biting my lip, I gazed at the azure blue sky and thought for a moment. "I can't avoid them forever. But . . . I was already planning to stop by Richard's this afternoon."

"Call him now," urged Deena.

I nodded and placed the call. When he answered, I got straight to the point. "Hey, Richard. I'm just leaving Sue Ellen's wedding and thought I'd drop by the B&B. Would that be okay?"

"Normally, it would be," he said. "But I'm on my way out the door."

"Oh," I said, disappointed. "I was actually hoping to catch up with Vince, since he didn't show up last night."

"Sorry, friend. But he's not here anyway. They all went to the fair. That's where I'm headed now."

"The fair, huh? Cool." I told Richard I'd talk to him later and hung up.

Calvin and Deena had heard my side of the conversation.

"I haven't been to the county fair in years," said Deena.

"It sounds kind of fun," said Calvin.

"What do you think?" asked Deena.

My mind weaved a myriad of possibilities. "I think . . . I'll call Rocky and ask him to leave Gus with our mom." I smiled at their bewildered expressions. "Then we can go on that double date we talked about."

Chapter 26

The county fairgrounds were located along a rural highway a few miles outside of Aerieville. Following a brief discussion, we decided that Rocky would drive, and the rest of us would leave our cars on the street in front of Deena's parents' house—which happened to be in a secluded subdivision out near the Country Club. Not that we were trying to be sneaky or anything. It was just a convenient place to convene.

After the short ride, Rocky parked his Jeep in an overflow parking lot behind the livestock barn. As we strolled past the cows, pigs, and goats—and the proud 4-H kids who had raised them—I felt a sense of peace wash over me. Something about the open air and change of scenery took me outside of all my worries and problems, at least for the moment.

The company was nice too. Rocky and Deena fell into an easy rapport. Walking side by side, they led the way toward the carnival grounds with Calvin and me following behind. We chatted companionably about inconsequential things. At some point, I swung my arm, causing my fingers to graze the back of Calvin's knuckles. He took the opportunity to clasp my hand, and we continued that way, holding hands like a real couple. It gave me the warm fuzzies.

Entering the amusement park section felt like stepping back in time. I took it all in with relish: the smells of deep-fried food and cotton candy, the sounds of children laughing and shrieking on the high-flying rides. My ears picked up the melodious tunes of a calliope, coming from an old-fashioned carousel. I promised myself I'd fit in at least one ride on the merry-go-round before the night was out.

We passed by several carnival barkers before Rocky decided to stop. The rest of us formed his audience as he tossed darts at balloons, quickly winning a stuffed pink rabbit for Deena, after only three tries.

Calvin gave me a sidelong glance. "I guess it's my turn now. I hope you won't think less of me if I'm not as skilled at this as your brother."

"You don't have to—" I broke off as he threw a dart, popping a balloon on his first try. I chose a fluffy unicorn as my prize.

Next we stopped at a food stand for corn on the cob and grilled kebabs. (Rocky refused to let us go anywhere near the elephant ears.) We finished off our meal-on-the-go with paper cups of fruity Italian ice.

Everywhere we went, I kept an eye out for any familiar faces. I'd thought I might run into Vince and get my chance to try to reason with him. But as dusk fell over the fairgrounds, I had second thoughts. I was having such a good time, I found myself hoping I *wouldn't* see anyone connected in any way with the murder investigation.

As it happened, less than a minute later, I recognized someone in the crowd: Officer Davy Wills. I froze when I saw him. Calvin noticed me holding back and signaled the others to wait. Standing under the canopy of the beer tent, I observed Davy on the other side of the pedway at a lemon shake-up stand. He wasn't in uniform. And he didn't appear to be on duty. In fact, he seemed to be engaged in a friendly chat with the person next to him. Then that person turned his head, and I saw who it was: one Richard Wales.

"Oh!" I broke into a delighted grin and tugged on Deena's arm. "Look!"

So Davy is Richard's secret boyfriend. That explained a lot—like why Richard was so certain he could keep the students from going on their planned hike. He must've asked Davy to come over and keep them tied up with questions about the investigation.

"Ah!" said Deena, following my gaze. "How wonderful and interesting."

Rocky turned to Calvin. "What are they talking about?"

Calvin shook his head. "No idea."

"Who wants to go on the Ferris wheel?" asked Deena, changing the subject.

"I'm game," said Rocky.

Calvin and I looked at each other. "Eh," we both said at the same time.

"Aw, come on," said Deena. "It's a tradition."

"You two go ahead." I took the pink bunny from Deena and handed it to Calvin. "We'll take our prizes to the car, so we don't have to keep carrying them around."

Rocky gave me his keys, and Calvin and I headed back to the parking lot. As we left the noise of the carnival, we could hear strains of live country music from the bandstand at the rear of the fairgrounds.

"You're not a fan of Ferris wheels?" asked Calvin.

"They make me nervous," I admitted. "I don't like

feeling trapped on those little seats, at the mercy of the ride operator. I don't love heights either."

"I guess that rules out the rollercoaster then. And all the other rides."

"All but the carousel." I smiled hopefully, and he laughed, throwing an arm over my shoulders.

We passed by a line of booths, where vendors sold everything from T-shirts and sunglasses to novelty toys and personalized spray-art paintings. I slowed down near a table featuring Southwest-style jewelry, my attention snagged by a pretty turquoise and coral beaded bracelet.

Calvin paused. "If you want to browse, I can take our prizes to the car and meet you back here."

"Are you sure you don't mind?"

"Not at all." He took my unicorn and Rocky's keys. "I'll be right back."

"Thank you!"

I perused the jewelry and found several items I liked. I was trying to decide between the beaded bracelet and a silver necklace with a lapis lazuli pendant, when a trill of laughter pricked my ears. Glancing toward the adjacent table, I gave a start when I saw who it was: April Finley, bouncing between her cohorts, Vince and Isaiah.

"Come on, guys," April said loudly. "We only have an hour before Ms. Washington is picking us up. I want to go on the rides!"

Vince and Isaiah exchanged a bored look. Then Isaiah draped an arm over April's neck. "I'll go on the Ferris wheel with you, if you go on the Tilt-A-Whirl with me."

Rolling his eyes, Vince snapped the collar on his leather jacket. "Alright, children. Let's go."

I didn't think twice. I set down the jewelry I'd been holding and followed them. I made sure to stay far enough back that they wouldn't catch a glimpse of me if they happened to turn their heads. Whenever possible, I walked behind other fairgoers while keeping at least one of my quarry in sight. In the midst of this game, I felt my phone buzz and knew it must be Calvin. I felt bad about not answering, but it felt too risky. He'd understand.

I wasn't sure what I was doing exactly. I had a vague idea that I'd keep eavesdropping and perhaps overhear something incriminating. Beyond that, I also had an uneasy feeling about things between Isaiah and April. If I'd been afraid of them going mountain climbing together, the prospect of them on a Ferris wheel was equally as concerning.

Then I had another strange thought. What if April was the dangerous one? She was the one who seemed most intent on keeping leadership of their motley little drug ring.

A chill coursed through me, and I shivered. There was one thing I knew for sure. At least one of them was a murderer.

April ran up to a ticket booth and leaned her elbows on the ledge. As she spoke to the seller, I hid behind a giant inflatable clown and reached into my purse for my phone. Maybe I could at least send Calvin a quick text. I'd just opened the screen on my phone, when I glanced over and saw that the trio was on the move again. I dropped the phone back into my purse. *Sorry, Calvin.*

They wound their way through the carnival, with me once more on their tail, and ended up at the Tilt-A-Whirl. April and Isaiah got in line. Vince said something to them, then sauntered toward the food vendors.

Now was my chance! I'd finally caught Vince by himself, at least for the duration of a Tilt-A-Whirl ride. I waited for him to buy a soda, then started to approach him. But he turned the other way, heading, not back to the rides, but toward the end of the row. To my surprise, he stopped, looked furtively from left to right, and disappeared through the opening between a tent and a generator truck.

What is he up to? Feeling like a spy again, I crept through the narrow passage he'd entered. He hadn't gone far. He was loitering next to the generator. As I watched, he dumped out half of his soda onto the ground. He then removed a flask from an inner pocket of his jacket. He proceeded to pour some of its contents into the rest of his soda.

I stepped forward and spoke casually. "Hey, Vince."

He jumped into the air, cursing, and splashed his drink on his hand.

"Jeez, lady! What's your problem?" He wiped the back of his hand on his jeans and replaced the lid on his cup.

"Why did you stand me up yesterday?"

"Stand you up? I never agreed to go out with you." His eyes roved from my dress to my bare legs, and he smirked. "Under different circumstances, I would. But I knew you had ulterior motives."

"I just want to talk to you. There's nothing 'ulterior' about it."

He took a long sip through the soda straw. "You want to talk, huh? Okay. Go on a ride with me, and we can talk."

I narrowed my eyes. "Why can't we just talk here? No one else is around." As I said the words, I became acutely aware of their truth. It was dark and shadowy back here. The loud hum of the generator muffled the carnival noises on the other side. Behind us a low fence separated the fair from a large area of scrubby grass, where a cluster of trailers provided temporary homes for the carnival workers.

He gave me a wolfish smile. "Indeed."

Taking half a step back, I crossed my arms in front of my chest. "Look, Vince," I said reasonably. "I have some information I think you'll be interested in, but I need you to be honest with me."

"I'm always honest." He cast about for a place to set down his cup. Finding none, he placed it on the dirt in front of him. Then he reached into his jacket pocket and pulled out a pack of cigarettes. As he did so, a plastic wrapper fell out of his pocket and floated to the ground. "What's your information?"

I opened my mouth to respond, but I'd lost my train of thought. Something about the wrapper had jumped out at me—probably the image of sunflower seeds on the plastic label. I reached down and picked it up.

"So, now you're the litter police?" said Vince.

Interconnected thoughts clicked in my mind like gears in a clock. There had been a receipt for sunflower seeds on the floor of the storeroom, right after the murder—a receipt Gus had, unfortunately, eaten. Then, as now, I realized the receipt was not exactly a smoking gun. The person who bought or ate the sunflower seeds was not necessarily the same person who dropped or tracked in the receipt.

Nevertheless, seeing it now was very interesting. And suddenly I perceived Vince in a whole new light. He was different from his classmates. More experienced and less eager. He seemed like a levelheaded sort of guy, willing to hang out with his ex-girlfriend and her other ex-boyfriend. April had gone to him when she was concerned about Isaiah, as if Vince had some influence over the younger guy. And, from what I could tell, Vince had no interest in carrying on Lowry's devious schemes.

Observing him in the gloom, I remembered a few more things I'd learned about Vince Gonzalez. Like the comment he'd made about death messing a person up. And the fact that he'd tried to get the trip canceled— ostensibly so they could go someplace different for a change.

I held up the empty sunflower seed bag. "Did you get these at Marla's Mini-Mart?" At his blank look, I elaborated. "The gas station on the western edge of Aerieville?"

"Yeah. So?" He lit his cigarette, took a drag, and exhaled out the side of his mouth.

"So . . . I think you dropped the receipt. In the storeroom at Flower House. After you hit Lowry on the back of the head."

He was as cool as ever. His eyebrows only went up the barest amount. "That's what you think, is it?"

"Yeah. It is. And I think I know why."

He gestured for me to go on.

"It was to keep Isaiah from doing it. You didn't want him to become a murderer. And the only way you knew to stop him was to do it yourself."

Now he looked impressed. He leaned back on the fence and, smiling a little, took another drag. "That's some information you have there."

"That's not all. I know what Lowry was all about, what he made you guys do. With the poppies and everything else."

For a moment, he looked out over the bare grass toward the workers' trailers. He seemed to be considering what I'd said, as he smoked his cigarette. Then his eyes slid back to my face. "And I suppose you're not the only one who knows this?"

My eyes might've widened a little at that.

He laughed. "I'm only kidding. I wouldn't hurt you." He pushed himself off the fence. "So, what are you, psychic or something? How do you know all this?"

"I'm just perceptive." *And determined and lucky.* "Are you admitting it's true?"

He shrugged. "I told you I'm honest."

"Not always," I countered. "You tried to blame Calvin for the murder."

"Yeah, well, somebody had to take the blame. I thought it would be the truck driver, but the cops never went for him."

"Bart was on his phone at the time, so he had an alibi."

"Ah," said Vince.

I felt my phone buzz again and ignored it. This dialogue was too fascinating. "Do April and Isaiah know?"

"Nah. April thinks Isaiah did it, and Isaiah thinks Calvin did it."

"And you let April believe that about Isaiah. Is he a dangerous person? Do you think he could harm April, or anyone else who stands in his way?"

Vince hesitated for a moment. "I don't think so," he said slowly. "It was different with Lowry. The professor got under Isaiah's skin. The way he used people and manipulated them. That's what got to Isaiah so much."

"And you too," I pointed out.

"I'm not sorry he's gone." Vince finished his cigarette and tossed the butt. "You probably won't believe me, but I didn't really mean for him to die. I thought I might put him in the hospital and get the trip canceled. Buy some time to find another way out." He squinted his eyes, as if imagining how things might have turned out differently. "He never even knew it was me. I told him Calvin had something on him, hidden in the back of that closet." He shot me a rueful look. "Oh, well."

My phone was buzzing like crazy now. Calvin had probably called Deena and Rocky. They'd never find me back here, but I wasn't scared. Vince seemed to have given up.

"I have one more question," I said.

"Shoot."

"Why did you lock me in the storeroom?"

He furrowed his brow. "What?"

"On Tuesday, when you guys rode Richard's bikes to the bakery."

"Oh, that was Isaiah. He wanted to search the shop. He thought Calvin might have a stash of unwashed poppy seeds he could steal. He was scheming to get ahead of April somehow. I told him it was a waste of time."

"That reminds me. What happened to Lowry's canteen?"

"He left it in the flower shop bathroom. April found it and tossed it out the window. She begged me to come back for it later." He shook his head. "The things I've done to keep that girl out of trouble."

I softened my stance. "You're not a bad guy, Vince. When the truth comes out about Lowry, that's sure to be a mitigating factor. You can plea-bargain. Maybe it won't be . . ." I trailed off, when he moved closer to me and touched my shoulder.

"I got priors, babe. Nobody's gonna go easy on me."

"For what?" My voice came out as a whisper.

"Theft. Vandalism. A few other things."

"Those aren't violent crimes."

He reached into his jeans pocket. Before I realized what was happening, he'd pulled out a switchblade and flicked it open. I gasped.

Laughing softly, Vince pushed me against the fence and leaned over my face. "You're quite the innocent flower, you know that?" Quick as a flash, he thrust his knife under the strap of my purse and cut it from my shoulder. Holding the bag like a football, he hopped over the fence. "See ya, babe."

Then he tore off into the shadows.

Chapter 27

I was breathless, unable to move, for several seconds. The entire exchange with Vince had been so astonishing, from start to finish. I feared no one would believe me when I told them about it.

Finally, my legs stopped shaking enough to allow me to walk. I staggered out of the makeshift hideaway and into the bright flashing lights of the carnival. I felt lost without my phone. For a few minutes, I wandered aimlessly, vainly searching for a friend among strangers. I also wondered what Vince was doing. Would he steal a car and drive all night? Or hitch a ride to the bus station? Maybe he'd just hide out at the carnival, then stow away with the crew whenever they traveled to the next county on their circuit.

Part of me felt sorry for Vince. I'd meant it when I'd said he wasn't really a bad guy, not at heart. But he'd done some very bad things. The more I thought about it, the more my senses returned. I realized he had to be caught. Not only for the sake of justice, but also for the sake of clearing Calvin's name. And mine.

Walking rapidly now, I headed toward an information

booth. I planned to borrow a phone and ask them to call
security. I was almost there when I heard someone shout
my name.

"Sierra? Are you okay?"

Spinning around, I searched the crowd and quickly
found Richard. He was still with Davy, who was now
clutching an oversized teddy bear. I jogged up to them, so
relieved I could've cried. The whole story spilled out of me
in a rush. Almost before I'd finished, Richard was on the
phone with Deena, and Davy was calling headquarters.

As soon as he hung up, Richard pulled me into a quick
hug and patted the top my head. "Didn't I tell you not to
chase after bad guys?"

"Yes," I mumbled contritely.

Davy gave Richard the teddy bear, then went up to the
information booth and showed his badge. After speaking
briefly with the head of security, he asked me to show him
where Vince had run off. Davy and the security guard,
flashlight in hand, climbed over the fence and headed
toward the dark trailers.

"Be careful!" called Richard. He then guided me to a
picnic area, where he'd told Deena we'd be.

She, Rocky, and Calvin were already there. They
rushed at me like bees to honey. Richard stepped aside,
and I braced myself for a scolding. I was sure they'd all
be upset.

"Sierra, thank goodness!" Deena wrapped her arms
around me. "We were so worried. I was afraid you'd been
kidnapped or locked up someplace or—"

"Nothing like that," I interrupted. "I'm fine." I
gave them the short version of my adventure, including
Vince's confession.

Rocky's face was flushed, like he'd been running.
"You sure you're okay, sis? That guy didn't touch you?"

"I'm okay, really. He stole my purse, but he didn't hurt me." I turned to Calvin, who hadn't said anything yet. His face was a mask of concern. "I'm so sorry, Cal."

He tried to give me a reassuring smile, but I could tell he was shaken. "It was weird," he said. "At first, I assumed you'd gone to the bathroom or something. Then I realized what must've happened. I knew you must've seen Vince and the others."

I reached for his hand and squeezed it. I didn't know what else to say. In truth, I'd probably do the same thing all over again if given the chance. But no one needed to hear that right now.

"Rocky probably covered every inch of this fair in ten minutes flat," said Deena, with a hint of pride in her voice. "While he raced all over the place, I got back on the Ferris wheel. I asked the operator to stop me at the top, so I could look around. You can see pretty far from up there."

"Smart," said Richard.

"Hey, maybe we should do that now," said Rocky. "We might spot Vince that way."

"Yeah!" said Deena. "If we see him, Richard can call Officer Davy."

Richard raised his eyebrows. "How did you—oh, never mind. I can't keep anything from the Bobbsey Twins."

Rocky gave me a questioning look. "What do you think, sis? Do you want me to just take you home?"

"No way. I'm too jumpy to go home." I glanced at Calvin. "I'm still not keen on the Ferris wheel though."

Calvin moved closer to me. "Feel like taking a spin on the carousel?"

"Absolutely."

It was agreed that we'd all check in with each other

in thirty minutes. Calvin and I strolled to the carousel, saying little along the way. The fair stayed open late, but many families had gone home by now. It was mostly teenagers and couples who remained. We had our pick of seats on the ride. Normally, I'd choose the fanciest, most colorful horse I could snag, but I was feeling subdued tonight. I went straight for the elaborately carved, painted wooden bench.

Calvin slid in next to me. As the ride lurched forward, jubilant circus music rang out, covering all other sounds in the park. It wasn't exactly conducive to intimate conversation. Still, after two revolutions without talking, I shifted in my seat to face Calvin.

"What's on your mind?"

He answered without hesitation. "You."

"Are you mad at me?"

"Mad? No. I think you're amazing. You've stuck by me throughout this whole ordeal. You never doubted I was innocent. You've been fighting to get to the truth of everything. I just—I can't thank you enough."

My heart melted. I reached for his hand again. "I think you're kind of amazing too."

"Oh, yeah?" He grinned, and his eyes took on a playful gleam.

"Yeah." I could've stayed there forever, bantering and flirting in our little merry-go-round bubble. Maybe there was no such thing as a tunnel of love anymore, but this was pretty darn close.

It was too bad I kept seeing something in my peripheral vision. I caught a glimpse of it every time we passed by the low concrete building housing the first-aid station. Two people were standing in the grass, one with a mass of curly yellow hair, the other with short, neatly trimmed dark hair. As the ride slowed, the recognition sank in.

I pointed them out to Calvin. "Check it out. It's April and Isaiah. They don't look very happy."

In fact, they appeared to be arguing. April kept looking at her phone, while Isaiah glared at her.

"Should I make some calls?" Calvin said in a low voice.

"How 'bout sending Deena a text. She'll alert the others." I stood up slowly and moved to exit the ride. "I want to try to hear what they're saying."

"I'm coming with you," said Calvin.

I looked back and met his eyes. "Of course."

We had to make a wide circle so we could approach the two students without being seen. Coming up from the backside of the small, square building, we paused at the front corner. Calvin stood behind me, with one hand on my shoulder.

April's whiny voice carried loud and clear. "Where is he? Why won't he pick up?"

"I have a bad feeling about this," muttered Isaiah. "He ditched us. He probably went back to Knoxville. It's what I should've done."

Calvin texted Deena, as I continued to listen. I'd finally gotten my chance to eavesdrop, and I was determined to make the most of it. I figured April and Isaiah wouldn't wait around for much longer. It was probably past time for them to meet Sheila.

Then I heard April squeal. "Finally!" She brought her phone to her ear. "Where are you? We've been looking—what?"

Isaiah tried to grab the phone from her hand, but she jerked away and continued in an incredulous voice. "What are you talking about? What tour bus?"

I glanced back at Calvin to see if he was catching this. He gave me a triumphant look. Grinning, I turned back to hear more.

"What, you're a roadie now?" said April. Then, "Oh. Just a free ride to Memphis. Like that makes it any better. I don't understand. Why would you—"

I didn't know what Vince was saying to her. Maybe a word of caution or maybe a final goodbye. Whatever it was, he'd made his last mistake. His final error in judgment would soon lead to his arrest. I imagined the police would locate him near the bandstand, with whatever short-lived friend he'd just made. They would approach him in much the same way two officers were even now approaching April and Isaiah.

Two weeks later, on the first of August, we held the soft opening of the Flower House café. It was a festive low-key party, exclusively for family, friends, and neighbors. The latter included Bill and Flo Morrison, who had sweetened their views on me when I decided to place a standing order with them. I figured their fresh-baked Bread n' Butter brioche would be extra delicious when paired with our rose petal jam.

Of course, the fact that the murder had been solved put everyone's mind at ease. The morning after the excitement at the county fair, Richard called me with an off-the-record update from Davy. He said Vince had been arrested and had given a full confession. The suspect had even returned my purse, which I took as a good sign.

April and Isaiah had been brought in as accomplices. Whether or not those charges would stick remained to be seen. As I learned later, my letter about Lowry's schemes had made a big splash on the UT campus. Everyone was talking about it, and everything was out in the open. The jig, as they say, was up.

I circulated through the café with a tray of edible flower hors d'oeuvres. We had crostini with herbed cream cheese topped with garlic and chive flowers, fried zucchini blossoms, rose water mini-cupcakes, and, of course, Deena's pansy cookies. Guests sipped on lavender-infused cocktails and honeysuckle iced tea.

Walking around, I heard snippets of conversation and saw plenty of warm smiles. It touched my heart to witness what an open, friendly bunch I had in my life. Deena chatted with my mom and Granny about recipes, Dad traded home-repair tips with Richard, and Calvin talked with Wanda about the history of Aerieville.

I was also heartened by the growth in business we'd seen over the past several days. I'd even had to increase our most recent wholesale order. On delivery day I'd geared myself up for another awkward encounter with Bart, but my angst was for nothing. The driver was new. Evidently, Bart had decided to take a long overdue vacation. I hoped he'd work on some of his personal issues and come back in a more relaxed state of mind.

Since everyone at the party was like family, in one way or another, I let Gus roam free among the guests. He was in his element. As a herding dog, he loved to be where the action was. It was cute how he kept trying to nudge everyone into the same room. He didn't like it when I stepped out the front door for a moment, but Rocky held him back. There was something I had to do.

When Granny had arrived at the party, she placed a heavy gift in my hands: a cast-iron horseshoe. "For good luck," she'd explained. "Hang it upright to keep the goodness from spilling out—and hopefully ward off any more bad fortune from entering this house."

Calvin held the ladder and handed me a hammer. As I attached the horseshoe above the entrance to Flower House, I told myself I still believed we create our own luck.

But why take chances?